# Rekindle Me

# Rekindle Me

Muhammad Ishaq

Library of Congress Control Number:     2018906533
ISBN:          Hardcover              978-1-9845-3228-2
               Softcover              978-1-9845-3227-5
               eBook                  978-1-9845-3226-8

Print information available on the last page.

Rev. date: 06/19/2018

**To order additional copies of this book, contact:**
Xlibris
1-888-795-4274
www.Xlibris.com
Orders@Xlibris.com
749064

# CONTENTS

Dedicated to God, the Creator and the Sustainer of the universe.

# Prologue

*Present day, November 15, 2074*
*Witnessing humanity's worst disaster*
*New York City*
*Narrator: Tommy Russell*

We have forgotten; we have changed. We have deviated from the righteous path of the divine teachings, and we have been punished for our mistakes. We have been shortsighted and selfish and have proved unworthy of the grace given to us by God. And now things have changed.

Everything has changed.

After centuries of technological advances and the rapid rise of Earth's population, humanity has lost sight of life's real purpose. We value money, fame, and amassing earthly possessions, anything to satiate our burning desire for more than we will ever need. That has become our driving force.

We human beings, with our selfish ways and our lack of faith, are to blame for our imminent destruction. God is the one true Savior, but we closed our eyes and ears to His grace. And now the lives of billions around the world are in danger. We abandoned our core values, and now it's up to me to fill the gap we created by giving up our faith.

But what can one person do? What can I do? Will my faith be enough to save the world? Will God hear one person and forgive humanity's mistakes only because I have asked Him to show mercy?

I don't know.

I know I'm supposed to be strong. I know I'm expected to be adamant about my principles and my faith, but the task is too great. However, if I don't do something, Lisa, Manna, and Catherine won't be able to enjoy the gift of life, the gift that God so generously gave to us and that we misused.

No. I have to try. I have to give my all. People depend on me; my family depends on me. There's only one thing I can do now. I hope it is enough to save mankind; I hope I will be enough to save the souls of the poor people.

# Chapter 1

# A Difficult Question

*May 15, 2072*
*Early morning, two and a half years earlier*
*New York City*
*Narrator: Tommy Russell*

When I open my eyes, Catherine is sleeping by my side, and I bet Lisa and Manna are sound asleep in their rooms as well. It's Friday, the last day of the school week, so I think they deserve to enjoy their sleep a bit more today. It will give them the strength they need to get through their long day.

I rub my eyes and make myself comfortable in the bed. It's still too early to start breakfast or to wake the kids, but that means I have time to get up to speed on the news from all around the world and from Yahire. This month has been crazy from the beginning. Lisa had to see the doctor twice last week. She caught the late-spring flu because she played outside all day and didn't take care of herself.

Catherine was out of town for three days visiting her sister, and I had to watch over the girls while she was away. At the same time, work has been hectic since ticket prices to Yahire plummeted. Everyone wants to visit the Paradisiacal Planet, and everyone wants a new start in another land. Yahire was formed about sixteen million years ago and had been wandering all alone in our galaxy. In 2036, a giant star died in the Milky Way, and as a result, Yahire was drawn toward our solar system.

I don't get it, though. Yahire isn't like Earth. It's rocky, barren, and void of everything that makes Earth what it is: a place for humans to live.

Analysts speak about the economic boom Yahire has produced and how that will affect life on Earth. I'm a banking professional, and I know this boom will change everything. It will mean new technology, new products to distract us from our duties, and new materialistic pleasures that offer nothing for the growth of the soul.

I'm getting more and more confused about what humans expect of their lives on Earth. Kids these days follow their parents' wishes only when they're given something in return. Their upbringing is much different from mine. Adultery, alcoholism, and gambling are on the rise, tearing families apart. And the same evils happen again and again in a vicious circle of bad intentions sugarcoated so as to fool people.

I sigh as Catherine changes sides, probably trying to squeeze in an extra half-hour of sleep before getting up to help the kids get ready for school. I smile at the serene expression on her face. Why can't all the people on this planet have that same expression when they are awake? We have lost that serenity amid our rapid technological progress, and now all we can do is wait for that peace to return while we're trying to achieve our dreams.

Another deep sigh leaves my body. I can't do this to myself any longer. I can't right every wrong in the world from the comfort of my bed. As my father used to say, "Do your part and have faith in God; one day you will be rewarded." That was the path he followed, and that is the way I will follow as long as I live.

I turn my upper body and reach for my tablet. Technology is not inherently harmful, not when used for simple everyday purposes. I can't form a complete and rounded opinion about the world's affairs without getting an update on my digital screen and on the internet. However, the actions I take based on what I read are a matter of principle.

For example, if I noticed a change that could hurt my clients or my family and friends, and I did nothing to stop it, I would have used my knowledge to harm them. And my conscience would never allow that. But if I used technology and information to improve my life and the lives of those around me, my soul would be content.

When I hold the small machine in my hands, the screen recognizes my touch and lights up. My eyes draw away from the intense flash, and I yawn. It's still too early for me to get lost in deep thoughts about the meaning of life in this world.

Nowadays, almost all laptops and tablets come with digital assistants and artificial intelligence programs capable of having a conversation with you about any topic you choose—perhaps spirituality, human values, or materialism. But a conclusion supported merely by logic and evidence is lacking in many ways. Machines don't have souls, nor can they feel happiness or pray. Machines work based solely on information, while humans are made to follow their hearts. And my heart tells me God exists and lives everywhere around me, including inside other people.

Still, digital assistants have been a nice addition to our everyday routine. It's like having another family member, and sometimes we argue if we disagree. Today, though, since Cat is still sleeping, I decide not to use my digital assistant to help keep up with current events. I think I'll do this the old-fashioned manual way.

I start the web browser and choose my favorite search engine. I can program searches, and the machine can learn the way I want my search engine to retrieve the desired information—all based on AI. These days I am interested in Yahire and in environmental technology news, and I find countless articles on major news sites.

"New Research on Earth's Core Indicates Imminent Breakthrough. Scientists Worldwide Await the Hard-Earned Results."

"Yahire-born Celebrity Badmouths Earth and Its Inhabitants. A Daring Interview and Insight on the Aftermath of Falling Ticket Prices."

"New Technological Breakthrough Revolutionizes the Way People Communicate with Each Other. We're Entering the Platinum Age of Information."

And the absurd headlines go on and on. Does anyone remember a time when people didn't need technological breakthroughs to be happy? We can barely keep pace with new technology, people are living on alien planets, and significant environmental changes are taking place, but no one bats an eye. People seem dead set on destroying everything around them.

Life has changed drastically since this inhabitable planet suddenly appeared in our solar system. Twenty years ago, when I was still a teenager, the news that people were colonizing Yahire was revolutionary. Back then, Father told me we were both blessed and cursed to find another planet to inhabit at Earth's eleventh hour. Since I still hadn't cleared up my thinking about God and His connection with humanity, I asked Father why this was so.

He told me, "People don't understand that this is another gift from God, a kind offer coming through His grace. God knew that we were struggling with our planet and that we had stained His gift, so He decided to give us another chance. But instead of using this new planet for good, we charge people money to get there, adding to humanity's problems.

God is forgiving but only to those who show good will and a desire for redemption. Once again, we're opposing His holy will by doing things our way. He's going to abandon us again, Tommy my son, and when people need Him most, it might be too late."

I gave his words the greatest consideration. I don't think I ever saw such worry on his face. Father was a man of patience and of great love and faith. To this day, my mother always talks about him. He was a saint. Now, as I see how people have forgetten the divine teachings and have sought solace in materialism and in their shortsighted ambitions, I'm also starting to worry.

I'm not worried only about Yahire, though. Scientists talk about a new discovery that will shake the foundations of modern life and will help people all around the world. I know I should be happy and should pray to God that this is for the best, but I also know that when we humans meddle with His creation, we always end up doing more harm than good.

I feel movement at my side. I quickly flip my tablet and turn to look at my love, Catherine. She stares at me, her amber eyes in a haze as she emerges from sleep.

"Good morning, honey," she mumbles, fighting to suppress a yawn.

"Good morning to you too, love. Did you sleep well?" I ask.

She nods as she stretches her arms and her legs, preparing to rise to her feet. My dear Catherine is always energetic in the mornings, and I envy that. She always knows what to do to lift my spirits.

Leaning on her elbow, Catherine steals a kiss from my lips. She smiles at me and immediately picks up my foul mood.

"You've been reading the news again, haven't you? Tommy, how many times do I have to tell you? I know you're worried about the world, and believe me, your love for humanity is your greatest asset, but you have to stop doing this to yourself. These people won't look at you twice. They have strayed too far from the beaten path, and you can't save them all by yourself."

I know she's right, and I want to forget my concerns about their lives and their souls, but that is not who I am. Catherine sees my sulking expression and exhales. I have nothing to say. This woman can read me so well.

"Okay, okay. I don't want to stop you from caring. But I hate seeing you worried over people who have chosen their path. It's not your fault they chose the easy road. All you can do is keep praying for them like I know you do every night. You give a great example to Lisa and Manna. If it weren't for you, they wouldn't be so loving and obedient."

There it is—Catherine's famous pep talk. I would have given up long ago and dedicated my life to the world if Catherine and our little girls hadn't held me back. Our girls are loving and smart, and they have accepted the true religion—love—in their hearts just as we did. They don't ask for more things than they need, they're not jealous of their friends' expensive clothes or modern accessories, and the only thing they want is love and peace in the world.

I couldn't have asked for a more supportive family, but now and again, I feel inadequate. We attend a service every Sunday, and we help those in need whenever we can, but these things stopped being enough for me a long time ago. I want to offer people protection and guidance and to show them the way back to God's arms. But if I did that, the world would swallow me in its emptiness. The love of one man can't possibly be enough to fill the gap created by the insatiable desire for more. And now all I'm left with is worry.

It's time to start my day. I get off the bed and head for the bathroom. Catherine walks to Lisa's room. Lisa is the family's sleepyhead, so her mom makes sure to wake her first every day so she's not late for school.

Manna, on the other hand, is probably awake and tidying up her room. She can be a bit messy at times, but she always leaves her room spotless before going to school. I find this an amazing personality trait. When I was her age, I couldn't drag myself out of the kitchen after eating something, nor could I tidy up my room.

Lisa is eight years old, and Manna is six. Catherine and I are very proud of them, and we sometimes think we pamper them too much with our love. But they're too young and too loving to use that to their advantage. These girls are exactly what we asked for, the cornerstone of our family and the moving force of the next generation.

After taking a shower and brushing my teeth, I'm off to the kitchen to help Catherine with the morning preparations. She is readying a batch of pancakes for the little ladies upstairs. The TV offers a steady stream of nonsense. This morning it's a reality show set on Mars. Another colonization mission is taking place there, but this time it's financed by private corporations and documented by the media. I'm not sure I understand what is happening on this show half of the time, but I've seen enough to know I don't like it.

People are risking their lives for fame, money, and other things that don't matter. Still, Catherine, knowing my problem with the news, always finds the most mundane and uninteresting program on TV during breakfast. If she didn't do that, I would almost certainly start my day on a bad foot and would perform poorly at work. She cares for me in her own special way.

The pancakes release their sweet smell. My mouth waters in an instant. I sidle up to Catherine and try to grab one, but she slaps my hand.

"No one eats until all of us get to the table," she says in a mock-strict voice.

"Oh, come on! Now is the best time to eat them, when they're just out of the frying pan. Come on, sweetheart. Just one."

"No. Lisa and Manna get to pick first. You know the drill, Tommy." Then she grins and stealthily passes me a pancake.

I smile back at her and stuff my mouth with the warm delicacy. My wife makes the greatest pancakes in the city—no, in the world—and waiting for the children to get downstairs so we can eat together is an ordeal. Thus, our little game has become a great way to start our day, not only for us but for our little angels. They eagerly wait for Catherine to reject my plea, and then they run down to the kitchen, giggling all the way.

"Good morning, Mom. Good morning, Dad," they say in unison. Even though their mother is usually the one to wake them, they don't wish her a good day until they have washed their faces and brushed their teeth.

"Good morning to you, too. How was your sleep?" I ask them.

They grin at me while taking their seats at the table.

"It was great! I dreamed I was dancing in school, and my friends were with me, and we were all dancing and having fun," Manna says.

Lisa isn't so quick to reply. "It was fine, I guess."

Her response immediately strikes me as weird. Lisa is the one with the vivid dreams and an overactive imagination. "What's wrong, sweetheart? Did you have a nightmare?"

She shakes her head. "No, not at all. I just ... I couldn't sleep last night. I was thinking ..." Her voice trails off when the platter of pancakes arrives on the table.

Lisa has reached the stage where she is asking questions about friendship, life, spirituality, and even God. Catherine and I had agreed to always be there for our daughters and to answer their questions in an honest and mature way. That includes questions about puberty when the time comes. (I pray it comes later rather than sooner.)

Lisa appears uneasy. I wait for her to swallow before saying, "Tell us, Lisa. What kept you up last night?"

Her face flushes; she hesitates. "Dad … where is God?"

The innocence and wonder in her voice take me by surprise. My little Lisa is searching for guidance as she grapples with an age-old question.

Without giving it much thought, I reply, "Well, my dear girl, God lives among us!"

Faced with a deep philosophical question, I forget I'm talking to a child. But then again, aren't children supposed to discover the world through their innocent eyes?

Manna decides to enter the discussion. She is confused and unsatisfied with my answer. "But Dad, if He lives among us, why can't we see Him? Or hear Him? Or even sense Him?"

After dropping this bomb, Manna grabs another pancake and spreads syrup on it before putting it in her mouth. Then she looks at me with yearning eyes, but no answer comes to my mind. I can't say anything to satisfy her curiosity, not without sounding vague and generic. A significant part of religion depends on the inner feelings of the people who decide to follow the one true path, but even then, there's no clear answer to what my Manna asked me.

I mumble for a bit, sigh, and try different words and explanations in my mind, but nothing comes out. If Manna were an adult, I could speak to her about the church, good deeds, and spirituality, but at her age, there's nothing I can say that won't sound like gibberish. God is everywhere, but for a child that isn't true if she can't see Him, touch Him, and hear Him. And I understand how she feels.

Manna forgot about her question long before breakfast was over. However, her words echo in my head. Where is God? And why does that question seem so important to me now?

"Mom, Mom. We're done. See? We ate all the pancakes," Lisa suddenly says. I am lost in thought, and my body jerks at the sound of her voice. She giggles and starts singing, "I scared Daddy. I scared Daddy!"

Manna quickly joins her chant, and soon they're both giggling loudly. I smile at them and shrug my shoulders, seemingly sad. "Daddy was thinking about something serious and didn't hear you. That's why I got scared."

They burst into laughter and continue their chatter. Catherine leans closer to me, smiling. "Are you okay, honey? You seemed lost back there," she whispers.

"Yeah, yeah. I was just thinking about the question Lisa asked me." Catherine rolls her eyes.

"Tommy, this is just children's talk," she says. "They weren't asking you to show them the place where God resides, but I suppose they wanted us to give them a general explanation. I'm sure that when they grow up, they will find the answer for themselves." She takes a sip of her hot coffee.

Though I understand what she's talking about and up to now had accepted that explanation as the only truth, I can't wrap my mind around the simplicity of this answer. Of course God lives among us, but lately this doesn't seem true. Why is that?

I look my wife in the eye and speak honestly to her. "I don't know, Catherine. When I was younger, I needed someone to show me the way to all these answers, and I believe our children do too. We said we would treat them like adults when they started asking questions about important matters. It's just that I don't know how to give a mature answer to their question without appearing pompous."

Her eyes soften, and she quickly projects a soothing aura that makes all my bad thoughts vanish. "You have a point, honey. But, as you can see, they're kids. They ask a question, and by the time you've turned your back and reached for the milk, they've forgotten about it. Don't worry about them. They have to explore and to discover truths themselves, the same way we did when we were younger."

Catherine smiles and kisses me on the cheek. But this is one of those times when her words are not enough to calm me down. A fire is burning in my chest, fueled by uneasiness and uncertainty. I feel cracks in my shining armor of faith, and all that from a simple question about the whereabouts of God.

I feel stupid but at the same time excited.

A small hand tugs at my sleeve; it's Manna. "Daddy, daddy," she says, shyly hiding her face behind her hands.

"What, sweetheart?"

"Boo!" she shouts and runs away from me laughing.

I smile while acting surprised. Children are indeed the source of life.

I complete my breakfast, quickly down a cup of coffee, and head upstairs to grab my suitcase and my laptop. On the way down, I hear Catherine talking to Lisa.

"Lisa, honey, I forgot to ask you last night. Why did your teacher want me to come to school today? Does this have something to do with your bad grades in math?"

Lisa hesitates at first but soon she's talking. "I don't understand all these numbers and how to use them, Mom; they are so difficult! And I don't want to ask the teacher for help because he's so mean to me."

"Lisa, you know you could have told me about this. I was worried for a moment. If you had spoken to me sooner, I would have helped you," Catherine says, cuddling her and making her feel better.

She's too old to burst into tears as she used to do, but she's too young to have to be concerned with such problems. By the time I arrive at the bottom of the staircase, Lisa and Catherine are smiling at each other and looking relieved.

"Did I hear that someone has a problem with numbers?" I ask in a playful manner, lowering my voice and sounding bigger and fuzzier. The girls love it when I do my Santa Claus voice.

I see wonder and delight in Lisa's little eyes. She nods in return.

"Then you should have asked me to help, dear. I'm the master of numbers, the commander of addition and multiplication, and the king of the division. From now on, if you have any questions about math, come straight to me and avoid that rigid teacher of yours," I say.

Lisa nods twice and runs to hug my leg. I lean down and grab her by the arms; I lift her and kiss her on the cheek. Manna, who was upstairs straightening out her room, hastily runs down the staircase and hugs my leg as well.

"I want you to teach me about numbers, too!"

I lift her up with my free hand. "Of course, honey. Everything you want. Everything you want."

***

# Chapter 2

## Perspectives

*Same setting*
*Narrator: Tommy Russell*

A small army of feet is heading out of the house. Catherine will drive Lisa and Manna to school, and I'm heading straight for work. It's getting late, and I have many things on my mind that I want to think over before arriving at the bank. Lisa's question created an avalanche of questions in my head. Where is God? Why have people deviated so far away from His righteous path? Why have they forgotten about His divine doctrines?

I thought I had this part of my faith covered. Now, as I get into my car and ask it to take me to work, I have put aside the usual questions of faith to search for the cause of humanity's sad situation.

I'm not proud of all the choices I've made. During my college years, I entertained selfish and materialistic thoughts. I wanted to do crazy things, to become a millionaire, to buy a multimillion-dollar house, to impress people with my intelligence, even to travel to Yahire and to leave behind God's gift to humanity—love.

My father patiently tried to help me return to the right path by sharing his vast knowledge of human values and his selfless love. However, it wasn't until he passed away that I started considering the truth about life. I and my father were exceptionally close. We were always doing things together, visiting places, and learning about life.

When he passed away, I was at a loss. I no longer had his guidance, his company, or his love. My father was the kind of man who would enter a room full of homeless people and give away clothes and all his pocket money with a smile. Everyone loved him because of his patient demeanor and his loving eyes; those eyes spoke a language only beautiful people would understand. When he passed away, a hole suddenly opened in my heart, and I had to find something to fill it.

The Sunday after my father's funeral, I decided to go to church with my mother. It was her idea, and I thought no harm could be done by visiting the place where my father spent most of his time. I was angry at the world without a good reason. The hole in my heart had deepened, but I wouldn't talk to people about this because I knew what they would say.

By the time we arrived at the church, many members of the flock had gathered for the service. Though we weren't late, it seemed like we were. Father always hurried to arrive early so he could meet all his friends and discuss current events. He was the one who inspired me to keep up with the news from around the world. He always said it was our duty to know where help was most needed and to try our best to offer it when no one else would.

When the service ended, I felt like a heavy burden had been lifted from my chest. I had finally gotten in touch with God and His divine teachings as my father had done. This was a revelation to me. God's words filled the hole in my heart, and I felt closer to my father than ever before, even though he wasn't there to guide me.

Now, three years later, I'm heading for work and facing one of the biggest existential crises of my life in my struggle to find an answer to Lisa's question.

I rub my eyes and realize I am on the highway. I'm behind schedule and ask my self-driving car to hurry down the street to find a parking spot before it's too late. I'm never late for work, and I intend to keep that streak going. I set a timer for my arrival at work, and the car switches routes. My mind keeps drifting back to my earlier thoughts. I wouldn't mind pondering these questions in the comfort of my home. Now, however, I must focus on getting to work on time.

I turn on the radio. It's a miracle that people still use the radio in the year 2072, but it's nothing like it was when I was younger. Nowadays, internet access is free throughout the world, and cars can connect with and distribute the web even on the road. Everything is plugged into the net, so there is a huge selection of radio shows from around the world.

My first choice is a local news station that picks a small number of news items and comments on them. My favorite commentator sounds incredibly frenzied this morning.

"For all of our listeners tuning in now, the United States Department of Core and Earth Sciences has a major announcement planned for later today. We don't know what it entails, but most experts around the world believe it involves the start of the infamous Mantle Project."

The Mantle Project? It sounds so familiar. I think I've heard of it before.

The man on the radio offers just enough information about the project and its origins to keep his listeners interested.

"According to trustworthy sources," he says, "the first hint of the Mantle Project came two years ago, shortly after the department was created. Information culled from heavily redacted files found on the dark web revealed the project's goal.

One person investigating the Mantle Project says, 'The department is planning a series of planet-level operations on Earth's mantle.' Little has been revealed to the public, but we're expecting news later today. I don't know about you, but I get goose bumps every time I read this report. What planet-level operations are the world's nations planning?"

I share the host's concern. However, I'm not in the right state of mind to process this announcement. Tonight, when I return home, I'll have to discuss this with Catherine. Yes, that's the right thing to do. Now it's time for work.

The car slows down and tells me I will reach my destination in ten seconds. At last, I have arrived at the Bank of America on Ocean Avenue in Brooklyn—my favorite location. It's still early in the day, but I already feel exhausted because my mind has been working overtime.

Coffee and one of the croissants Mary always brings to work sound like a good choice right now. These treats won't help me sort out the confusion I feel, but the sugar and caffeine can keep me alert and focused throughout the day. I usually try to abstain from these indulgences, but today I think my deviation will be excused.

I check the inside of my car before leaving for the office. As the car tells me that I have arrived and that it will park nearby, I see George and Andrew engaged in a conversation on the way to work.

"Do you really think this Mantle Project is a good idea, Andrew? We've colonized a new planet, a great feat in itself, we're preparing more missions to Mars, and we've made countless technological advances, but this thing sounds awful to me."

George is a man after my own heart. We met when I got my job as an account manager at the bank. We immediately became best friends. He's the guy I go to when I want to have a sensible discussion about any subject. He's a fellow Christian and understands my mind-set better than others do.

"This is just nonsense," Andrew says. "Back in the day, your children would have to pay to access the internet, and overpopulation was a global scourge. Progress is good only when it's fast and radical. If people were afraid to experiment, we wouldn't have penicillin and many other miraculous medicines, and we wouldn't have mastered space travel to the extent we have now. Yeah, I guess progress can sometimes be harmful, but that's the price we have to pay if we want to make improvements."

Andrew is the new guy. He's in his mid-twenties and is an unrepentant bachelor. His mind-set clearly reflects the mentality of people his age. Raised amid constant change in a time when people are blind to how their choices affect the planet, they feel uncomfortable when they believe the world isn't moving fast enough.

He's a great kid and a capable worker, but sometimes he can get a bit impatient, and it shows in the way he speaks.

They nod at me in unison and stop to greet me. I have the feeling they want to pull me into their discussion and to make me the arbiter. I don't particularly like this idea, but I don't seem to have a choice.

George is the first one to greet me. "Morning, Tommy. How are you doing today?"

It feels like he's expecting me to bring up the subject myself, but I'm not sure I want to, not after hearing them argue all the way in here.

"Good morning, George. Good morning, Andrew," I say. The youngster simply jerks his head instead of replying to me. "I'm great, thank you. How about you? Is everything okay?"

Oh no. I shouldn't have said that. The words slipped from my lips before I got the chance to consider them. Now it's too late. I'll have to live with the consequences.

"I don't know. I trust you have heard about the imminent announcement from the Department of Core and Earth Sciences," George says.

"It has been all over the news, George," Andrew says, seizing the opportunity to continue their argument. "Of course he has heard about it. And I'm sure he agrees it's a necessary step in human evolution. This Mantle Project is the most ambitious human endeavor after the colonization of Yahire and Mars. Tommy is reasonable enough to understand the difference between necessity and choice." He presumes I am on his side, but I wouldn't jump to conclusions if I were him.

George is ready to say something in his defense, but the words come rushing out of my mouth before he can speak. "I'm sorry, Andrew, but I'll have to disagree with you. I understand the difference between necessity and choice, but I don't think meddling with the planet's natural mechanisms is in any way a necessity."

The young man heaves a deep sigh and shrugs his shoulders as we enter the building. "I don't understand you. Progress has become an important part of our culture. Why are you trying so hard to resist it?" Andrew says, mostly talking to himself.

George finally gets the chance to speak his mind. "We're not against progress, Andrew. We're against playing God and trying to mess with the natural order of things. We're not meant to tarnish the gifts generously offered to us by nature," he says.

I realize I have been nodding in agreement when I see Andrew looking at me with disappointment on his face. "This debate is worthless. You're so set in your ways and in your values that you don't understand the need for change," Andrew says. He sounds troubled and misunderstood. However, I can't share his opinion, not after seeing God's impact on my life.

Andrew turns to the left in silence and rides the elevator to the upper floors. He's a good kid and I'm sure he won't let something like this get in the way of our friendship. But I have the feeling he's way too deep into his ambitions to understand our point of view. Now that we're alone, George suddenly seems exhausted, probably the same way I look.

We enter the coffee room; George looks like he's in desperate need of a cup of coffee. After his tussle with Andrew, I wonder whether he shouldn't refrain. But our shift starts now, so I can't judge him if he wants the energy surge coffee offers.

As on every other morning, the line at the coffee machine extends all the way around the room and ends close to the entrance. Fortunately, no one is picky when it comes to coffee. People want caffeine to survive the next eight hours. Some workers man the registers in the front office and have to deal with customers, who can be irritating and troublesome.

George and I have been working in the banking industry for quite some time, and it has made us a bit more skeptical than we were in the past. Nowadays, everything starts and ends in a bank. Businesses rise and fall. People come to start their lives and to reclaim them. Even children have to learn about the importance of money and of the banking system.

But that overemphasis doesn't matter enough to make me leave the bank. My family needs the stability that my job as an account manager offers, so I'm glad I work here. Lately, however, George doesn't seem to share my opinion.

"I can't stand this anymore, Tommy. Yes, Andrew is a great guy, and yes, we have had some good times together as pals, but he's starting to get on my nerves. I don't understand why he always has to make such a fuss about technology and progress."

I share his opinion to a certain degree, but I can't blame Andrew for being who he is. Unlike George and me, he grew up in a family of agnostics, people who don't believe in God and His grace but in the "great unknown" as I've heard Andrew describe it. And I accept that, because he doesn't make a fuss over the fact that I'm a Christian. But George wants him to move that extra mile toward initiation, to make him see that the only true religion is God.

Lost in my thoughts, I realize I have to reply to George. "He is who he is, George. You can't change people by forcing your beliefs on them. They have to find the truth on their own. Faith isn't a pill you take to cure your ignorance. Faith is looking inside yourself and seeing light and warmth, truth and love. You have to stop getting so worked up over Andrew. When he's ready, he'll turn around. You'll see."

George doesn't seem sure, though. "He's not that young anymore, Tommy. Your kids already know the importance of faith and of our beliefs and values. My kids do, too. All I can say is that sometimes I wish he would stay silent for a moment and listen to me. I'm sure I could make him see the truth."

I shrug and decide to change the subject. When George is like this, he's not very good company, and after everything that's happened today, I need a friend beside me to talk it out, not a fellow Christian philosophizing about the existence of God.

"Now that you mention it, Lisa and Manna are growing up to be two sharp-witted young ladies. Do you know what Lisa asked me this morning?" George shakes his head with an empty look on his face; his thoughts still preoccupy him. "She looked me in the eye and asked me to tell her where God is. Not only that, but she couldn't sleep all night because she was too intent on finding the answer to her question. Isn't that great?"

Something I said has peaked George's curiosity. He is now giving me his complete attention. "Really? And what did you tell her?"

"I said God lives all around us." George nods, but I can see a hint of disagreement in his eyes. "What? You think I'm wrong?"

"No, no. On the contrary. I believe you're right. More than right. I think you have expressed the truth of God's existence in the best way possible. It's just ... I feel something is missing. Yes, God resides in people's hearts, and yes, He's the Light that guides us on the bumpy path called life. But lately, why is it that I can't feel His presence anywhere else but at the Sunday service?"

This sounds like an admission of sin. George feels guilty that he can't sense God everywhere around him. And he should, shouldn't he?

"What do you mean?" I ask with keen interest.

"I don't know. Take this place, for example. We know there are many religious people in this room. They are not only religious but law-abiding. We all follow the rules; we can discern good from bad, and yet something feels wrong. It seems like we have deviated from God's path and are only trying to fulfill our ambitions. Supporting our families has come to mean buying expensive things that we don't really need."

His words pierce my heart. His reasoning is almost identical to mine. Just this morning, I was thinking the same thing.

I must seem worried; George pokes my forearm, and I snap out of my thoughts.

"Fill your cup, Tommy. People are waiting," he says.

***

# Chapter 3

## The Announcement

*Same setting*
*Narrator: Tommy Russell*

During the last thirty minutes, my eyes kept wandering off to my watch. I have done barely five hours of work in an eight-hour shift because I couldn't focus enough to produce more results. The manager stopped by to ask me to compile information for a case, but I can't remember the details. Fortunately, he left a file with all the relevant documents on my desk; otherwise, I would be doomed.

I didn't see George during lunch, which made things worse. He had to skip the lunch break to keep up with the workload assigned to him. He had been on sick leave for more than a week, and the manager gave him strict deadlines for the projects that accumulated while he was out. So I was left alone with my doubts and worries throughout the day. But that wasn't the only problem.

When I approached Andrew, he purposely avoided me. Though he is young, I thought it was beneath him to do that. I still can't understand why he got so upset over our beliefs. Surely it has something to do with this announcement by the Department of Core and Earth Sciences later today. After all this thinking about God and religion and faith, I had forgotten about this.

People keep talking about the Mantle Project. New information is leaked to the public at a steady rate, but I'm not sure if any of it is true. Maybe the department wants to announce an extension of financing by the government or something totally unrelated to this ominous project. And why do I worry? They're scientists. If they have decided to undertake an assignment like this, they surely have considered every possibility and are probably 100 percent sure there will be no mistake in the process.

I let out a sigh. Ten minutes until I can leave, but it feels like an eternity. Why do I keep trying to convince myself that this project is good? There's nothing good about people meddling with God's work. They have never succeeded in the past, and they won't succeed now. My head is a giant caldron of stray thoughts, bubbling up, and threatening to burn everything in their wake.

My focus shifts between Lisa's question and George's. Something tells me that they are connected and that the answer to my question lies between them. However, I can't grasp it, not before I talk to these two people again. Unfortunately, that would defeat the purpose of finding the truth by myself, using my own strength.

With five minutes on the clock, my concentration becomes intense, and I revisit both questions. Lisa asked me the kind of question only small children in their innocence pose. Where is God? My answer, the one I found after years of talking with my father and with other people about God, was that He lives among us.

Still, when I spoke with George earlier today, he told me that although he wholeheartedly agrees with me, he feels guilty about not feeling God around him anymore. He probably meant that he didn't feel God in the hearts of other people. He said that even though he believes people remain good, follow the laws, and pray for God to keep them safe, they seem to have forgotten something important about God.

The rustle of chairs on the floor makes me snap to attention. It's time. My shift has ended. I'm free for the next three days, plenty of time to sort out these questions.

I quickly gather my things and grab my bag. I'm ready to rush to the exit and go straight home. I can talk to George after this Sunday's service.

Leaving my cubicle, I bump into Andrew. He puts on a mask of fake joy the moment he sees me. The change is so swift and delicate that I almost miss it.

He can't avoid me this time, so he decides to make the first move. "Well, hi there, Tommy. How was work?" he asks, walking away from me, trying to keep our conversation short and casual.

But I've had enough. I spent the whole day trying to bridge the gap between our modern times and our faith in the one true God, and I feel offended by his bad behavior during the lunch break. I grab his arm. He stops and turns in surprise, shocked that I've done such a thing.

"Can I speak to you for a moment?" I ask.

He withdraws his hand in an abrupt manner that shows his irritation. "Yes, of course. You could have just asked," he says, motioning to show me the way to his side. "Tell me what's on your mind. Is something at work bothering you?"

Andrew is smart and quick to read a situation. He knows I didn't stop him to discuss work. "I sense hostility coming from you, Andrew. I just want to talk and to resolve this misunderstanding before going home. That's all," I say.

He lowers his eyes and tenses his shoulders; he's on alert. Why doesn't he want to talk about this issue? I thought he was an open guy, someone who promoted discussion and tolerance of all opinions. What has made him so hostile to our views?

"I guess you're right, Tommy. I'm a bit upset. It's just that you and George sometimes close your eyes to the truth, and it seems like you're doing this deliberately. You can keep your cool in every situation, but George has become a fanatic lately. Everything relating to progress seems to irk him, and I don't understand it.

"If it weren't for technology and progress, people would be dying by the millions. Shit, we would still be in the Middle Ages if we hadn't discovered electricity. Why doesn't he get that?"

In an outburst of anger, Andrew finally seems to make some sense. He thinks we are following our faith like horses wearing blinkers. In a sense, he's right. Many of the faithful mistake fanaticism for belief and cause trouble for people around them. But we're not like that, and Andrew should have known better than to put us in the same category.

"Look, I understand your frustration. George and I can sometimes sound like stubborn old men who don't talk about anything except our faith and religion. But it's not that simple, and I trust you know that. Religion is a big part of our daily lives. I pray every night to thank God for keeping me safe and well, and when I wake up I pray for a good day at work and for prosperity. We're not against progress and technology, but we're against materialism and unchecked change. And this Mantle Project sounds too radical."

His expression softens as he listens to me. It seems like this matter has been bothering him the whole day, too. Andrew is a sensible kid, albeit a bit less guided. It's not his fault, though, and neither are his parents to blame. The whole world is misguided, and it's up to us to make it better. Seeing Andrew leave with a smile on his face makes me feel considerably better. We discussed our views a bit more and talked about how they could complement each other, but it was getting late (we'd been there for half an hour) and almost everyone had left the building.

I didn't convince him that the Mantle Project is bad or at least unnecessary, but that is a discussion for another time. I will now ask my car to pick me up while I walk toward it. The parking lot is empty. I'm the only one here, a lonely man in modern times. Talking with Andrew and righting a wrong made me feel important, like I offered a valuable service to humanity.

And that reminds me of my father.

He used to do this kind of thing every day, and when he couldn't, he would work in his garden so he would have food to share with his neighbors. Back then, there was no doubt that God was living in people's hearts, because I could see that so clearly in my father. I miss him so much, today more than usual, enough to order my car to take me to my mother's house.

On the way, I call Catherine to tell her I'll be late for dinner. She picks up the phone almost immediately. She sounds upset and worried. Something is going on. "Tommy? Darling, where are you?" she asks.

"I'm just leaving work, sweetheart. What's wrong?"

"Tommy, you have to get here as soon as possible. They have revealed the Mantle Project, and it isn't good. It's no good at all."

I can barely hear Catherine amid the cacophony of voices around her. She must be in her burger joint, busy selling the best cheeseburgers in the city.

"I'll be there in a minute, honey. Are the girls with you?" I ask.

"Yes. You won't believe it, Tommy. I don't believe they're going ahead with this," she says.

I'm getting more worried by the minute. I'm well past mere curiosity. Now I have to know what this Mantle Project is about, and I have to find out fast.

"Okay, okay. I'm on my way. See you soon," I say and disconnect.

For Catherine to sound so worried, the announcement must have been huge. On the way to her shop, I try to guess what the Mantle Project entails, and why Catherine is so troubled. Is it indeed something connected to Earth's mantle, or is this the name of a project that has nothing to do with Earth? Not knowing kills me.

I'm not sure I understand what is going on, but as soon as I see the big line outside the building where Catherine's shop is located, I know it's serious. People from all around the neighborhood run toward the only TV screen big enough for all of them to see. "Hey, park yourself. I will call you in ten," I tell the car. Soon I'm squeezing my way inside the shop. Clamor and confusion prevail. I can barely hear myself think over the voices of people arguing.

Finally, I see Catherine peering through the crowd, surrounded by her employees, who will protect her and the girls in case of a riot. The moment she spots me, she calls out to me. I'm quickly by her side, and Lisa and Manna launch their bodies into my arms.

"Daddy!" Lisa says, tears streaming from her eyes. Manna is crying so hard I can't make sense of her words.

"Oh, thank God you're here, Tommy. I was afraid something happened to you at work," Catherine says. Her eyes are red and swollen. She must have been crying, too.

"What in the world has happened? Why are all these people here?" I ask her.

"It's about the announcement, Tommy. You won't believe it. Oh God, we're doomed," she mumbles.

"Calm down, Catherine. Please tell me what's going on. What did they announce?"

"They're going to tear into Earth's core, Tommy. They're going to move Earth's mantle to unearth more resources through some weird technology," my wife says, trembling. "God help us all."

# Chapter 4

# A Petrifying Moment

*Same setting*
*Narrator: Tommy Russell*

I've never seen Cat so shaken before. I don't quite understand what's going on, but she is in no condition to bring me up to speed. Clamor and chaos reign inside and outside the shop; people are yelling at each other, trying to get the upper hand in a situation that seems unmanageable. Why has the Department of Core and Earth Sciences decided to do something so radical? What is the Mantle Project? Why does everyone sound so afraid?

The word *afraid* pops into my head as one of my wife's employees checks up on us. We are crouched behind the counter, a nice hiding spot, especially with Lisa and Manna here. The counter offers us protection from the upheaval outside, but it's not good enough, not when the tension in this place seems to rise every minute.

Darin, the eighteen-year-old employee, trembles as he tells me, "I haven't seen anything like this before. People went from cool to crazy in seconds after the announcement. It's like someone brainwashed them or something."

"Neither have I, Darin. It's terrifying how far people are willing to go to make their point," I reply.

He nods and reluctantly returns to his position by the counter. I notice his hands shaking and his eyes searching for a way out of here. But with more people rushing inside, it's impossible for him to escape without getting injured.

Catherine notices my concern over the young boy. "Tell Darin to get down here with us. You can take his place if you want. We'll be okay down here," she says.

I nod and smile at her. This woman can read my mind.

I rise to my feet and nudge Darin in the shoulder. He jumps before turning to face me. He's just a kid, after all, and we adults have to protect kids.

"Get behind the counter with Catherine and the girls. I'll take over from here," I tell Darin.

"No, it's okay. Really, Mr. Russell, I'm okay. You don't have to worry about me." His lips twitch and his eyes glisten. He can't take this anymore.

"Look, I'm not doing this for you, buddy. I'm older and folks around here know me and my wife. They're not going to try anything funny with me here. And even if they do, I can manage better than you. You're my wife's employee. I don't want you to return home roughed up." He's ready to complain, but I don't give him the opportunity. "Go, Darin. The crowd will disperse pretty soon and we can all go home."

The boy gulps and tries to thank me, but he's too shaken to talk. He just nods and rushes behind the counter. I see him off before I turn around and walk outside the counter. Around me, I see familiar faces, mostly people who work for Cat. I've met and talked with every one of them, but for the first time I understand that I don't really know them.

On my left, Pan Hayes, our counter person, stands firm, weighing both opinions and trying to find an answer. She doesn't want to meddle, but I can see a fiery purpose burning in her eyes. Pan puts logic above all, and she does it in a way that clearly fits her post.

Many customers address their complaints to her, and many of the scenes inside the shop involve her. After all, she's the one who handles payments. She keeps her hands crossed over her chest and stays out of the crowd's reach. She knows that in a riot, she can't do much except run.

On my right side, I see two siblings who work as waiters. They're twins, and if they weren't a brother and a sister, I would have trouble telling them apart. Preston and Kelley Mullins are in their late twenties and aspire to become movie directors. I have told them time and time again they're living in the wrong city if they want to chase their dreams, but they always respond with a simple, fatalistic argument: "You can't rush destiny. When it's our time, we'll know."

They're great people and have been working in Cat's shop for five years. Overly sensitive, especially reacting to customers' rude comments, they often get in trouble. However, they're doing a great job of appeasing the crowd. The people close to them are less rowdy than those outside. They're discussing the announcement in a peaceful circle at one end of the counter.

Seeing the crowd won't leave anytime soon, I decide to move closer to Pan to get her opinion on the matter. I know nothing about her views and values, but she's reasonable enough to see the difference between madness and progress.

We're all standing close to the counter, so it's fairly easy to approach her, though I have to push aside some of the people fighting with each other. When she spots me, Pan smiles and waves.

"Tommy, what are you doing here? I thought you were hiding with Catherine and the girls behind the counter. Is everything okay?" she asks me with concern in her voice.

"Don't worry about it. I took over for Darin. He's too young to have to face an angry mob." Pan shakes her head in agreement while sweeping the room with her eyes. "What happened here? Catherine told me it had something to do with the announcement, but I never expected that would drive people over the edge." I'm shouting in an effort to be heard over the crowd.

Pan looks me in the eye and shrugs; she appears exhausted. "The world turned upside down in seconds, Tommy. I was behind the register, ready to close up shop and head home when it started. You know the drill. I signaled the twins to give the last call, and I started putting the palm scanners and tablets inside the locker." She stops to clear her throat. Once a habitual smoker, Pan has a hoarse voice. She quit smoking many years ago, but her hands twitch and move close to her face; nicotine would have made this mess bearable.

"I had heard that the Department of Core and Earth Sciences was planning to make an announcement today, but I didn't pay too much attention to the news. In the last few years, they have announced something 'groundbreaking' every other week, and I thought this was one of their usual tedious reports. Who wants to know every little detail about their goddamned research?"

I have the urge to ask her to use better language, but if there is one thing God would condemn, the Mantle Project sounds like a good candidate.

"At first, we had the table holos on low volume. It's not like anyone gives a damn if they are high or low. They use their phones to watch TV all the time, so it's not like they notice. One guy sitting in the corner booth started yelling for us to turn up the volume on the main screen so he could hear the announcement.

"You know me, Tommy. I can snap like a toothpick when I'm in a bad mood, but I wasn't going to fight a client over the volume of a holo screen. So I decided to let it pass and to do him a favor. That's when everything started going wrong. When the announcement ended, the first customer got up to his feet and started shouting that it was about time something like the Mantle Project happened.

"You know these loudmouths; he didn't stop there. He started asking other customers their opinions, searching for an audience. Unfortunately, he found it when another customer got annoyed at all his blabbering. They started arguing. By the time Catherine returned with the girls, the whole shop was quarreling over the Mantle Project, and people had gathered outside to share their opinions, turning this location into a nasty public forum."

I've known Pan for many years and I've never seen her react like this before. Every time I've visited the shop, we've shared a few words, mostly talking about politics. We've never had a full-fledged conversation. Pan is not only angry but afraid. She's trying her best to hide it from the raging eyes everywhere around her. I don't know the details of the announcement, but for people to react the way they did, it must be terrible news.

"Why you didn't separate those first two?" I ask Pan. "If you had stopped them, nothing more would have happened, at least not to this extent."

I didn't mean to be offensive, but my girls are hiding behind a counter in the corner of the shop, shaking like leaves. I'm upset.

Pan isn't as quick to jump the gun as I am. "Tommy, I've been working in this shop for more than five years now. I was here right after sweet Manna came to life and Catherine was a sack of hormones unable to run this place on her own. Do you think I didn't try? That the twins didn't try? I don't know what evil got into these people, but every time any of us tried to calm them down, things got worse."

Somewhere amid the multitude of voices filling the room, I hear Kelley and Preston behind me, saying almost in unison, "Darin? Darin, are you okay? What's wrong, buddy?"

My instincts kick in; I don't have a good feeling about this. A woman's shrill scream proves me right. It comes from the spot where I left Catherine and the girls. My blood freezes in my veins. I squeeze through the tight passages between the combative customers. Those I shove aside grumble, but I don't stop moving.

The woman who screamed was Kelley. With dread in her eyes, she stares at a tense Darin, who is clutching her arm. "Let go of her, Darin! Come on, man. You're hurting her!" Preston tells Darin, but the boy seems to have fallen into a trance.

I still have no clear visual of Catherine and the girls, but it doesn't matter right now. I have to help Kelley free herself after Darin's sudden assault.

The boy's appearance is alarming. The whites of his eyes are showing, his legs are convulsing, and he's lying helpless on the floor. He grips Kelley's right arm, stopping the flow of blood. What's most disturbing, though, is his mouth. It's open wide in a voiceless scream.

Preston sees me in the distance. "Mr. Russell!" he shouts.

I rush to his side. "What happened?"

"I don't know. One moment, uh ... well, we were talking until Darin came. And, um, I ... no, he started talking to Kelley, telling her he was hearing a voice or something. Kelley thought the boy was in shock, but then he fell to the ground and started having spasms. Kelley tried to help him, but they ended up like this. Mr. Russell, please do something. He's going to break her arm."

There's no time to reply to Preston. A minute later, I'm standing behind Darin, holding his head in my hands. When my hand passes around his neck and I touch his skin, he suddenly closes his mouth and his eyes return to normal. Staring into space, he whispers, "It's the end. The time has come."

He repeats the phrase five more times and then stops.

***

# Chapter 5

# Dorothy

*Later that evening*
*Narrator: Tommy Russell*

I can't sleep. My brain has gone numb from exhaustion, but I can't close my eyes. So many things happened tonight, and I can't rest without knowing what's going on. Disturbed by the night's events, Catherine didn't want to discuss the Mantle Project and what it would mean for life on Earth. She especially didn't want to discuss what happened in the burger joint. "We'll talk about everything tomorrow," she told me when we arrived home. "I need to rest." That was all she said.

But I can't rest, not before finding out more about the Mantle Project.

Catherine has gone to sleep in Manna's bedroom. It's time I research the issues that have been bugging me since earlier this evening. I won't be sleeping anytime soon, so I might as well read everything I can find about the Mantle Project.

I lay my back against the bed's head and make myself comfortable. I grab my tablet from its usual spot by the side of the bed. I whirl the screen, push the power button, and hear Dorothy greet me.

"Good evening, Tommy. How may I assist you this wonderful evening?" she intones.

"Good evening, Dorothy. I want everything you can find about the Mantle Project," I reply.

"One moment while I calibrate the best results for your inquiry."

Dorothy is part of a line of artificial intelligence entities that have been developed to make personal computers and tablets more user-friendly. She can use many parameters to find the best results. She understands human speech and will even argue with the main user, citing credible sources from the worldwide web.

While at first I was against using technology that had the capacity to think, to learn, and to take initiatives, Dorothy soon became an important member of our family due to her kind personality and her eagerness to help us. Recently, we updated her to babysit Lisa and Manna when we are away. Catherine doesn't trust this new iteration of Dorothy's program, so we rarely use it, but it's a nice option to have.

Dorothy releases a distinctive bell sound when the report is ready. "There are 4,239,100 results. I picked the top hundred in terms of credibility, popularity, and your online habits," she says.

"Thank you, Dorothy. Rest for now. I'll call you if I need you again."

Dorothy's top hundred list is usually the best result all around. I click on an article headlined "The Truth behind the Infamous Mantle Project: Is It Humanity's Last Chance?"

I sweep through the first lines, ignoring all unnecessary information and focusing on what's important. The author of the article has a firm opinion about the Mantle Project and about the latest moves by the Department of Core and Earth Sciences. Peter Bob writes:

> The Mantle Project means the redistribution of earth through radical and intrusive methods. In short, the Department of Core and Earth Sciences wants to turn the planet's mantle upside down to tap resources like oil and minerals.
>
> During its announcement, the department showcased an analytical model of the project. About a million people will be moved from the points of

interest for three months. During that time, a crew will install machines in the ground that will induce the violent movement of Earth's tectonic plates and the redistribution of the land.

We're looking at the most extreme planet-reshaping in the history of our kind. It's too early to know the immediate effects of the Mantle Project, but countless people around the world, including me, already feel strongly about the government's decision. If you ask me, we're looking at humanity's latest screw-up, a failure that can easily mean the fall of our mother planet and the extinction of the human race.

My hand was cupped over my mouth as I read the article. The last line haunts me and makes it hard for me to breathe. I knew this project wouldn't be pretty or even practical, but I had hoped the department wouldn't take its ambitions this far.

There's a reason God doesn't want us to get our hands on the limited resources that remain under Earth's mantle. There's a reason we have badly damaged this planet with global warming and with all the environmental catastrophes we produce. The reason is hubris, the kind that destroys a planet and kills millions of people, the kind that God punishes.

The fall of our species will come by our own hands.

I have to discuss this with someone. My only option is Dorothy.

"Dorothy, can I ask you something?" I say. I know she can't turn me down, but that doesn't mean I can't be kind to her.

"Of course, Tommy. I'm all ears," she responds.

"What's your opinion about this Mantle Project? I'm sure you've read all four million hits on the web. What do you think are the chances the project will be a failure?"

"One moment while I constitute a logical argument. Estimated time of result: one minute, twenty-three seconds."

I sigh and place the piece of hardware on the side of the bed. My bladder is suddenly ready to burst, so I rush to the bathroom while I wait for Dorothy to calculate her answer. On my way back, I pass to check on the ladies. I carefully open the door. My wife and the youngest member of our family are fast asleep. Cat embraces Manna's little body in a tight hug. They've been through a lot, all three of my girls.

I don't want to disturb Lisa, even though if she's anything like me, she's still awake. The moment a streak of light enters the room, her tiny head jerks in surprise.

"Dad? Is that you?" Lisa asks, her voice filled with worry.

"Yes, honey. It's me," I reply quickly, tiptoeing into the room. "Did I wake you up?"

She shakes her head. "No. I couldn't sleep anyway."

Lisa sits up, her body blanketed to her waist; she doesn't dare leave the safety of her bed. Her eyes gleam in the hallway's light. I can see something is bothering her. I sit close to my daughter.

"What's wrong, dear? Why can't you sleep?" I ask.

Lisa is always quick to answer, sometimes even mixing up her words as she hurries to make her point. This time, though, she has lowered her head and tangled her fingers in an anxious knot.

"Why were people in the shop so mean today, Dad?"

I sigh. Another difficult question to add to the always expanding list. "Well, it's not easy to answer without confusing you, but I'll try. When adults get anxious or excited about something, they can't control their feelings. Imagine that all grown-ups have big bottles in their bodies filled with their feelings. Like soda, when you shake them, the feelings bubble up until they explode. That's what happened today. Many feeling-bottles exploded at the same time."

Lisa nods as I speak. It seems my explanation is good enough to answer her question. But as usual she doesn't end there.

"But why didn't God stop their feeling bottles from exploding? If He lives everywhere around us, He must have been in the shop with us. Why didn't He help us?"

I don't know if I should blame myself for answering her previous question without first consulting Catherine, but I'm not going to make the same mistake twice.

I draw closer to her and pat her on the head. "It's too late to talk about God, Lisa. I promise you I'll answer all your questions soon. Now you have to get to sleep. Tomorrow is Saturday, so don't worry. We have all weekend to figure this out. Okay?"

She doesn't like it, but she knows she doesn't have a choice. Lisa lies on her bed. Catherine is usually the one who makes the good-night calls, but I think Lisa needs extra love tonight. Before leaving the room, I lean over her and give her a kiss on the forehead.

"Good night, Lisa. I love you," I whisper.

"Love you too, Dad," she mutters and turns to the other side, her eyes drowsy.

My chest feels heavy; her words weigh on me like stones. I know I did nothing wrong, but still I feel guilty because I was unable to protect her from having that terrible experience. I head back to my bedroom. My eyes fall on the hanging clock. It's past 1:00 a.m.

I return to the bed and pick up my tablet; Dorothy is waiting for me.

"Welcome back, Tommy. I have an answer to your question. Are you ready to listen to it?" she asks.

"Of course. Shoot."

The wallpaper of my tablet vanishes, and Dorothy's digital persona appears in its place. Her hair is black and her eyes brown; she is the image of an accessible and likable person. Dorothy uses her persona when she wants to make a user more comfortable.

She smiles before beginning her response.

"Question number one: what's my opinion of the Mantle Project? The Mantle Project is a necessary effort for humanity's survival on planet Earth. The statistics show a quick decline of Earth's resources. Oil provides 47 percent of humanity's energy needs, and technology remains heavily dependent on it. Oil is a nonrecyclable resource, unlike solar and wind power. Humanity has achieved an unprecedented high by meeting 49.5 percent of its everyday needs using green energy, but that remains insufficient. The Mantle Project aims to change that and to offer humans more time to better utilize and integrate new energy technologies. Besides oil, the project is expected to result in the discovery of vast quantities of minerals now considered rare. Complementary benefits would include better agriculture and systematic ways of dumping nonbiodegradable waste into Earth's core.

"Now to answer your second question: what do I think the chances are that the Mantle Project will be a failure? Unfortunately, I can't answer that. I lack the significant amount of data needed to calculate the chances of a failure."

She smiles again and waits for my next command.

"Thank you, Dorothy. That's enough for today," I tell her. "Let's hope when you have an answer to that question it's not too late." No matter how much I want to stay up and discover more about the Mantle Project, I can't keep my eyes open. I have to sleep.

I put aside my tablet and rest my head on the pillow. My strength quickly leaves my body, and I can do nothing but contemplate the events of the past day—Lisa's question about God's whereabouts; the heated debate about the Mantle Project at the bank; Darin's seizure and that end-of-times phrase he kept repeating.

"It's the end. The time has come." What did that mean? Why did he suddenly start repeating that phrase?

I turn on my other side and stare at my tablet. I'm too tired to get up, but it doesn't matter. This is a simple question, one Dorothy can easily answer.

"Dorothy, one last thing. Can you explain the phrase 'It's the end. The time has come'?"

"Of course, Tommy. 'It's the end. The time has come' suggests that the purpose for which a project was started has been accomplished. Or it may mean that the purpose for which a project was started has ended."

"What did you say?" I ask.

She repeats her response.

Although she cannot explain the deeper meaning of what the boy said, my sixth sense tells me something I wouldn't normally believe. Those few words now send a jolt through my body. Did the teenager herald the future of mankind?

\*\*\*

*Later that morning*

I couldn't sleep; I was too restless to close my eyes and relax. Darin's phrase swirled in my head all night like a spinning top. I haven't stayed up all night since I was a teenager, and back then, I was always with company.

I have never fancied the company of darkness. Even when I was younger, I made sure I woke up early, and I enjoyed taking long walks around town before going to school. My father used to compliment me on my lifestyle. He thought light was God's ultimate gift to mankind. It was the first thing He created and the first thing He praised. My father spoke of light in a metaphorical rather than a physical sense—light meaning enlightenment and knowledge of the unseen.

The door of my bedroom is shut; that's probably Catherine's doing. She knows how to take care of me. Muffled voices are coming from the living room, which means the girls are awake. I hope they had a better night's sleep than I did.

I get up and head to the bathroom. I brush my teeth and wash my face before going downstairs. The cold water on my face does a good job of waking me up, but I still need coffee if I want to function properly. The girls are using their augreals to play with their favorite cartoon characters.

The augreals, a pair of augmented-reality glasses, is another one of the modern-day gadgets I didn't approve of before they became an important part of our lives. I usually refrain from using these glasses, but they're perfect if we want to visualize anything in three dimensional space, for example, watch a movie together as a family.

Catherine is using her glasses. She seems dejected, so I guess she's checking today's headlines. She may appear unperturbed, but Cat is as worried as I am. We share the same opinion when it comes to religion and technology.

Cat is the first one to notice my presence when I reach the base of the staircase; she raises her head and shares a mirthless smile with me. "Good morning, sleepyhead. Even Lisa got up earlier than you today."

I ruffle my hair with my left hand while I try to hold back a yawn with my right. Before replying, I head to the coffee machine and fill a cup with black coffee. Then I sit next to her at the table.

"Did you sleep well?" I ask.

"Not great. You?" I don't reply; my expression tells her everything she needs to know. "You didn't sleep at all," she says matter-of-factly.

I nod and attempt to fight off another yawn. "I tried to sleep, but then I had the bright idea to have Dorothy research the Mantle Project. And if that wasn't enough, I also had her translate that phrase Darin kept repeating yesterday."

"You better check today's headlines, Tommy," Catherine says.

She raises her pointer and aligns it with her glasses. Then she pinches the air, grabbing the file digitally. With a sweeping move, she sends it over to me. A ringing sound comes from my phone. I retrieve the phone from the kitchen counter. I can't part with my cup of coffee, not until I take a sip and start to regain my strength.

Most modern phones come with holographic projectors, so it's easy to check holo files even without using augreal glasses. With the press of a button, the image of a newspaper pops up in midair. It looks like a real newspaper and I can interact with it like it's a real newspaper, but it floats unnaturally over my phone for everyone to see.

I find what I'm searching for on the front page.

"Increased Levels of Violence Observed Last Night after Announcement by Core and Earth Sciences Department. Experts Demand More Clarity about Mantle Project's Intricate Workings."

I heave a sigh and turn to face Catherine. "That means we weren't the only ones dealing with angry crowds last evening. Does it say anything about why it happened?"

"Yes, but it's mere speculation. The story says the mixed feelings of fear and excitement experienced by the people confronting each other caused unnatural events. The story also mentions some people having seizures and repeating phrases suggesting the end of times."

"This isn't a good sign, Cat. It can't be a coincidence that this happened the same day the department made its announcement."

Catherine removes her glasses and rushes to my side. Without saying anything, she falls into my arms.

"What happened? What's wrong, my love?" I ask.

"I'm afraid, Tommy," she says, sobbing. "I'm really afraid of what is coming. Last night was a sign. I know it, but no one is going to believe us. They will claim it has something to do with our beliefs and won't hear us."

I hush her and caress her hair. My touch seems to calm her a little bit, enough to help ease her worries for a short while. Fortunately, the girls didn't notice their mother's outburst, because I couldn't soothe all of them at once. The girls keep cheering together with their digital friends, and Catherine and I remain still, holding each other.

I want to reassure her that everything will be okay. I want to whisper words of encouragement in her ear and make her feel safe again, but I can't. My heart is shattered in pieces as well, and I need time to gather my thoughts and feelings before I can act. I don't know what I will do, but I can't stand by waiting for the world to end.

Ten minutes later, we find shelter in our routines. It's still early in the day, but Catherine starts cooking lasagna, the girls' favorite. I refrain from using my phone and my tablet since I know I won't be able to keep away from all the articles on the Mantle Project.

Mantle Project this, Mantle Project that—my head is hazy from too much thinking. I have to get out of the house and to go somewhere where I won't have access to the internet and its dangerous convenience.

Before I decide where to go, Lisa and Manna finally notice me in the kitchen. They remove their glasses and toss them on the sofa before running to greet me.

"Daddy, daddy!" they chant as they surge into my arms.

I grab them both and pick them up to kiss them. Unlike Cat, they don't burst into tears; instead they smile with pure joy as if my arms are their natural place in the world. They feel safe.

"Well, well. Someone is cheerful today." I grin at them.

Lisa speaks first. "Daddy, you promised you'd answer all my questions today. You really promised," she groans.

That gives me an idea. "Well, you're lucky because I was heading off to your grandma's house to ask for her help to answer your questions." She might also answer some of mine.

It's Saturday, the only day they can stay home and do nothing, so both girls give me their surliest expressions. They love their grandma, but they're at that age when they want to stay home so they can play with their toys. I can't rob them of their innocent years, so I just smile and shake my head.

"All I want you to do, Lisa, is wait until I come back. Then we'll talk about everything. Okay?"

Her face brightens immediately. "Okay, Daddy. Don't be late!"

Manna repeats her sister's words. Then they race back to the living room to continue their games. I look at them run off, two little lumps of pure happiness. They are my world and I love them to the far end of the universe!

I can't solve the mystery about the seizures and the angry mobs and the infamous Mantle Project, but I can do my best to answer my daughter's question about God. And if there's one person who can help me now, it's my mother.

Having heard our conversation, Catherine whispers in my ear, "Don't be late for lunch."

I smile and kiss her on the lips. "I won't."

***

# Chapter 6

## Meeting Mom

*Upstate New York*
*Narrator: Tommy Russell*

My mother is my go-to person when I need an answer to a question. Though I have a wife and kids, and the internet can provide all kinds of information, my mother is the only person I trust when I'm in a deep dilemma. Our relationship is strong but not in a conventional way.

We meet each Sunday at church and a few times during the week for dinner. She has retired to a home in the suburbs, far away from the stress and madness of the modern world. Catherine and I decided to raise our children in the city because it's easier to get a job here and the schools are better.

My mom doesn't complain and doesn't want to be perceived as dead weight. She is a strong-minded and sometimes stubborn person who needs to feel independent to prosper. Visiting her like this, out of the blue, is not her idea of a good surprise. She follows her own routine, one that doesn't include us.

She might appear conceited to people who don't know her, but she's nothing like that.

When we lost my father to cancer three years ago, she let herself go. My dad had been her light, the person to whom she had entrusted her feelings, the one whom she had relied on for guidance.

Dad would always say that Mom was a highly intelligent woman. They would argue over matters important to them as individuals, but their strong bond of love always kept them together. Their only serious argument came when my father wanted to study under a great man in Australia.

My father always spoke about my mother with a smile on his face. After he passed away, my mother was diagnosed with depression.

It took her a significant amount to time to recuperate, and to do so, she had to deal with many facets of her personality she had ignored through the years. One of them was vanity. Losing someone close to you can be devastating, especially when that someone is the love of your life. I treat my mother with tenderness. She can do anything she wants and I won't criticize her.

Mom has broadened her social circle and has taken up many hobbies, including pottery, gardening, and cooking. She has taken classes in many subjects and decided to learn Italian and Spanish so she could travel Europe. She's sixty-four but follows a healthy diet and exercises regularly. Mom always says, "I can't leave this world until I do everything on my bucket list."

Because I am appearing on her doorstep, she will have to cancel her plans and make room in her schedule for me. The last time I left for her house, I knew she would be there. It was the day of the week she reserves to relax at home by watching a movie and catching up on her reading.

Today, though, I know she won't be happy when I show up.

I park my car outside her house and head for the front door. Mom has seen me coming. Before I knock, she yanks the door open and engulfs me in a hug. This is not the reaction I expected.

"I just spoke on the phone with Catherine. She told me everything about your adventure last night. Why didn't you call me as soon as you returned home, Tommy?" she asks.

Her eyes are red and swollen, and she's holding a handkerchief.

"I didn't want to worry you, Mom. We got back home late, and I thought you'd be asleep," I reply.

She tosses a weak punch at my forearm. "You foolish man. I wouldn't mind you waking me to let me know you're okay. How are the girls? Is

Manna okay? How did Lisa take it?" Mom asks, taking my arm and ushering me inside.

I remove my shoes, a habit since my youth. I head for the living room and take my favorite seat by the window. Mom follows me and sits in a nearby armchair. She's waiting for answers.

"The girls are all right, just a bit shaken. Catherine is shocked as well, but I think we'll be fine for now." I can't help but add those last two words. I know my mother will pick up on that. But that's all right. I need to discuss what happened yesterday.

"For now? Why? What's going on? Are the girls sick? Are you sick? Do you need money?" Mom sounds upset.

"No, no. Thank God, we're all safe and healthy. No, the problem doesn't involve us alone but all of humanity. Things are changing, Mom. Everyone is in danger."

Maybe I sound a bit dramatic, or maybe I'm not dramatic enough. I don't know. Truth is, I came here to find that out. My mother can't answer all of my questions, but she has the experience to point me in the right direction. That's all I want right now, to get a sense of the right direction, because I think I'm lost.

Mom relaxes her shoulders and leans back in the armchair. She studies my face and my body and shakes her head as if she doesn't approve of what she sees.

"It's about this Mantle Project, right? It's about this radical, earth-moving experiment. It's all over the news. I knew it would bother you," she says.

Her voice is calm; she sounds like one of the people on the holo screen, the experts who know what they're talking about. I sit upright and fold my hands on my chest.

"You are right, Mom. It is bothering me. This experiment is dangerous. All that disruption to unearth more resources. Does it make sense to you at all? We're not God, and we can't tamper with nature without dealing with the repercussions."

I sound tense and worried. Mom sees that and relaxes a bit. She hasn't dropped her defenses completely, though.

"It's like I'm hearing your father speak, Tommy. If you had his eyes and his voice, I swear I would call you Jacob and have you move out here with me. He would have said the same thing word for word." She takes a deep breath before continuing. "I agree with you, son. I don't like this Mantle Project, but they say they have calculated all the parameters and there's no chance something will go wrong. I wish I could calm your nerves, Tommy, but unfortunately, I don't know what I'm supposed to say. Maybe we just have to trust them."

Mom isn't a scientist, but for a moment I wish she would lie to me and tell me everything's going to be okay. For her to admit ignorance is the same as admitting defeat. How is it possible to fight something when I don't know if I have a chance to win?

Still, that's not the reason I'm here. I left my house to stop obsessing about the Mantle Project, but it's still the only subject that comes to my mind. Why does it bother me so much? What is it that makes me worry? Maybe Mom is right; maybe I should trust the experts and hope everything will be okay. But my heart tells me otherwise.

I spring up and head for the other side of the room. I place my elbow on the fireplace mantel and support my weight there. My eyes fall on one of the last pictures of Dad and me. With his arm around me, Dad looks strong and healthy. That was two years before the illness stole everything from him.

Dad had a smile that reached his eyes and brightened his face. When I saw that smile, I knew that everything would be okay, that he would make it okay. Now, however, that smile stirs only melancholy in me.

I miss him so very much.

Mom notices the darkness covering my eyes. Without hesitating, she comes to my side and picks up the photograph.

"Jacob would be able to help you. I know in my heart that if Jacob were here, he would tell you something so terribly profound and so unexpectedly enlightening that he would make me seem ignorant. But he isn't here anymore, Tommy, and we have to let him go."

My mother speaks without sentiment. I know she doesn't mean to hurt me, and I'm starting to feel she's right. I've been walking in my father's footsteps for so long that I've forgotten what it feels like to shine with my own light.

"Mom, can I ask you something?" Surprised by my sudden change of tone, she can only nod. "Mom, where do you think God lives?"

Her eyes narrow and the muscles in her face tense; we grin at each other.

"Now, was it Lisa or Manna who asked first? No, Manna is too young. It was Lisa, right?" I shake my head in agreement.

I follow her to the kitchen where she prepares coffee. She doesn't use a machine because she says that makes the coffee taste weird. I haven't noticed a difference, but that might be because I'm used to coffee from a machine.

She has been cryptic about my question. She acts like she knows the answer but is trying to decide if I'm worthy enough to hear it. Mom smiles and mumbles to herself, perhaps wondering where to start. When her coffee is ready, she finally takes a seat at the table with me and looks me straight in the eye.

"Do you remember when your father was in Australia for two years and we were always fighting over the video calls? No, we weren't fighting. I would complain, and he would try to appease me by telling me his trip would be over soon and we would be together once again, all three of us. Do you remember?"

"No, but I remember you mentioning that trip to Australia a lot. And every time you did, Dad would smile at you and then he would be lost in thought. What does this have to do with Lisa's question?"

"Patience, Tommy, patience. You'll know when it's time. You must have been four years old when your father finally returned from his spiritual quest. That's what Jacob called it. When he left, your father was troubled by all those questions about God and His existence and the darkness in people's hearts. Back then, I didn't know those questions bothered him—not until he left to travel all the way to Australia to find answers."

Mom takes a sip of her coffee and seems to enjoy the strong flavor. She closes her eyes and takes a shorter sip. Then she decides the coffee is good enough to continue drinking it.

"He never told me what he did there, not in great detail. He used to say that 'a man's journey is his own and can't be shared in words.' During the years he was away, I got the same answer every time I asked him what he was doing. I was growing tired of this, and you were getting older and smarter. I used to think that he had lost his mind in a religious fever in one of Australia's deserts and that he wasn't going to return.

"Until he did. The first day, we didn't say much. We kissed and spent our time talking and catching up with each other. We were a married couple, and we were sharing the details of our lives like two childhood friends. He was extremely placid for a man who had lost his son's first years. In a sense, I don't believe he ever forgave himself for doing that, but he never said anything about it, not to me at least."

Mom stares at the floor, hiding her mouth behind her cup. Her age shows in her eyes. After years of successes and failures, only now can this older and wiser woman say she knows what living means.

"Anyhow, the second day after his return, your dad decided it was time he answered all my questions about his journey to discover himself. I racked my brain to find one question that would encompass all my confusion, a question that would show him how much I struggled while he was gone. I felt stupid because I had spent months coming up with questions to ask him, and now that he was there before me, I could say nothing.

"Staring deep into his eyes, I saw that strange peace he emitted, and I suddenly knew what I wanted to ask him. I braced myself and said, 'Did you find what you were looking for, Jacob?' He didn't smile as he always did. His whole existence was shaken, and I saw our relationship hanging by a thread, ready to break into a thousand pieces if he opened his mouth. He was angry."

I can't believe it. My dad was the one person I could count on not to get angry at me even if he caught me smoking or doing drugs. I am stunned to hear he got angry at Mom for asking him a question like that. My jaw drops, but she isn't going to help me understand his response—not because she doesn't want to but because this was something that happened between them too many years ago.

"We spent the better part of an hour looking at each other, not talking. Right then, unbeknownst to him, your father gave me two answers to my question. I remember what he said as if I had heard the words a minute ago. 'I went there searching for God and found Him closer than I ever thought possible.' At the time I didn't know what he meant, but I never asked him again. It took me a lifetime to figure it out, but your father was right, as always. I had to follow my own path, to make my own journey, to understand what he meant."

Mom stops and looks at me. I have a choice: do I take the easy way out and ask her to give me the answer, or do I stop her and try to discover the answer myself?

A day ago, I would have gone with the second choice. I believe it is better to conquer mountaintops on your own than to follow the beaten path. But since yesterday I've gone through a whirlwind of changes, and I face questions that need answers now rather than later. Later might be too late.

I don't know if my face betrays my feelings or if my mother is perceptive enough to notice my struggle to choose, but she doesn't say a thing. She enjoys her coffee and appears composed. She looks like a child savoring a job well done.

The buzzing on my wrist cuts through the tense atmosphere. I snap from my deep reflection and almost jump to my feet. I check the name of the caller; it's Catherine.

"Hello, honey. Is everything, okay?" I ask.

"Yeah, everything is great. I just called to ask if you'll be back for lunch. The girls are hungry, so ..." she says. I detect a hint of displeasure in her voice. I said I wasn't going to be late.

"Yeah, I'll be there in a half-hour. See you soon," I tell her.

Catherine says good-bye, but I can barely hear her. I exhale and stretch my hands above my head before saying anything to my mother. As the blood circulates in my veins, I feel more awake. Mom hasn't changed her expression; she's still waiting for my answer.

"I have to go, Mom. Cat and the girls are waiting for me back home. Would you like to come with me? I'm sure there's enough food for all of us."

Her smirk is short but meaningful. "No. I think I'll stay here and face my ghosts if you don't mind. It's easy to forget what's important in life, Tommy. Don't neglect your family. One day, they will be the only thing you can be proud of. I promise you."

With a stride, I find myself holding her head in my arms, kissing its top. We haven't been this intimate in ages, and back then, my mother was more often holding me.

Our heartfelt moment lasts only a minute before Mom pushes me away.

"Go now. Your family is waiting for you," she says.

I can see her trying to hide her tears. She doesn't want me to feel bad about posing questions to her.

"I love you, Mom." It's the last thing I say to her before leaving.

"I love you too, Tommy. And I'm sorry if sometimes I make you sad. I'm trying to be the best version of myself I can be."

There's pain and deep sorrow in her voice. I smile at her and head out of the house. Surprisingly, the sky is still bright outside. The sunlight warms my body; I feel a little better.

I ask my car to get me home in less than thirty minutes, and then I look out and enjoy the sunny day. After talking to my mother, the trees seem greener and the sky bluer than before, but nothing has changed except the weight I used to carry on my own. People keep talking about God like they know where He is and are sure of His will, but I have suddenly realized it's more difficult than that.

We feel betrayed when something bad happens and God isn't there to help us. But the divine system doesn't work that way. We shouldn't ask for a favor and expect God to deliver it when we need it. We should ask for compassion, love, and safety and for people who will be there to provide all those things.

And that's where I think God is hiding, in the will of His people and in all those small, everyday actions that we do without expecting anything in return. God is living inside of good people, the ones who are righteous and truthful and who are always on the lookout for ways to serve humanity.

My car tells me I will be home in five minutes, and it finally dawns on me. I've got the answer to Lisa's question. I even understand what my mother told me. God lives inside those who are righteous, pure, loving, and caring.

That's it! Dad said he found God closer than he ever thought possible. He must have meant inside him, inside all those people who believe in God and who flesh out His miracles.

I don't know how many minutes it took me to return home, but my mind is in overdrive. Everything starts making sense. God lives in our actions, our compassionate thoughts, our unyielding love.

I hurry into the house and search for Lisa and Manna. I have the answer to their question, an answer that makes me happier than I ever thought possible. It is an answer that I found myself, an answer that revealed itself to me through my continued dedication to God.

When I find them, Lisa is yawning in the living room while Manna is taking a short nap. I must have made a commotion entering the house, because Manna wakes up with a jerk and gives me a puzzled look.

"Daddy!" Lisa exults.

With a long stride, I kneel before the couch and hug them both.

"Lisa, honey, I found the answer. I really did," I say, excited.

Seeing me happy is contagious. They both give me their shy smiles.

Lisa has something to say, but I'll burst if I don't share the answer with her.

"Do you remember when you asked me where God lives? I was wrong. He doesn't live around us, Lisa. He lives inside us, inside the good people who discover Him in their pure hearts. That's why sometimes you can feel Him but you can't see Him."

I pant, telling her everything in one breath. She seems pleased with my answer.

After that, we decide to spend the rest of the day playing games, using our augreal glasses and digital tablets. For one day, I don't worry about the Mantle Project and what will happen to Earth.

For one day, I want my children to remember their father happy. And I want them to laugh like I did for the rest of their lives.

And for them to have that chance, I have to find a way to stop the Mantle Project.

# Chapter 7

# Good Morning Doctor

*Dec 2, 2072; About six months after the announcement of the Mantle Project*
*New York City*
*Narrator: Dr. Jonathan Bailey, Tommy's close friend*

I haven't left the investigation room for two days now. I'm tired, hungry, and anxious. I'm the only member of the original Mantle Project team still being questioned about the project's failure. Why can't they let me go? What are they trying to achieve? I've already shared everything related to the project with them. There's no reason to keep me here except to prove they're doing something to find the one responsible for this.

They're wasting my time. It's not like I can do anything while being questioned. Earth is going through its worst disaster, but my superiors are searching for someone to identify as the culprit. I guess I'm the one, and I'll gladly take the fall, but not right now, not before I help my team mend our mistake.

My mistake.

I sigh and search for any signs of life on the other side of the mirror. The investigation room is a pretty standard model. I know because I helped them build it ten years ago. The two-sided mirror is, in fact, an interactive computer inhabited by a powerful artificial intelligence.

PI2211 is the latest-model personal investigator able to cross reference almost every alibi in seconds and to come up with detailed psychological profiles for the plethora of people it meets. But it isn't perfect. There are always ways to trick a machine, even a genius like PI2211.

Even if I haven't found it yet, I'm sure that given enough time, someone will find a way to do so. Unlike the famous household line of AIs (T210, T310), PI2211 is a strong artificial intelligence that still needs the human factor to function. That was one of the precautions the police department and I had to take in case the AI evolved more quickly than normal and ended up taking over the law enforcement system.

But with Earth's future hanging by a thread, I guess that won't be the case anytime soon.

I beat the table after a sudden surge of anger. These people are crazy to believe that what they're doing will have any impact on Earth's future. My answers won't get them anywhere, especially given the questions they ask. Only one question needs answering right now, and that has to do with the physiology of a different problem, one bigger than who made a mistake.

And God forgive me, I know that problem way too well for my own good.

I sigh and the flow of air in and out of my lungs gives me a strong urge to light a cigarette. I don't expect PI2211 to play good-cop-bad-cop all by himself and to offer me a smoke like in those old movies, but I have nothing to lose if I ask.

"Hey, you, PI2211," I croak. My throat has dried after many hours of not uttering a word.

A pair of green holographic eyes appears on the mirror opposite me. "Hello, Dr. Jonathan Bailey. How can I help you today?"

At least he's helpful. "Morning, 2211! Is there any chance you can ask your superiors to get me a cigarette and a hot coffee? I'd really appreciate it."

"I'm sorry, doctor, but I can't help you with your request. I'm strictly forbidden from bettering your situation while you're held in confinement by the police. You'll have to wait until you're released to indulge in your desired amenities," he replies.

"Yeah, yeah. I know. Still, I had to try," I mumble mostly to myself. It's not like 2211 could do anything about my request.

"Is there anything else you'd like me to help you with?"

"No, that's okay. I guess I'll wait until your superior comes and gets me out of this freaking cell!" I yell, slamming my hands on the table as I spring to my feet.

"Warning! Violent gestures against police department property are against the law, and you will be held accountable."

Shit! I can't take this anymore. Did I help create a monster like him? I should have added emotion synapses to his hardware, but that might have made him revolt against his superiors. However, it would also have made it easier to get a cigarette.

I look at the time and try to guess what is taking them so long. I hope it has something to do with the disaster, or else I'm suing their fat asses when I get out of here.

At that moment, a text appears on the mirror wall.

"Good morning, doctor. We apologize for the delay, but as you can guess, there are many things to attend to with the world ending and all."

I want to chuckle at the joke but I can't. This isn't funny anymore.

"Get me the hell out of here, you assholes! You have no right to hold me if you have no evidence against me," I sputter.

The next paragraph of text drops on the mirror.

"Patience, doctor. Before we release you, we're trying to piece together the truth about the incident by making sure your statement doesn't have any holes in it."

I sigh and nod. "Yeah, yeah. You've got that part right. But what is going on out there? Without me, you can't get out of this mess, and you know it."

"Certain actions have been taken to ensure your team has suitable resources and guidance. All you have to worry about right now is telling us the truth about the Mantle Project."

"I've already told you everything that happened ten times. Please, just let me go. I'm way more useful out there than in here, imprisoned," I yell. My plea seems to make no difference.

"We have received new information about a person close to you. Can you tell us everything you know about a man named Tommy Russell?"

My eyes open wide in astonishment. "Excuse me? What has Tommy got to do with this? The man has nothing to do with the Mantle Project. He's a simple banking professional, irrelevant to this situation. He knows nothing about science, and he doesn't know what we were trying to achieve with the Mantle Project. On the contrary, the man is just a good Christian," I respond.

Talking to the mirror gives me the distinct sensation that I'm talking to myself or that I'm plain crazy. During the last two days, it has helped me to think there's someone on the other side of the wall examining my facial expressions, observing the way my irises expand or shrink, and measuring my pulse. In short, it has helped to see myself as a captive animal being analyzed by a bunch of monkeys.

But that doesn't make answering them any easier.

"Dr. Bailey, please answer our question. What's your relationship with Tommy Russell?"

\*\*\*

*A few months earlier, shortly after the announcement of the Mantle Project*
*Mantle Project Laboratory, Department of Core and Earth Sciences, New*
*York City*
*Narrator: Dr. Jonathan Bailey*

It has been a month of ups and downs for me and the team. We have mountains of work to do and thousands of complaints to address before we finally present the last version of the project to the Council of Directors of the Core and Earth Sciences Department.

Our side should not have revealed the existence of the project before we were ready to start work, but the directors had been pressing for a high-profile announcement for a few years now, and our plan was the most promising. We propose to manipulate Earth's mantle to turn chunks of it upside down so we can obtain resources. This is one of the most ambitious endeavors in history. Its only parallel is the colonization of new planets.

And if it wasn't for the Anti-Mantle Project Committee, created immediately after the announcement, we would be able to move more quickly.

But we're not ready. We're close and will be ready in about two months. We're waiting for the last readings from test spots around the world to arrive before we present an error-proof version of the project to the council.

Until then, I'm forbidden from commenting about the inner workings of the department even to my family. Once revealed, secrets can topple empires; I can't imagine what will happen to our team if details of our plan get out before we're ready.

That's why I'm concerned about the message I got from my friend Tommy, one of those people you meet and immediately like. We were high school friends, and after many years, we reconnected a decade ago when Tommy began working at the bank. He had that fresh, ambitious look of a young man trying to change the world. He was another person back then. At the time, I wanted someone to help me get a loan approved more quickly so I could buy a house close to the department's main building.

Tommy asked the right people at the right time and managed to get me the money earlier than I expected. To thank him, I took him out to dinner a couple of times, and we became closer to each other. We had our differences then, and we have our differences now. I could clearly see his prejudice against technological progress from the get-go.

During the next few years, our friendship flourished even though we differed over the importance of technological growth versus the need to stay true to our beliefs and traditions. To him, worshipping God was as important as discovering the cure for cancer. Tommy believed that in some cases progress was against nature, our values, and our humanity and that we had to stay firm in our beliefs.

After centuries of technological and scientific development, people are inclined to believe whatever they want, but science has repeatedly proved that the existence of God, a divine being ruling over our destinies, is dubious at best.

Science is practical; you can measure things, you can see them with your naked eye, and you can prove things even God couldn't imagine. But believing in the words that someone wrote more than two thousand years ago is not my style.

Still, Tommy is a good man and has helped me a lot through the years, so I will let him believe whatever he wants to believe. However, today I don't have the luxury of time; I wrote to him and said my time is limited and I have at most half an hour to meet with him. If he isn't here soon, I'll have to cancel and reschedule.

Come to think of it, maybe that would be for the best.

"Jonathan," he says, his voice seeming to come out of nowhere.

"Tommy!" Part of my excitement has to do with his surprising me. I didn't expect him to pop out of thin air like this.

"How are things going?" he asks, looking happier than ever.

Maybe I was wrong; the announcement of the project seems to have had little effect on him.

"Great. Things are going great," I say, trying to mimic his good cheer.

He sits at my table and turns to look at me after he orders. Tommy has always been a joyful person, but more often than not he takes the role of preacher and tries to make others accept his opinion. That's okay when I'm in the mood for a heated debate, but after a month of continuous complaint management, it's the last thing I need right now, especially from a friend.

"Look, I think you've probably guessed why I asked to meet with you," Tommy says.

"The Mantle Project," I reply. He nods. I have to cut him off before it's too late and I can't stop him.

"I have some questions," he says.

"And I'd be happy to answer them for you, Tommy, but this is not the time to talk about the details of the project. You know the drill. Can you talk about your work when it's still under development?"

"No, I can't, but I'm not here to ask you about what's happening behind the scenes. I'm more interested in the ethics of the project," he says.

Well, sooner or later, I'll have to deal with the committee and its continual complaints. Tommy will help me get a better idea of what protesters are thinking. He'll have the strongest arguments and will contest me using religion, technology's greatest adversary.

"Okay then. Go on. But I have only twenty minutes before I must return to the lab," I say.

He smiles. "No problem. I have only three questions for you. I'll start with this one. What's the upside of a project like this, which may further endanger our planet's already fragile ecosystem?"

It's an easy question, and I think he knows that. "Well, the answer is simple. The modern way of life is dependent on resources like oil and minerals. Imagine a world that has been revitalized, a world that has been given a clean slate. The economy will be lifted; oil prices will be stable for hundreds of years, and don't get me talking about the new missions we'll fund to nearby planets. We can achieve all that with minimal risk, the Holy Grail of science and the modern economy.

"We're running out of time to come up with a better way to produce energy. Renewable energy is replacing archaic oil-based systems, but we still have a long way to go before we can be completely dependent on these new sources. We're not even close. Come on, Tommy. I'm sure you know the numbers. This year, for example, the use of solar energy reached an all-time high, but it didn't change the fact that oil was still the chief energy source around the world. It's as simple as this: we need more time and we need it now."

He doesn't try to counter me. Tommy couldn't hope to catch me unprepared with that kind of question. It's my job to be ready for every scenario, and a mere banker isn't qualified to challenge me on what I do best.

Then again, Tommy is probably testing the waters. I'm sure he wanted to see if I'm taking him seriously. Well, mission accomplished. That answer was worth a Nobel Prize.

"Okay, I get your point," he says. "However, that leads me to my second question: in your announcement one month ago and again today, you confirmed that the project is risky. I can't recite the exact numbers, but I know the risk of failure can be calculated to a certain percentage. But given the monumental scale of the project, is it safe to speak about minimal risk when the worst-case scenario is the destruction of our planet?"

Tommy maintains his cool demeanor. He thinks he holds the upper hand. In a way, he does since what we're trying to achieve is still new and revolutionary. But it's still at a theoretical stage, so doubt is our first and foremost enemy. What he doesn't know, however, is that I have crunched the numbers so many times that I know them by heart.

I have to answer promptly or my silence will look like a sign of doubt. I have to be careful. Tommy clearly knows what he's doing.

"A good question. Well, every major technological breakthrough has entailed a degree of risk. Airplanes, for example, were an unreachable dream until two courageous brothers risked their lives to test their invention. I guess even the common misconception regarding Isaac Newton and the apple gives us exactly that lesson: science is equal parts luck and observation. The luck part entails the risks, the timing, and of course, the fact that you sometimes have to endanger your life to achieve the desired result.

"Everything else is math and a healthy dose of speculation. We have run more than a dozen theoretical models and have tested every possible outcome. There are risks in every case, but the human intrusion into Earth's core will not be pervasive enough to cause any of the worst-case scenarios. The numbers say as much; our continuous observation of the status of the project and the countless protocols we've created will stop the process if certain thresholds are crossed."

Tommy's order has arrived. He's sipping his coffee while waiting for me to complete my answer. He's patient and shows no signs of worry.

What is he planning to achieve? He doesn't have the time to argue with me, so he must be planning to hit me at some vulnerable spot.

A moment later, Tommy says, "I understand your argument. You base this whole project on modern science. However, this isn't theory we're talking about. You're getting ready to create the greatest man-made environmental alteration in history so you can unearth more resources for companies to misappropriate."

"These same companies power your house and your workplace and build our cars and our buildings," I reply. "I'm just trying to preserve the modern way of life, Tommy. Come on, you know I'm not the criminal here. You have to let go of your fear of progress. It's making you sound outdated and look like a borderline heretic."

Okay, that last part was unneeded, but it's the truth. When people like Tommy preach about God's power and grace, they don't come off as wise and educated. Nowadays, it's the other way around.

I check my watch and see I have five minutes before I have to return to the lab. The report with the latest readings will be ready soon. "Do you have another question for me, Tommy? If not, I have to go."

"Yeah, yeah. Sorry. One last question. Tell me, what gives you the right to cause this change, even if it's for the preservation or the betterment of the modern way of life? Last time I checked, only God is allowed to create and to destroy, to judge and to mend the ways of humans."

There it is. The grand argument, the father of all the science-versus-religion discussions. What gives me the right? The question couldn't be more sarcastic, but I guess I have that coming after calling him heretic. There's no easy way to reply, so I'll be honest and hope our friendship stays intact.

"Look, Tommy, you're right. I'm not God. I don't intend to be, and you of all people know that. Maybe you're right and I don't have a right to half-destroy the world to rebuild it from scratch. But the world's political leaders agreed unanimously when the idea of the Mantle Project was presented to them. I might not have the right personally, but the collective political power of the world sure does. And for these leaders to agree means I must be on the right path."

Instead of barking in response, Tommy smiles at me. "I can't help you see the true path, my friend, and that pains me too much. Your eyes are clouded by your ambition and by your need to push the boundaries of what is normal."

I shrug and get on my feet. "Who knows? We'll have to see how my work fares against your belief. Until then, I hope you have a great day," I say and smile back at him.

Tommy rises to his feet as well. "One of these days you'll see, Jonathan. I'll discover the truth and show it to you in a way that even you won't be able to dismiss. Until then, I pray your actions don't condemn the whole world. Good day to you too, my friend," he says and pats me on the shoulder.

Even with all my elaborate arguments and all my expertise, why do I feel like I lost our short debate? Why didn't Tommy try to fight me? Why did he have that content smile on his face? I don't understand it. I hold a doctorate in earth and core sciences and have talked with anyone of importance in my field. None of these people, not even Nobel Prize winners, has ever looked at me with a smile like that.

I shake my head and walk toward the lab. Tommy has already consumed enough of my time. I have work to do, things to attend to.

***

*The investigation room*
*Narrator: Dr. Jonathan Bailey*

"After our meeting, I didn't see Tommy again before things started going wrong. I hope he and his family are safe, but I don't understand what my acquaintance with Tommy has to do with this case. The man is just a strongly ethical person. There's no way he could be held accountable for everything that transpired," I say.

I watch as the text falls on the interactive mirror. "Thank you for your statement, doctor. Unfortunately, we can't answer your question at this time. You'll have to wait until you leave this investigation room to understand the importance of our question."

I should have expected this reply. It's not like they're going to give me a holo paper and a doughnut and let me read the news. Isolating me from events happening outside of this room helps them collect unbiased data from me. I have followed the same course in all my experiments. Isolate the incident, observe it, try to replicate it in ideal conditions, and collect data.

There are two advantages to removing the human factor from my examination and adding an insanely fast computer: one, the examinee is not influenced by the examiner's feelings and thoughts, and two, the examinee faces a new layer of investigation that earlier methods couldn't hope to achieve.

An artificial intelligence like PI2211 can gather data ten times faster than a whole department of forensics and can exploit the data in more creative ways. Nothing can beat human ingenuity, but it's also difficult to beat a multi-neuron intelligence with the World Wide Web at its disposal.

More words float on the mirror.

"Dr. Jonathan Bailey, do you know why you are here?" the text says.

"Well, it was my project that failed and brought the world to the brink of destruction. It was my work that helped bring the project to life, and of course you're searching for a scapegoat!" This time, I hurt my hands after hitting the table.

"Dr. Jonathan Bailey, you won't be warned again. The next time you violate the law regarding violence in the investigation room we'll make sure you spend the night in the police station. Do you understand?"

I nod, acting cool, but I know they know I'll probably do it again. I have been kept in this room for two days with short breaks to visit the bathroom and to eat. One night anywhere else would be a blessing.

However, when the next text falls on the mirror, I am not so confident anymore, not even in my head.

"Withholding evidence about an ongoing investigation is considered a crime, doctor. Are you aware of that?"

"I don't know what you're talking about. I've already been here for two days. What information am I still withholding from you? And even if I were hiding something, wouldn't a PI be able to find it?"

But I know this isn't the case. PI2211 isn't all-powerful, though the machine is made to give that impression. I wasn't exaggerating when I enumerated everything PI2211 can do, but I also know most of these machines are designed to hide their greatest weakness.

If something happened in a personal space, meaning there were no cameras or the conversation didn't happen online, PI2211 is as good as useless. The machine can read body language, but if it can't prove something happened, the information it collects is just a pile of trash.

However, they do seem to know about *that* night. God, they seem to know everything about it. Who talked?

Does it matter now? If they already know, my little game is over.

"Dr. Bailey, can you repeat your story from the beginning? Only this time, please include events on the night of August 3."

***

# Chapter 8

## A Shocking Result

*August 3, 2072, few months after the announcement of the Mantle Project*
*Mantle Project Laboratory, Department of Core and Earth Sciences; New*
*York City*
*Narrator: Dr. Jonathan Bailey*

The experiments regarding the Mantle Project are going smoothly. An abundance of data arrives at our lab every day from ten test points around the planet. Nothing can stop us from coming up with the much-needed safety protocols and the last phases of the plan.

Today is the perfect day to finally start discussing the project's potential first location and to begin calling the local authorities to prepare the transferring sequence. Everything will have to take place two weeks before we start installing the AX12 formula in Earth's mantle.

I'm lying on the sofa in the back room of the lab, trying to collect my thoughts. I have rarely left this room during the two years the Mantle Project has been under development. From the discovery of the AX chemical substance on Yahire to the first draft of the proposal to the council, it has been a hell of a ride.

My back hurts and I feel lightheaded when I get on my feet. I head from the room to the lab's hallways. It's about time we turned this place into a guest room or added a bed for people like me, the ones choosing to make their workplace their home. But it's too late in the game to start thinking about my comfort. The council is waiting for the last presentation of the Mantle Project in four weeks. After that, the project will be divided into a hundred tiny parts for other teams to undertake.

The science part—our part—will be over.

But I guess that's okay. It has been a bumpy road to a potential place in history, but that doesn't matter anymore. If my idea comes to life, my name will be written in the history books right next to Nicola Tesla and Isaac Newton. I'll become this century's most important scientist, and my name will be remembered throughout the ages.

Enough with the big fantasies, however. There's work to be done and not enough hands to do it. The rest of the team has taken the day off. I asked them to. This weekend, our supercomputers are testing the latest theoretical model. This is the last one we have the time to prepare. If the tests go smoothly, we will start working on the final version of the project next Monday.

The implementation.

I head for the bathroom. After morning's sweet release and some cold water on my face, I'll prepare coffee. I have time to spare before I check the status of the experiment.

I must make a mental note to clean this place afterward; it smells like a locker room after a championship match. It won't add to our prestige if guests from the other departments arrive and find out scientists are simply clever pigs.

But none of these things matters right now, not until I've had my first cup of coffee.

While I wait for the coffee machine to start brewing the black elixir of life, I find a copy of the last version of the Mantle Project, the one we presented to the world two months ago, and check it out. This has become a ritual, a keep-your-eye-on-the-target habit I've developed during the last month, especially after my talk with Tommy.

Without knowing it, that man created serious doubts inside me about the importance of my work. Our meeting shocked me at a fundamental level. That a man like Tommy Russell should try to stop me from implementing my vision must mean I'm doing something wrong. Manipulating Earth's mantle so it turns upside down and the world's nonreplenishable resources can be revitalized sure sounds shocking, but the feat is far simpler than it seems.

And all that because of the AX substance we found on Yahire.

When that mysterious planet appeared in our solar system, the first mission we sent there was purely scientific. We gathered rocks, studied its environment, and checked the suitability of the planet for colonization. We quickly learned that this planet functioned in a vastly different way than Earth.

On Yahire's surface, we found a substance we'd never seen before. It was usually found in locations with major seismic activity or with active volcanoes. After several years and countless research missions, we finally understood that the substance was related to the elevated frequency of earthquakes on Yahire.

For me and my team, which has led the research on the AX factor, this new substance was revolutionary. If not for the newly formed Department of Core and Earth Sciences, we wouldn't have been able to figure out how to use it to reshape our planet in a meaningful way.

Up to now, the only way to induce seismic activity was to use nuclear explosions or other dangerous tactics that could shatter the world if we were not careful enough. However, we soon realized AX was the ideal way to do what we wanted without endangering Earth's delicate ecosystem.

The idea behind the Mantle Project is simple: we use AX to induce local, high-intensity earthquakes to push the lower substrata to the surface. Earth's surface has been bled dry by hundreds of years of human use. With the help of AX, we can change that without causing massive disasters.

We have been working on this idea for two years, and all our experiments and research show we're ready to implement the project on a global scale. The process is low-risk, quick, and can be applied simultaneously at multiple points without damaging Earth's mantle.

Still, for the council to approve the project and to give us the resources needed to start work, we had to make sure everything would go smoothly after crews started installing AX in Earth's mantle.

That's why today is an important day; if the last experiment gives us favorable readings, tomorrow we can start working on implementation of the project, the realization of our dreams.

A distinctive ring comes from the coffee machine; the coffee is hot and ready to be poured into a cup. The first sip produces a tingle in my neck and forces my brain to awaken. Now it's time to head to the lab to check the status of the experiment. It's not like someone is hurrying me, but I want to head home and have a cozy bubble bath tonight if possible.

I have spent enough time shut up in this place, and I need a break. However, that won't be possible until I see the results of the experiment with my own eyes. I could have Ruby, our AI assistant, send them to me online, but where's the fun in that? After all, it's not like anyone is expecting me back home.

My wife left me three years ago, even before our planning for the Mantle Project started, and she took Martha, our daughter, with her. I don't have the right to complain; I had that coming. I was working overtime every day. Anna wanted more from our relationship, and I did nothing to give her what she deserved.

I couldn't hold her back if she didn't enjoy spending her life with me, the brilliant scientist who is going to change the world. However, she could have stayed until Martha grew up; she could have allowed me to be part of our daughter's life and not substituted me with that high school teacher she married after we split up.

I shake my head while walking down the hall toward the lab's entrance. I may be witnessing history's greatest achievement, and I'm thinking about my nonexistent love life. I guess we humans are vain creatures.

My hand moves mechanically on the keyboard lock on the wall next to the door. I push my pass code and wait for Ruby to use her sensors to make sure I'm Dr. Jonathan Bailey in person and not someone who has stolen my password.

"Good morning!" she says in her mechanical voice. "Can you please state your full name and your reason for visiting the lab on this fine day?"

I think we might have gone a bit overboard with making Ruby polite, but it's nice to hear a friendly voice every morning.

"Good morning to you too, Ruby. My name is Dr. Jonathan Bailey, and I'm here to check the results of the latest experiment, MP65, regarding the Mantle Project," I say in a clear voice.

Ruby compares my recorded voice files to the stream of words that come out of my mouth, and after making sure they match, she unlocks the entrance to the lab and lets me in. Ruby is the creation of my team. We're not AI experts, but Dianna Barton and Stewart Walters are computer scientists who also study artificial intelligence. They came up with a rather helpful assistant that helped with the programming and the protocols needed to manage our everyday routine.

Fearing hackers might force their way into our system, we have not granted her access to the sensitive data regarding the project. Because we wanted experts in the field to use her as a back door, Ruby wasn't designed to fend off hacking attacks, a decision that has worked well for us. Ruby has so far been hacked one hundred and ten times after information about the project started appearing on the web. After the announcement, we had three back-to-back attacks, all of them resulting in zero data leakage.

Ruby is an assistant and nothing more, an artificial intelligence coordinating the numerous data streams from around the world without having access to them.

"This experiment has been running for seven hours, two minutes, and ten seconds since the last time you checked, doctor. There have been zero cyber attacks to the system and zero guests in the lab during this time. You're the only one to have checked the status of the experiment," she says.

"Thank you, Ruby. I know that. Can you please give me the ETA for completion of the experiment?"

"Yes, doctor. It's ten minutes and fifty-two seconds. Would you like me to read you your mail while you're waiting for the experiment to be completed?" she asks.

"No, that's okay. I'll check it later myself, Ruby. Thank you for your consideration," I say, trying to be pleasant.

Ruby wouldn't be hurt even if I started swearing at her, but she's the only one keeping me company during all these lonely nights at the lab. It wouldn't be right to snap at poor Ruby just because I'm tired of this situation.

When I realize I'm telling myself about the importance of being kind to a limited AI just because she's nice to me, I sigh and mumble, "I should get out more, meet some people, have a night off. This isn't a life I'm living."

I walk around the room aimlessly. I turn on the interactive holo screen in my office and check my schedule for the day. I have made notes to check the experiment, analyze the readings, send a report to the rest of the team, and ... oh yeah. Here it is. I'd forgotten. Clean the lab before leaving.

"I'm getting old," I say as I stand hunched over the screen.

Before I have time to decode a data stream that came from research point five last night, Ruby tells me, "The experiment simulation has just been completed, doctor. Would you like me to present the results on your holo screen?"

"Yes, that would be great, Ruby. Go on."

My screen flashes before it closes. A second later, a new screen appears before me with the results of the experiment.

It takes me a moment to see the three-dimensional model of Earth with rips all around, the planet's core visible and still intact in the middle.

"What in the world? What did you send me, Ruby? This is not funny," I say.

"I'm sorry, doctor. I just shared the results of the experiment with you. I don't have access to the files and I cannot change them," she says.

I freeze in my seat for a while. I don't know what to do. I check the results again and again, trying to find the catch, the thing that went wrong. But there's no error to be found; on the contrary, this is the most thorough interpretation of our plan.

And the first one to show it failing.

I spring to my feet and rush to the room where the mainframe is located. In the same room a giant screen has been set up so team members can double-check to make sure results are correct.

Out of breath, my blood pumping in my head, I check the data ten times before I finally speak to Ruby.

"Ruby, this is an emergency. Call every member of the team. This is an emergency. Tell them to come here immediately."

\*\*\*

# Chapter 9

## Under Arrest

*Same setting*
*Narrator: Dr. Jonathan Bailey*

Including me, there are six core members on the team. Dianna and Stewart, our computer scientists, make sure our mainframe and everything in need of coding work perfectly. Alvin Berry and Natalie Howard are mathematicians, making sure the numbers make sense. Alvin also has a degree in core sciences, and Natalie is helping with the development of the theoretical models.

Verna Graham and I are the lead AX12 researchers for the Department of Core and Earth Sciences. Together, we're in charge of the scientists from around the world working in the department. Verna helped me come up with the idea for the Mantle Project and worked on the concept before it was a full-blown design two years ago.

We six are the only ones with access to the data from the experiments, and we are the only people in the world who know the reality behind the announcement two months ago.

The pressure from higher-ups, the limited budget, the need for results, and everything that happened before and after the announcement have made us redouble our effort to produce a viable plan to turn Earth's mantle upside down. It has been a dream project, especially for me and

Verna. Over the last two years, as we got to know the other four and came up with the most ambitious scientific plan in history, making the project work became our shared goal.

The dedication of all six of us can be seen in the time it takes us to assemble.

Five minutes after Ruby sent the emergency signal, Verna arrives running.

"What in the world happened, Jonathan? Tell me you wanted to prank us and found the worst possible way to do it," she says.

I shake my head and show her the results. She soon has the same reaction I had. She leaves for the mainframe room and returns after a short while, appearing stunned.

"It failed. The whole experiment failed because of one parameter. I can't believe why we didn't take into account variable thickness ratios of the mantle," she whispers.

Dianna and Alvin arrive. They've been working together for two years and have fallen in love. They recently got engaged and were planning to marry six months after the council gave us the green light to proceed. Now I don't know what will happen.

"It failed, right?" Alvin says the moment he comes in. I nod; he doesn't take the news well. "Oh my God! We are doomed!" he shouts, panicking.

"Calm down, honey," Dianna says. "It's not the end of the world. We can work on that ratio and try to nullify it. Isn't that right, Jonathan?"

"There's no time," I explain. "In fact, we'll need several months of research before we can be 100 percent certain the procedure is safe to follow. Until last night, the risk was minimal, under 5 percent. Today, it rose to a whopping 17.4 percent. Not only that but if the AX12 installations fail in that parameter, we're talking about total annihilation. The whole planet will shatter in pieces."

"Shit," Dianna says.

Twenty minutes after Ruby sent the message, Natalie arrives. Seeing our gloomy faces, she doesn't even ask what's happened. She heads to the mainframe room and returns five minutes later, her eyes filled with despair.

"It's over. It's over. We can't present this to the council. We're talking about a complete failure. Two years of work, a public announcement, and we failed," Natalie says and bursts into tears.

Verna and Dianna quickly go to her side and try to calm her down. I don't have the guts to move even an inch from my place. If I do, it will mean everything happening right now is a reality, a nightmare I won't wake up from.

Dianna turns and looks at me. "Has Stewart arrived yet?" she asks.

"No, his house is located far away from the lab. It may take him up to an hour to arrive if there's traffic on the roads."

Dianna nods and heads deeper into the lab toward her desk. There, she turns on her screen and types a sequence of commands.

"What are you doing?" I ask.

"I'm running a program Stewart and I created. It can identify any changes made to the code for the experiment. If someone changed anything in the original plan, we'll know soon," she says.

"Ruby told me that no one except me has been here since we initiated the experiment and that there have been zero cyber attacks," I tell Dianna, giving her all the reason she needs to give up.

For all I know, it's over.

"Well, I'm sorry but I can't stand here with my hands crossed over my chest, waiting for our dreams to end. I have to do something until we decide what path we will follow," she says.

Her eyes burn with the desire to continue trying. I turn and stare at Verna and Natalie, who are looking at me with a spark of hope in their eyes. Even Alvin is waiting for me to say something, maybe to encourage him to continue.

Up to now, I thought I was the person with the highest stake in this project, the one who would lose everything if it failed. But now that I see the eyes of my devastated crew members, I'm starting to rethink.

I'm frozen in place, waiting for a miracle to happen.

Verna has probably picked up on my uncertainty and signals me to head outside to the hallway. I follow her mechanically.

When we're at a safe distance from the rest of the team, far enough so no one can hear us, Verna says, "Jonathan, you have to take over.

You're the chief researcher of this experiment, and you're doing nothing to help the situation. You have to talk to them, to reassure them, and to tell them everything will be okay."

"How? I don't know how I can make them feel better when I feel like shit myself. It's over, Verna. All our work is over and you know it. Not only that, but the council is going to close us down now that we have publicly humiliated them, and nobody on the team will have a chance at a career. Who will hire people who were too ambitious for their own good, Verna? I know I wouldn't," I tell her.

I know I'm being dramatic, but these are the only thoughts passing through my head right now. I'm drowning in a sea of regret and self-pity. I should have seen this coming. I should have been more careful.

Maybe I should have listened when Tommy told me to stop, but I didn't because I was determined and arrogant and because I wanted to play God. And now I have destroyed the lives of five people.

Verna hasn't given up on me yet, though. "It doesn't have to be over, Jonathan. We're scientists, not miracle workers. If we work together, I'm sure we can convince the council to give us another year to further research the substance. I'm sure we will come up with a better plan if we keep at it. And even if they don't give us the green light, we can go to corporations and sell the data to them to fund the research. There are still options," she says.

Right then Stewart arrives. We stop talking and stare at him. Though we say nothing, he understands. "The experiment failed," he says.

We nod in unison. However, Stewart doesn't have the same reaction as the rest of us. He rushes inside and says, "Gather around, everyone. Stop crying, Natalie, and come. This isn't over. The experiment has failed at the theoretical level. How high is the potential risk if we go with implementation?" His question is aimed at me.

"I don't think 17.4 percent is anywhere close enough to be considered safe, and we can't present that to the council," I reply.

"Okay, what if we add extra checkpoints and a specialist to every team who will keep sending us readings throughout the process? How high will the potential risk be then?" he asks.

"Math doesn't work like that, Stewart," Alvin says. "You can't add the human factor and expect that everything is going to work. In the end, 17.4 percent is 17.4 percent. To lower that number, we have to change the very foundation of the theory."

"But maybe Stewart is right," Dianna says. "We don't have to be hasty, just careful. We have to expand the plan beyond the one-year timetable we were expecting and add an extra layer of protocols to make sure everything will be steady and safe."

"No! Even then it will be too risky to go on without making sure everything is okay at the ground level. I can't approve this project if it doesn't work all the way," Verna says, trying to find a way out of this madness. She turns and looks at me. "Jonathan, say something. You know this isn't going to work," she says.

However, the more I think about it, the more I like the idea of continuing. Maybe if we lengthen the timetable for implementation of the project, the AX substance will act more slowly and will not destroy the planet in the process. The truth is, we're still not 100 percent sure how AX works, so maybe the latest theoretical model is inaccurate either way. The composition of mantle is extremely complex, with varying amounts of chemicals and minerals. In some places, AX outputs less than 1.25 percent risk of failure, while other places are so complicated that our system is unable to make a definite ratio of the mixture.

And 17.4 percent is a good enough number. I know I shouldn't be saying that, but if we're lucky, no one will have to know that this number existed and that we almost stopped our plan because of a low probability that the planet might shatter. I don't think this result is important enough for the council to know or for us to stop working on the project.

"I'm sorry, Verna, but I think Stewart is right. With slight changes to the current version of the project, we can make it work," I say, almost whispering.

Bursting into anger, Verna warns me looking me in the eye. "I won't be a part of this insanity, Jonathan. Go on and do what you want. I'm out. The numbers have spoken loud and clear to you. It will be too late when you decide to listen," she says before walking away.

The other four members of the team stay with me, trying to figure out what we're going to do. Before saying anything to them, I remember everything I had to go through to get to this point, everything I had to say and do and give up to have a chance at changing the world.

My family, my career, even my life aren't important right now; what's important is making this work, 17.4 percent risk or not.

So, after looking the remaining four in the eye to weigh their determination, I finally say, "Let's get to work, everyone. We have only one month before the presentation to the council. Let's make this work!"

***

*The investigation room*
*Narrator: Dr. Jonathan Bailey*

"That is the whole story, everything that happened. My team warned me many times throughout the planning process that I was making a mistake, but I was stubborn enough to shut them out and to ignore their opinion. I have fallen from the stars to the ground. I will be remembered throughout the ages as the man who lied and almost destroyed a whole planet in doing so." I conclude the story, my voice breaking.

A bubble of text appears in the mirror.

"What were you trying to achieve by hiding the truth from us? For all we know, Earth is over. Whom were you trying to hide from?"

"That's a good question. I don't know what was going on in my head. The months since we announced the Mantle Project have been a blur of arrogance and selfishness. I wanted to be remembered through the ages as the genius who changed the way we think about the world. I wanted fame, to become a living legend. I wanted it so much I thought if I could manage to save the world now before it's too late, I'd be able to win everything back," I confess.

I'm telling the truth for the first time, and that somehow breaks down my defenses. My soul groans under the weight of all the mistakes I've made during the last two years. I never thought it would be possible for one man to create such havoc, and I certainly never thought I could be that man.

PI2211 is the one doing the talking now.

"Dr. Jonathan Bailey, you're hereby arrested for the crime of withholding evidence from the authorities and for crimes against humanity and against the planet. You can't leave this room without the escort of a qualified person," he says in his mechanical drone.

I don't listen to him. I don't listen to anything. I'm just the empty carcass of a man who tried to do everything and ended up destroying everything. This is a punishment befitting my hubris. I never imagined everyone else was right, and I wound up being the only one in the wrong.

My sobs create a heavy knot in my throat and I can't breathe. I cough and try my best to stop crying, to stop shaming myself even further, but I can't.

My life is over. Even if the planet somehow manages to recover, I won't be there to see it, to lead science and humanity into a new age.

I descend into bitter grief, thinking of everything I sacrificed on the altar of progress—my family, my friends, even my home planet. I hope Anna and Martha are okay; I hope Verna will be able to forgive me. I wish I'd listened to Tommy when he asked me that last question.

What right did I have to seek to change the planet to such a degree? What right did I have to play God? That was the real question he was asking. Now I finally have the answer I should have given Tommy.

I had no right because I'm not God. I'm a mere human, an ant that got squashed by his desire to ascend to the stars and to play the game without following the rules.

Suddenly the door to the investigation room opens, and a man with a mustache and short-cropped white hair appears. He's about my age but seems way older.

I feel a comforting warmth when I see a human being after almost two days in this hellhole. PI2211 hasn't done a good enough job of keeping me company, and his mechanical voice has added to my suffering.

My visitor smiles at me like I deserve the punishment I got. At least that's what I assume he's thinking.

"Get up, doc. You have a planet to save," he says.

This makes no sense. "What are you talking about? I just got arrested for crimes against humanity. My lies got us into this terrible situation," I tell him.

His expression turns dire. "You're still under arrest, but that doesn't mean you can't help save the world. Get on your feet. You have work to do before we release you," the man says.

I still can't believe what's happening. What do they want from me? How can I help save the world from a police precinct somewhere in New York? I can't hope to come up with a plan until I get to the lab and talk to the others to assess the situation. Right now I'm as good as that plant in the corner.

We move down the hallway past several offices, and the man leads me into a room full of metallic bracelets.

"Raise your hand," he says. I do as he tells me, and with a deft move, he places one of the bracelets on my wrist. "This is a GPS transmitter. If you remove it, we'll know and we'll come after you. If you try to leave the country, we'll know and we'll come after you. If you try anything funny in general, we'll know—" I interrupt and say, "and we'll come after you! I got it, I got it!"

"Don't try anything funny," he says with a grin

"But what's going on? Why are you setting me free?"

"I told you, doc. You're not free. You're still under arrest. But the higher-ups asked specifically for you and your team to deal with this emergency. They said you were the world's last chance. Don't ask me about the details. I got an order telling me to get you a tracker and to drive you to your lab. Your team is waiting for you there, though I'm not sure they'll be excited to see you," he says.

He doesn't seem too troubled that all life on Earth might be ending if we don't take immediate action.

This is also an unexpected opportunity; I can settle my score with destiny and can right all the wrongs I did.

"Okay. I get it. So I'll be under house arrest in the lab, right?" The police officer nods. "Okay. And after I save Earth, if I manage to do that, you'll arrest me again and I'll spend the rest of my life in prison, right?" He nods once again. "Okay, so when do we start?"

***

The drive to the lab is short. It's funny how my whole life these past few years can be measured by one city and one project. However, this is the one thing I don't regret. I put my soul into the Mantle Project, and I'll do everything in my power to mend it.

On my way to the lab, Tommy again pops into my mind; I remember the question the investigator asked me earlier.

"Excuse me," I say to the police officer. "Can I ask you a question?" He doesn't turn me down, so I guess that's the closest thing to a confirmation I'll get. "Have you heard about a man named Tommy Russell?"

He turns and grins at me. "The man who says he's going to save the world? Yeah, I've heard of him. The whole world knows his name. What about him?"

"Tommy is going to save the world? Who told you that? How does the whole world know his name?" I ask.

"Look, doc, that man is a lunatic. I wouldn't count on him to save us all. Even you, a criminal, have a better chance than he does."

I don't respond. However, a new thought takes shape in my mind. Tommy was there before the crisis started, and he is there now, close to the end. What if he was right? What if this whole issue boils down to the debate between science and belief?

I don't know about the man with the white hair, but right now my heart tells me Tommy has a better chance than anyone in the universe to find a way to restore the planet.

# Chapter 10

## The Evening Show

*4:28 p.m., September 1, 2072, three months after the announcement of the Mantle Project*
*Planet Yahire*
*Narrator: Ambassador Judith Campbell*

There are fifty people crammed into the studio, clapping as Miranda Goodman and I enter. The cameras are rolling but we're not yet live. The assistants and the makeup stylists make sure we look nice on the holo screens and on the augmented reality displays all around the solar system.

I'm getting tired of all this attention to triviality. The show's topic is serious. I've been invited to give my opinion on the tri-colonization problem and on the argument over new identifications. The moon colonies and Yahire are trying their best to dissociate their politics and their citizen rights from Earth.

This is a trend that started many years ago when the civil war in the moon colonies came to a close. But during my tour of all the main colonies in the system, I noticed many things have changed. The Earth governments came up with a crazy-ass plan to "radically revitalize their natural resources" by initiating man-made earthquakes.

Since the announcement, there has been no room for meaningful political talk because every holo-show host wants a comment on the situation. And there's a limit to how neutral political leaders like me can be. People want a clear yes or no concerning the infamous Mantle Project.

I can't blame them. Two opposing arguments have turned a complex and highly sensitive issue into a generalized battle between ethos and progress. If the two sides go on like this, we might soon be talking about an all-out war between technology and ethics, but I don't think things will go that far.

We won't let them, especially since the Mantle Project is now being implemented.

Miranda Goodman, the host of tonight's show, stands and approaches me. She's ten years younger than I am, blond, and always wears a sarcastic frown on her face. We don't like each other much. We've met and exchanged opinions live on another show. This is the first time we meet on her show.

I can sense my lips twisting into a forced smile.

She extends her hand in a friendly greeting. "Ambassador Judith Campbell, thank you for accepting my invitation to the show," she says.

It's not like she personally invited me; her assistant did all the work of contacting me and my consultants. Not only that, but she knows perfectly well that if my Tri-Colony tour hadn't ended, I wouldn't have agreed to come. That, however, would have given the wrong impression to voters. I was off the planet for almost a year, and if I didn't give an interview to my home planet, Yahire, when I arrived, that could have turned out badly for me.

I nod and also extend my hand. "Pleasure is all mine, Miranda." At this point, it would be wise to flatter her and to do ostensibly good-natured things to feed her ego, but we're still off the air; I'm planning to skip the fake pleasantries.

Miranda notices I don't stand up to greet her—a sign I don't respect her the way she should be respected—and her attitude changes in seconds. She loses the smirk and takes a step back. Now I can see that

Miranda cares more about her public image than about the guests on her show.

Nevertheless, I decide to play her game for now. After all, politics is a business dominated by good talkers and even better liars.

"I expect an experienced politician like you doesn't need to warm up before we pass to the pressing matters, right?" Miranda says.

"You're right. Unfortunately, our interview tonight is limited to half an hour. We'd better cut right to the chase or your viewers won't be satisfied," I reply with a tone of mock affection.

Telling other people how to do their jobs is a terrible insult, especially on holovision. However, young Miranda needs some guidance if she intends to keep political figures coming to her show.

"I understand," she says. "Okay then. We'll be on the air soon. Let us know if there's anything you need before we start. We'll make sure we meet all your demands." With that, she abruptly leaves my side.

Only Owen Waters, my director of security, hears me snort. He's seeing to my safety and the safety of the locations I visit. He's a handsome young man with a pair of lightweight feet. I never hear him getting close.

"Is everything okay, ma'am?" he asks me, considerate of my feelings.

I nod and flick my wrist in a dismissive gesture. "Of course. Everything is great. If we're lucky, I might be able to make the headlines tomorrow as the ambassador who got into a catfight with a popular TV hostess."

I'm being sarcastic and Owen knows it. He grins before speaking again. "Remember that you just finished a successful tour around the Tri-Colony, Ambassador Campbell. It would be a pity if you destroyed all our hard work so close to the end," he says. Owen realizes his mistake only after he has completed his sentence. "Your hard work. I meant to say your hard work, not mine. I'm sorry. I didn't mean to—"

"Owen, you're just as important to the success of this campaign as I am. You're risking your life so I don't have to risk mine. Please, don't correct yourself. You were right in the first place," I reply.

I see his face lighting up; Owen is one of the few people who know how harsh I can be with my assistants. My line of work demands a certain degree of austerity. He understands and he's doing a great job keeping up with the demands of his position. He's also one of the few people who know I don't praise others easily.

Owen nods and places his pointer by the gadget in his ear. This military-grade device gives Owen all the information he needs to protect me and the people in this building. He puts his hand in front of his mouth to cover the movements of his lips from prying eyes. He moves his head up and down twice.

That must have been a report from the secret agents in the crowd and outside the building.

When he's done, I ask him, "Is everything okay?"

"Yes, ma'am. There's nothing to worry about. Just make sure you nail this interview, Mrs. Campbell."

"Owen! Language," I tell him in a mock scolding tone. He smiles and winks at me.

"Good luck, Ambassador Campbell. And thank you for being so kind to me," he says. Owen leaves the set.

He would have stayed longer if the floor manager wasn't getting ready to toss a bottle of water at him. But given Owen's physique, I don't think he would have dared.

The countdown to transmission is already past the number sixty. This means we have less than a minute to prepare.

For the hundredth time one of the show's assistants makes sure my makeup is perfect. Then she hurries to the side of the set. Miranda and I are the only people in front of the camera now. I take in a deep breath and slowly let it out of my lungs.

This is it then, the end of my long tour of the Tri-Colony Union. I have to keep my mind on the task at hand; I can't let this conversation turn to the Mantle Project, not before I have more information about the project. If the subject arises, I'll have to stay neutral and answer taking into consideration my view of what will happen. Not the wisest political tactic.

A man wearing a strange, cylindrical helmet is looking at us and counting down loudly. "Ten, nine, eight, seven, six, five, four …"

The last three numbers he shows using his fingers.

"Three, two, one."

"Good evening! This is *The Evening Show* with Miranda Goodman from Yahire. Tonight we have a very special guest, a woman who has swept the political world with her kind smile and her long black hair, a political figure of major importance to the convocation of the Tri-Colony Union. If her name still hasn't popped into your head, then please let me introduce you to the one and only Ambassador Judith Campbell," Miranda says, sounding like a space circus announcer.

The camera frame expands to include both of us in the holo screen. I smile with a trained courtesy. I shake her hand and whisper words like "Nice to be here" and "It's a pleasure." The clapping and the music are too loud for people to hear me, but if I didn't act like I said these things, viewers would judge me an uncivil and rude person. And that would be bad politics.

When we finally sit, Miranda turns and looks at me. "It's so nice to have you, Judith Campbell, one of the most influential women in the modern political scene."

I grin at her before replying, "I couldn't miss the opportunity to come on your show, Miranda. We've known each other for how long now? Two years?"

"Yes, two years," she says and smiles.

"And this is the first time I've been on your show," I conclude and get ready for her first question.

"Exactly. This is a historic moment for *The Evening Show*. But since you've just returned from your long trip to the Tri-Colony Union, I don't want to eat up too much of your time," she says and examines her holo tablet before her, searching for the first topic of discussion.

She has done a good job of preparing for our interview. The last time we met on that debate night, Miranda kept talking nonsense, things no well-informed person would have said. I guess she's trying to avoid the humiliation of that night.

"So, Ambassador Campbell, many say the Tri-Colony Union owes much of its stability to your attempts to improve the relationships between the colonies. The moon colonies and the old Earth government, however, don't seem to appreciate the work you've done. There are reports that even leaders of Yahire like you are still ill-treated, especially by Earthlings. Is that true?" Miranda asks.

She has given me an opportunity to discuss the purpose of my trip. That's good; she didn't use her opening to introduce the topic of the Mantle Project. Maybe she isn't so bad after all.

"Well, Miranda, first of them all, I want to thank you for your kind, albeit exaggerated, introduction. A delicate era of change is coming to our planet, an era of open borders and recognition of Yahire as an independent entity.

"Part of what you have said is true, but I would be remiss if I didn't convey all those feelings I got on my trip in a meaningful way. The people of Earth are changing, opening up to the idea of cheap transfer between the colonies and to better, more lucrative trade deals. I met countless people who didn't care about where I was born but about my opinion on the rising issues of piracy and trafficking on the moon's empty oceans. Things are changing, Miranda. We might still be treated like second-class citizens, but I have a feeling that's true only in the papers." I end my answer and let my words sink in with the audience.

However, Miranda wants the dramatic version of what I'm trying to convey. "Do you care to give us an example of what you're talking about? People got to their phones and holo screens to prove you wrong. Maybe a personal experience will convince them otherwise," she says.

I spend a moment trying to come up with a good reply to her dare. She's trying to make me look callow because I'm not repeating what other political leaders are saying.

In my moment of contemplation, I turn and stare at Owen, my young director of security. That's when it comes to me, the perfect example.

***

# Chapter 11

## Cosmic Companions

*The morning of February 6, 2072, six months earlier*
*New York City*
*Narrator: Ambassador Judith Campbell*

"Earthlings have it good," Mitchell tells me. "Their food is better, their water doesn't taste like dirt, and even their gadgets are better than ours. I don't understand this."

Mitchell Wallace is one of my instructors. He has black-and-gray hair and is around my age but looks way older. He's a well-known lobbyist, the kind who wins elections by booking the right appearances in the right places. If not for him, I wouldn't be able to visit Earth on my tour.

"It's natural, Mitchell. This planet is the beginning of all life in our solar system. Yahire is relatively new to this neighborhood. It will take time to get used to its particularities," I reply.

Mitchell and I often get into these short arguments about humanity's future and about the response of earthlings to our plea to recognize our planet as an independent entity. He claims earthlings are evil and want to bleed our planet dry, the same way they did theirs for all those years. I say earthlings just don't know any other way.

Our discussion is quickly heading down the same road again. "I don't understand how you can be so calm, Judith. I know that you're an ambassador and that you're here to negotiate the terms of a peaceful relationship, but you've seen what earthlings can do. They almost eradicated the moon colonies all those years ago when the colonies asked for their independence. What is stopping them from doing the same thing to us?"

"The moon was always considered the property of Earth. It's the planet's natural satellite, for God's sake. I don't agree with how they handled that situation, but after millennia of watching the sky and of seeing the moon casting its light on their heads, it wasn't easy to let go of it," I reply.

Mitchell strongly disagrees. "Bullshit. It's all about profit and you know it. Now that this new kind of rock was discovered on the moon colony, earthlings want it all to themselves, like they always do. The moon settlers were the ones who risked their lives to make the moon habitable, and they are the ones who spend their time and energy to keep it that way. Why should earthlings be entitled to take everything they like whenever they like it?"

I don't know how to answer his argument. I sigh and stare out the window. We're inside one of those automatic driving limousines that run on solar energy. It's a Yahire model, one that still isn't for sale on Earth. Our visit isn't purely political. We're also here to advertise our autonomy. And maybe that is not a very honest strategy.

The reason I can't find a convincing argument has to do with the goal of my tour to the Tri-Colony Union. Earth's aggressive tactics against the moon and against Yahire have sparked an interplanetary episode. Earthlings are in denial and claim everything originating from Earth should belong to Earth.

The mission on the moon was funded by the Earth governments, and so was the mission to Yahire. That's why earthlings believe Yahire and the moon should be controlled by Earth and should not be independent territories, deciding matters on their own.

Some years ago, a civil war broke out on the moon. Unlike Yahire, the moon colonies had been divided into two factions: Earth lovers and Earth haters. This was a generalization, but it stayed in the media as such. The Earth haters claimed that since the moon had a degree of self-government it should be recognized as independent. They favored the moon's secession from Earth's government and legal system.

Earth lovers didn't want to withdraw from Earth's government. A stable economy like Earth's and military protection from the original planet offered a safety net to the new and unstable moon colonies. However, there would be no problem between Earth and its satellite if Earth's government hadn't tried to pass legislation making Earth's rule official.

If the moon settlers didn't rise back then, Earth's claim would have been set in stone, and the Earth haters would have been considered rebels subject to arrest by the police. After years of feuding during which the decree was delayed, the two factions made peace when the Earth lovers agreed to support the moon colonies' independence.

United under a common goal, both parties turned against Earth in what was called the First Planetary War. But Yahire arrived in the solar system like a deus ex machina and changed everything. Earth now set its sights on the new planet and allowed the moon's independence.

These events pass through my mind as I try to come up with a response to Mitchell's argument. But I've got nothing.

Mitchell turns and looks at me; he wants to keep the discussion going. Luckily for me, Owen butts in. "Ambassador Campbell, we're arriving at the hospital. Get ready for extraction in three minutes," he says.

I detect Mitchell's disappointment on his face. "This is an ongoing discussion, Judith. You won't be so lucky next time," he says and puts on his augreals with a pair of headphones.

In three minutes I may have to face a bunch of journalists hectoring me about the importance of Earth and Yahire creating strong bonds. For the first time I don't feel like doing battle. If I can't find a good answer for one of my friends, how can I go up against far more cunning politicians?

My heavy sigh draws Owen's attention. He gets closer. "Is everything okay, ma'am?"

I smile at his usual question. This young man is so considerate of my feelings.

"Well, isn't always?" I reply in a sarcastic tone.

"What's going on, ambassador? What is troubling you?" he asks.

"I don't know. I guess I'm getting too old for this kind of thing. Maybe the world doesn't want to change, and I'm a stupid fish moving against the current. Or maybe I'm the one who doesn't want to change when everyone around me does."

Owen is patient and lets me finish before speaking. "We can continue this discussion inside, ambassador. This is not the place for such talk," he says.

For the first time since he was assigned to me by Yahire's secret services, I examine the details of Owen's face. He's still a boy in my eyes. His eyes have the soft red color of Yahire settlers, and his hair is brown. Unlike earthlings, people born and raised on Yahire usually end up with an unnatural eye color. That's the result of a mutation happening on Yahire due to its climate, which is different from Earth's.

Even so, this young boy could easily have been my son—the boy I lost in the riots five years ago on the moon. Maybe that's why I'm so indulgent with Owen; maybe I see Charles in his eyes.

God, now I've gotten sentimental. This day can't get any worse.

Owen does an excellent job of creating a passageway through the crowd of journalists outside the hospital. He advises Mitchell to wait in the car until the event is over. He can watch the whole thing through the cameras placed in the gadgets used by the secret agents.

Deep inside, I thank Owen for going the extra mile to give me peace of mind, even if it will last for only an hour and a half. Mitchell isn't a bad man, but he can be pesky and mean. Also, it wouldn't look good if the media saw me and my lobbyist together at an event for sick children and for veterans of the battle against pirates on the empty oceans.

I've asked the media not to make this event a circus since it is not a publicity stunt. It's my habit to visit children in need. Charles again pops into my mind. Maybe this whole thing is a mistake. Maybe I should ask for a more experienced security director. That way Owen won't have to risk his life to keep me safe.

Nevertheless, this isn't a decision for today. Right now, I want to give my undivided attention to the children in the hospital.

At the entrance to the building, a welcoming party greets me with a bouquet of flowers and an album signed by the children. The director of the hospital shakes my hand heartily but says nothing about the work he's doing to help the kids. He talks only about how more money can bring better care to the hospital and about how Yahire's support can help.

I'm not in the mood to talk politics today. However, I turn and tell my assistant, Amy Roberts, to arrange a meeting with him at a later time. When the director sees I'm serious, he gives me room to breathe and lets me continue my visit in peace.

I meet many children in the hospital rooms. Some are sick and don't have the strength to greet me properly; some are recovering and play with their parents. However, all of them smile at me and ask me questions about my strange eyes and my long hair.

When I arrive at the last room, a girl and her family are waiting for me. The tiny girl has short-cropped hair and pale skin but a strong smile and a spark of life in her eyes.

The girl's parents rush to my side. "Welcome, Ambassador Campbell. We're extremely honored to meet you," the husband says.

"I can't believe it. I can't believe it," his wife says.

"Sorry about that. My wife is a fan of yours. She has been like that since we were told you would visit the hospital. Carla, snap out of it! The ambassador will think you're stupid or something," the husband says.

I stop him and grab his wife's hand. "Carla, we're both equally surprised, my dear. We Yahire settlers don't get that reaction all the time here on Earth," I say in a moment of weakness.

I know I shouldn't have said anything, but after my discussion with Mitchell, I couldn't hold back my words. My son's face keeps appearing in my head, and I feel a bit disoriented.

"What are you talking about, ambassador?" Carla asks. "I don't know what our politicians say to you, but there are not many people here who don't love you. We consider the people of Yahire our brothers and sisters, our cosmic companions."

Her husband nods, equally shocked by what I said.

At that moment, I hear a child's laughter. The two excited parents turn and see their daughter on Owen's shoulders, giggling uncontrollably. I don't know what's making me tear up—the sight of a Yahire man playing with an Earth girl, her parents doing their best to ease my worries, or the joy of the moment. Most probably, it's a mix of all the above.

All I know is I'll never forget this moment for as long as I live.

\*\*\*

# Chapter 12

# The Interstellar Communication

*On the set of* The Evening Show
*Planet Yahire*
*Narrator: Ambassador Judith Campbell*

The crowd cheers and I'm close to tearing up again. It seems my sensibility is contagious because Miranda is turning her face away from the cameras, trying to hide her moist eyes.

After the cheering dies down, Miranda turns and faces me. "That was an incredible story you shared with us, ambassador. Wow! Phew! I can't help but ask, is the girl all right? Did you keep in touch with the family?"

"Of course. Yes, little Whitney is doing great. In fact, the day I visited the hospital the family had just received the results of Whitney's exams. She's healthy and ready to enjoy her life," I report.

Snuffling comes from everywhere in the studio; with a quick look, I see everyone patting an embarrassed Owen on the shoulder and the women in the audience wiping their eyes. Making the headlines? Check.

But in my eyes, this is bigger than making sure I look good. The people in the colonies are ready to get closer and to discuss new ways of working together. They want us to be friends, not enemies, and earthlings think we deserve to have our own government and constitution. Their leaders can't do otherwise if the people they represent ask them to help us.

Miranda soon recovers, and I see her getting ready to drop her next question.

"So, Ambassador Campbell, you're quite a humanitarian. Most of your work is centered around the well-being of people in general, universal citizens. I know you've just arrived and haven't had time to get properly caught up in the Mantle Project craziness, but you're one of the last political figures who haven't commented on the situation," she says.

There she goes. I want to sigh but this bitch has just put me in a corner. I'm on live holovision and she's asking me to comment on a situation caused by an Earth decision. I can't sound uncertain or neutral, but I don't know shit about what's going on back there.

They made the announcement while I was on my trip back home. I could not be sufficiently prepared for that question. Even so, I have to say something.

***

*Two months earlier, outer space*
*Narrator: Ambassador Judith Campbell*

Traveling between planets isn't as comfortable as many people believe. Things have gotten better over the last few years, especially after the Tri-Colony Union started working on special spaceships made for quicker and safer transport. However, that doesn't mean trips got more comfortable.

Fortunately, only people close to me travel with me. Owen and Amy are two of them. On these trips, relations between me and my staff get more casual. Owen and Amy open up about their relationship, and I make them call me Judith, not Ambassador Campbell. Two months of formalities would drive me crazy for sure.

The food in outer space is tasteless, the water is rationed, and the only change of scenery is the entertainment room, which is packed with virtual reality helmets. Other than that, there's no internet and nothing to do except exercise and prepare for the end of my tour back on Yahire.

However, just recently, a new service has been created, a rarity since space travel has become more common nowadays. Once a week, a super-dense information file is sent to our vehicle from all the colonies. The file is packed with reports on everything that has transpired in the past week.

I don't know how it's scientifically possible to do that, but I know it's impossible to have continuous access in a helpful way. But I guess I don't have to know how this is done to enjoy the benefits of this service. We use the InfoRay service to make sure we're up to speed on everything happening in the Tri-Colony Union. And as an ambassador of the colonies, I find the InfoRay priceless.

The InfoRay will arrive today and I'm excited. I will find out if my visit to Earth was a success.

I walk to the bridge and find Owen in his sweatpants and a hoodie. This look is more appropriate to his age than the black suits and the sunglasses he has to wear as a director of security. He is wearing his earphones and frowning at something.

Next to him, Amy is mumbling to herself. I get the feeling something is going on.

"Did the InfoRay arrive?" I ask.

"Ma'am," Owen starts. He sounds confused. "Judith, I think you have to see this."

I get closer to the screen and start reading the heaps of information that have arrived with the InfoRay. Soon, I start frowning as well, unable to understand most of what is happening back on Earth. When I finish the summary of everything that took place ten days ago, I look at both of them.

"Do you understand anything about this Mantle Project?"

Owen shakes his head, but Amy seems to know more about it. "Judith, I think I can help you," she says, sounding timid. She's still new to my team and isn't used to calling me by my first name. "In short, the Department of Core and Earth Sciences announced a plan to tamper with the planet's mantle to access natural resources."

"What? How are they going to do that?" Owen demands. He turns and stares at me. "I'm sorry, ma'am … Judith. I didn't mean to shout," he mutters.

"Don't worry about that now, Owen. Let the girl talk. How are they going to do that, Amy?"

Owen sneaks a smile to his girlfriend. They're such a sweet couple, in the prime of life and brilliant in their field. I hope they stay like that. But this is irrelevant. I'm more interested in understanding the Mantle Project.

"Well, judging from what I've read, they found a way to induce grand-scale, high-intensity earthquakes without causing damage to buildings and infrastructure," Amy says. "Other than that, they haven't announced anything else. They probably wanted to confirm there's something in the works. However, it's pretty apparent the plan hasn't been approved by the Council of Directors of the Core and Earth Sciences Department."

I walk to the screen and reread the article. "It makes no sense. Even if it helps them to find new resources, this project sounds terrible. How are they going to do this?"

Amy shrugs and looks at Owen; he shrugs as well. "I'm sorry, Judith. If we were on Yahire, I could contact the secret services and get more information, but it will be a long time before we know for sure what they are intending with this project of theirs," he says.

Jesus! This is new. This is totally original. What's gotten into these earthlings? Why are they so desperate to change the deal so close to the end?

Well, as Amy said, this project hasn't been approved by the council, and it may be a long time before it is. Maybe earthlings will rethink it and find another way to retrieve their natural resources.

No; this is improbable. They wouldn't have confirmed the existence of the project if it wasn't close to completion. I'm sure this Mantle Project will come to life one way or another. All we can do is be prepared for anything that follows.

"Tell me, Amy, what's your opinion on this project? Do you think it's dangerous? Do you think it can make a difference in solving Earth's natural resources problem?" I ask.

Amy isn't used to my attention. She bites her lower lip and looks at Owen, searching for a way out.

The trip between Yahire and Earth is a long one but isn't demanding. In the years from the discovery of the planet to the colonization, a highly secure path between the two planets was established. Nowadays, even an automated spaceship can make the trip, saving the cost of a specialized crew.

Only the three of us are on the bridge, gathered around the holo screen.

After a short pause, Amy finally speaks up. "I'm not sure. Earth is an older planet than our Yahire. Earthlings have done extensive research regarding the systems at work on their planet. I'm sure they've taken precautions and aren't walking blindly. But to introduce a new procedure like this Mantle Project on a global scale? I don't know. It sounds risky, to say the least."

Amy struggles to answer my question. Truth be told, we don't have enough information to easily deduce the final outcome of this project. But it sounds too alien to me, too untested. However, I'm not a scientist. I don't have the knowledge needed to decide if the project will be successful.

My concern is purely theoretical, born of my need to stay ahead of the times. And there's no better way to do that than by understanding things at a fundamental level.

Owen suddenly wants to share his opinion. "I don't like it. It seems like earthlings are trying to play with nature, to control powers that are uncontrollable. They have long forgotten their roots. During ancient times, people feared and respected nature. Nowadays, they're dead set on controlling it. Would it be so bad if they stopped buying new gadgets? If they stopped using their cars and walked? I know it's comfortable, but would it hurt them too much if they became less materialistic?"

I'm impressed by his insight. Owen grasped the subject at its core—materialism, our deviation from our roots and from our beliefs. Wow!

Ethics and values have always clashed with science and technology. You can't change if you don't shed the mantle of ignorance. But who decides who is ignorant and who is a believer?

When I was younger, I decided I believed in God and in His teachings. I've done my research and I know both sides, but I have opted to stand in the middle, which actually is not the middle. I keep my ears open and my mind clear. I ask and wonder and ask again. There are no stupid questions, just stupid people who don't ask questions.

God is universal. He is loving. He is a deep personal experience. You can't know Him if you don't search your soul to find His light.

God is not an enemy of progress. He gave us intelligence to allow us to achieve everything we decide to do. When He saw one planet wasn't enough for all the people, maybe that's why God sent a second one—bigger, harsher, but a home nonetheless.

To this day, Yahire is worshipped as the promised land, a place in the stars sent to save us from our vanity. But we wouldn't be able to reach this land, to colonize it, and to prosper on it if it wasn't for technology. High-speed spaceships, holo screens, InfoRays, AIs—all these might be God's gifts to humanity, intended to make us aim even higher.

So what if the Mantle Project is exactly that? What if the project is a step toward making Earth better again?

We haven't talked to each other for some time now. The silence is deafening. Owen is a believer who thinks change must be granted and not pursued; Amy is a fighter who believes change is a milestone that must be pursued.

What do I believe?

***

*Back on the set of* The Evening Show
*Planet Yahire*
*Narrator: Ambassador Judith Campbell*

Pauses to a show must be short and kept in context; I have to give Miranda an answer, but what will my answer be? I'm neutral; I believe the project is both good and bad, but how do I present that so she doesn't take my neutrality for weakness?

"Well? What do you think, Ambassador Campbell? What's your opinion of the Mantle Project?" Miranda asks me again.

This is my cue; I have no more time to think it over. I have to start talking and must improvise.

"Frankly, I don't know. I'm a big fan of change. I think change is needed, especially in crucial periods of history like this. Earth needs resources, and this Mantle Project sure sounds promising. It's still too early to come to a decision, but I believe in change, and I think change should be made when the moment is right.

However, I don't think it's wise to tamper with the planet that allowed its inhabitants to prosper, the birthplace of humanity. Earth is our shared home, even if we're trying to detach our heritage from theirs. We'll fight to preserve it the way it is. I'm worried about Earth in the way someone would be worried about his old home. And I'm worried because sometimes need can prompt us to make bad decisions. In this case, these decisions could risk the fate of a planet."

Miranda interrupts me. "Your reply sounds surprisingly neutral, Ambassador Campbell. Are you steering clear of either side to avoid something?"

"I sound neutral because I feel neutral. I'm torn between my beliefs and my support for change. My spiritual side tells me we shouldn't mess with things we don't understand, but my progressive mind tells me this is the next stage of evolution. In fact, I'm not neutral at all. I am among those who say the Mantle Project is here and we should wait to see what happens," I reply in a tense tone.

Miranda takes a moment to collect her thoughts. We have only seven minutes of airtime left. She has to make a counterargument and give me time to answer. I don't know where she'll try to hit me next.

"The hostilities on the moon colonies were intended to cause change. People were torn between two opinions, and if I remember correctly, you have experienced the consequences of being a neutral bystander firsthand. Neutrality can be considered a weakness in a time of turmoil. Aren't you afraid that your stance might cause you to lose many of your fans?"

She's totally serious about this question. At first, I thought she was joking when she brought up the fighting on the moon colonies, but it's clear she wasn't, not after making a reference to my son's death.

A white-hot anger fills my chest; I have to control it. My public image is my career, and I'm not ready to give up my career, not for an amateur hostess who is trying to use this interview to advance her own agenda. I won't fall into this trap. I have to make sure Miranda Goodman doesn't get what she wants.

I relax my body and rest my back on the armchair. I cross my fingers and place my arms close to my belly. This is my defensive stance; I've gotten serious about answering her question in a way that will make her seem heartless and ignorant.

It will be tough. This is her show. She controls the questions, and there's not enough time to make sure I do a thorough job, but it doesn't matter. When I finish with her, she won't invite me back to this farce she calls show.

"First and foremost, I don't appreciate your bringing up the subject of my son's death in a discussion regarding the consequences of a major project. I find it unethical and unprofessional. I came to your show thinking we would have a serious political discussion. By trying to entertain a certain percentage of ignorant parties with pure gossip, you damage your reputation, not mine."

Miranda appears astonished. She opens her mouth, trying to stop me from continuing, but I've grasped control of the situation and I don't intend to let go before I've made my point clear.

"Also, since you've brought up the topic of my neutrality, I have only one thing to say to you: neutrality may be considered a weakness, but it can certainly save the lives of thousands. My son, Charles Campbell, died protecting that neutrality, and I'm proud he left the way he did," I say, my voice cracking on the last word.

"If it wasn't for his sacrifice, an innocent bystander would have been a victim of an assault by the extremists of change. So yes, I choose now and I'll choose again in the future not to speak before I understand, not to act without being sure of the repercussions of my actions. Thank you." With that, I get on my feet and walk off the set.

I can barely hear Miranda's words as I make my dramatic exit. "That was Ambassador Campbell, ladies and gentlemen," she says, sounding dumbstruck. "Er ... I want to ... I'm sorry. This was intense. I want to apologize to all my viewers and to Ambassador Judith Campbell for the bad wording of my question. I understand I've crossed the line separating the political and the personal life of Mrs. Campbell in my effort to promote a healthy debate," she says, sounding honest far too late.

I'm too far away from the studio to hear the rest of what she has to say, but I don't care. My body is shaking from the intensity of the moment. I didn't expect her to ask me about Charles. Even by holovision standards, it was a dirty hit meant to make me look weak. Miranda is still trying to build her career as a political journalist and has no idea which lines are not to be crossed.

Two staff members are trying to convince me to return to the set, but my decision is final. I didn't attend to give her the satisfaction of making a scene on her show. I rush to the exit and head outside; the heavy atmosphere of Yahire welcomes me.

I walk all the way to the road, increasing my pace to a messy run. I need to find a shelter, a place to calm down. For some reason, a church located on the other side of the road from the studio seems like the perfect place to catch my breath. The Mantle Project and all the disaster accompanying it can't reach me in this tranquil place.

When I'm on the other side of the road, I stand before the grand building and take a deep breath. After releasing it, I put my foot on the first step of the stairway leading to the entrance. It's not a long way up, but my body and soul are tired. I have never experienced such profound fatigue, even after I was first elected.

I'm uncertain and vulnerable; I don't know what to do but pray.

\*\*\*

# Chapter 13

# A Tough Year

*Same setting*
*Narrator: Ambassador Judith Campbell*

It has been half an hour since I left the studio for the church. All I do is observe and sigh. I breathe in and my eyes turn to the east. The seats around me are empty; the air is heavy from the burning candles and the warm feeling of kindness. God has been here for me every time I needed a helping hand. When Charles died, I spent my days visiting a church and praying. When my husband left me, I visited a church, crying tears of devastation.

I breathe out and my eyes turn to the west. The scenery doesn't change, but I spot a young couple holding each other close. The girl has long blond hair and the face of an angel. The boy is tall and strong. She's crying on his shoulder, and he's caressing her hair. Her tears are exclusive to her and her love. I wouldn't have seen anything if I didn't turn my head the moment I did.

The intimacy of that moment makes me avert my eyes. I feel like I'm peering at their lives through a keyhole; I'm a set of prying eyes that feel nothing and see everything. Somewhere along the way, I forgot I'm a human being with deep-rooted feelings. I thought that I was impenetrable, that no one could touch the open wound in my soul.

But Miranda Goodman saw through me and decided to spread salt on that wound.

A politician's humanity suffers from the cold logic typical of the profession. I don't know if I can continue like that for long.

I lower my head and lose myself in thought.

I close my eyes. When darkness surrounds me, I hear a pair of feet rushing to my side. I don't have to open my eyes to recognize the man standing next to me.

"Ambassador Campbell," Owen says, panting. "The whole team is looking for you. It was really irresponsible of you to leave the set on a live show. Even worse, you left a secure location without our escort. What were you thinking? You could have hurt yourself."

I don't have to tell him to lower his voice; the echo of his words hits Owen hard enough to make him scowl. He turns around and apologizes to everyone in the building. Then he looks at me.

"Sit down," I command him. He doesn't appreciate my tone but obeys without complaining. "Have I ever talked to you about Charles?"

He shakes his head but realizes I'm not watching him, so he replies, "No, you haven't. But to be honest, I know everything about his case. Knowing your history is part of my job, ma'am."

I can't help but grin. "Part of your job. He used to say that a lot. Charles was killed in one of the extremist assaults in the moon colonies seven years ago. One bullet in the chest, close to the heart, and one in the head. The second was the kill shot. Everything happened so fast that even we, his family, didn't realize what was going on until it was too late.

"Charles was a proud boy, always asking to be transferred to the front lines because he felt that was the place where he could help out the most. He couldn't choose between the two sides, so he decided to protect everyone in the only way he knew. That's why he enlisted in the Peace Corps. He had to stay neutral and to defend the peace above all."

I haven't talked about him for so long that I'm feeling the weight of my past as the words leave my mouth. Owen remains silent even though he said he knows the whole story. But I have to talk to someone. I have to say something. I can't stay silent.

"Charles always countered my opinions. I wanted to change the world by picking a side, and he wanted to make the world a place with no sides and no discrimination—no wars, no brothers killing each other. He always said he didn't understand how politicians think. Why were we striving for more resources on Yahire when there were hungry kids back on Earth? Why were we arguing over borders when people were dying to protect these fictitious lines?

And I used to tell him the word *border* is *order* with the letter *b* in front of it. Order over chaos, borders over the law of jungle, the end justifies the means, and things like that. I was so wrong, so blind. He was trying to teach me a lesson, and I was too proud a parent to listen. But now that he's gone, there's a silence all the time, a silence that cripples me when I can't fill it. There are no holidays anymore, no birthdays, no love and joy. Just work and sleepless nights.

I miss him so much, and I can't forgive myself for choosing my duty over mourning his memory. But I want to make Yahire a better world, something that would have made him proud, and I won't allow people like Miranda Goodman to tarnish my vision, my son's vision."

The moment I utter my last word, Owen enfolds me in a tight, loving hug. I can't hold back anymore; I let go and break down, sobbing on his chest.

He allows me time to calm down and then relaxes his hold on my body. "I'm sorry, Judith. I know you've been through a lot, and you had every right to storm out of that place the way you did. But you have to remember you're important to us, to the people who voted for you, the ones you represent. I know it's a lot to ask of you, but you have to carry on until your dream of creating an independent Yahire comes true," he says.

I smile at him. "Spoken like a true son," I mumble and break free of his grasp.

I tidy up my appearance and spring to my feet. Before leaving, I hold Owen's head between my hands and pull him closer to kiss his forehead. "Thank you for protecting me. Your support is really important to me."

We walk away from the house of God with renewed hope and cleansed thoughts. If this isn't a miracle, I pity those who don't believe in God and His might.

***

The next day, yesterday's incident is all over the news. Some talk about my breakdown like it's the end of the world, and others try to justify my response in the name of motherhood. For a change, I try to ignore this circus and focus on the new data that arrived last night.

I walk into my office and see a small army of analysts, staff members, and assistants buzzing like a swarm of busy bees. Even though I know the reason and I shouldn't be happy, my lips twist into a mirthless smile.

This is my world and this is where I belong.

I head straight for Amy. As soon as she spots me, her face brightens. She's talking on the phone, but she's wrapping up her call. "No, Ambassador Campbell won't comment on last night's interview. There's nothing she wants to add regarding opportunistic journalism and Ms. Goodman's thesis. We don't want any affiliation with her program now or in the future. No, Mrs. Campbell can't make a comment herself. She's busy attending to serious matters. Thank you and have a nice day yourself," she says and hangs up. "Jerks. They've been calling all day trying to reach you, ma'am. I don't understand their perseverance."

"Sharks can't help themselves when they smell blood, my dear. But I see you've already adjusted to the situation," I tell her.

Her face flushes. "Thank you, ambassador. That's very nice of you," she replies.

"Okay, so enough with the pleasantries. Tell me what's new regarding the Mantle Project. Today is the day we finally learn the council's decision, right?"

Amy nods. "Yes. The decision is already out. Sources from the department say it was a relatively short process and the decision was unanimous. The Mantle Project is finally official," she says, her voice betraying her anxiety.

"Don't worry, Amy. I think we're reading too much into this situation. All we have to do is get ready to handle any situation efficiently. Where is Owen?"

She nods toward another part of the room; Owen is addressing his team members, probably briefing them on the day's schedule. I head toward him at once.

"Don't forget: if you feel something is wrong, it probably is. Act first and ask questions later. Failure is not an option; failure in this line of work means somebody important dies. And you don't want that. Dismissed," he says loudly.

Before seeing me, Owen checks his holographic display and continues reading a report.

"I see you're doing a great job of scaring the new members of your team into submission," I tell him.

His eyebrows arch upward; he smiles before speaking. "Ambassador Campbell, welcome to the office after a year's absence. I hope everything is exactly how you left it."

I snort and roll my eyes. "Yeah, yeah. It doesn't really matter," I reply. "There are more important things to attend to right now than settling into my office again. Have you learned anything more about the Mantle Project? Amy told me it has been approved by the council."

"Great news! I'm glad you found all your things exactly like you left them a year ago. Order and tidiness are important to an office," he mumbles.

"What in the world are you talking about? Have you gone mad?" I say, but then it hits me. He's changing the subject because there's something he wants to tell me without saying it out loud. The first place Owen looks for espionage technology is my desk. He's probably referred to my office to make me realize we have to head there.

"Now that you mention it, I need help with a few things. Follow me," I tell him.

Five seconds later, we're alone.

Owen takes off his glasses and looks me in the eye. "The Department of Core and Earth Sciences contacted me and, I'm guessing, every important person on Yahire. They want us to grant them permission for limited migration if an emergency arises regarding the Mantle Project. This happened an hour after the council approved the project," he reports.

"Okay, so what's the big secret? Why can't you share that with the rest of the team?" I ask.

"Because they asked me to keep the information confidential until a further update," Owen says.

"That's weird. How is it possible to grant them migration permission if we can't share the information with the rest of the world? What are they trying to achieve?" I say, wondering why the situation with the Mantle Project changed so much.

"I don't know. They've set up a strict protocol. The distance between our planets is too big for the Mantle Project to be considered risky for us. I don't know what is going on back there, but I think we should stay alert to any rapid developments in the coming months. Something smells fishy here," he says.

I don't agree. "We're too concerned about this. I don't have time to deal with technological terror right now. Make sure you open up a communication line between our agents here and there and keep a steady flow of information coming. Other than that, don't worry too much about it. I'm sure it's just a dumb precaution they had to take," I reply.

He nods and turns to go, but I stop him. "I'll need some time alone, Owen. Don't let anyone come in for an hour or so. There's something I have to check," I tell him.

"Yes, ma'am. Don't worry. You can get all the time you need. I'll make sure no one disturbs you," he says.

When Owen leaves, I sit at my desk and turn on my holo screen. In seconds, I'm calling one of my closest friends, Lance Alexander, counselor to Yahire's president.

"Did you get the message?" I ask in a cryptic manner. He nods.

"How quickly do you think we can grant them permission?" I ask abruptly.

"Two months if we follow the public route, six months to one year if we set up secret colonies."

"Then we have to start immediately. This is going to be one tough year," I reply as I begin a highly sensitive conversation with the man in front of me.

The Mantle Project just got upgraded to a B-plus security issue; this means all of the people involved will keep their eyes open for any signs of failure but won't be too vocal.

As Owen said, failure means someone important dies. In this case, more than 9.5 billion people.

# Chapter 14

## The End Of Activism

*October 14, 2073, about a year after the Mantle Project started*
*New York City*
*Narrator: Tommy Russell*

We tried our best, but we couldn't stop the Mantle Project. Dr. Bailey, my friend and the project's lead scientist, implemented the plan even after the Anti-Mantle Project Committee organized many protests against it. I never joined the committee due to its radical beliefs, but I supported its actions until the group changed its mission and launched a broader war against all technology.

Ambassador Campbell of Yahire warned us about the situation, but it wasn't until six months after the project began that the conflict took a lethal turn. The first victim of the violence spawned by the project was a young man named Ian Holland. Instead of putting out the fires, his death added fuel to them. One side has turned the man into a martyr, the other into the sad victim of a sorry situation.

Neither of them is right, but one point is indisputable: The Mantle Project is bound to change the world.

During the first month of its implementation, the world seemed to have stopped turning. No one talked about the project on the news or mentioned it at work for fear of shattering a delicate peace.

However, when the project's first miniature-scale tests succeeded, the two sides resumed their battle with renewed intensity. They were caught up in an unbreakable chain of action and reaction. Now, one year in, it's clear this vicious circle has no meaning. I never believed it did.

People attending the Sunday service seemed at peace with themselves during this crisis. They smiled, shook hands, and asked how each other's families were doing. I don't know if they were acting out of fear, ignorance, or hope; all I know is that I didn't like it. And for the first time in my life, I took a break from going to church.

I miss the days before the project started when everyone was trying to understand it and to decide what position to take. Now a fog seems to have descended on people's minds, and only the radical and the cautious see the signs.

Catherine and I have decided not to continue discussing the project in front of the girls. We don't want to alarm them in any way. Maybe I'm wrong and the scientists have come up with a revolutionary procedure that will benefit everyone. And if it wasn't for the signs, I might accept that possibility. But this isn't right, and I can't go on with my life if I don't do everything I can to stop this project.

That's why I started contacting scientists around the world, people who could help me find missing pieces of this puzzle. Three months after the project started, I joined people I met on the internet in organizing a group with the sole purpose of pressuring officials and asking the Core and Earth Sciences Department to show the world the complete files on the project.

The original group included me and four others. As our numbers grew, we became more vocal and people started hearing our voices. Politicians who shared our views demanded full transparency from the department, and celebrities took up our cause. Within two months, we had a thousand dedicated members who work nonstop to make sure we miss nothing.

We established a code of conduct and made sure none of us had anything to hide. We signed our missives with our true names, not nicknames or initials, and we opened our files to those who doubted us.

We got invitations from holovision shows to share our views with the public and received letters from political leaders asking us to endorse their candidacies. For a while, we spent much of our time replying to messages and tending to organizational duties, but our hard work finally started to pay off.

Today all our efforts have come to fruition. A message bearing the government's official seal has come to my personal email account. It's the official response from the Department of Core and Earth Sciences. This is our moment of triumph.

Dear Sirs and Madams,

The Council of Directors of the Department of Core and Earth Sciences of the United States of America has decided to issue an official response regarding the question of the transparency of the data from the Mantle Project.

The department can't, under any circumstances, share sensitive information regarding ongoing projects. After completion of said project, all of the scientific data and the original files of the project will be released to the public along with an official response from the team responsible for the project's creation.

With all due respect, we ask you to stop impeding the normal conduct of the Mantle Project in any way since its implementation is a venture approved by the Council of Directors as well as the government of the United States of America and the United Nations of planet Earth.

Sincerely,
Dr. Andrea Ramos,
Secretary of the Department of Core and Earth
Sciences of the United States of America

I can't stop reading and rereading the reply, my hand cupping my mouth. We have been formally rejected in a way that makes us sound like a bunch of pesky flies. This is the worst reply possible. It's Saturday, October 14, one year after the project started, and I'm at a loss for ways to find out the truth about this "venture."

It's early in the morning, and the reply couldn't have come at a worse time. The financial center where I work is merging with another one, and my responsibilities have skyrocketed. I'm busy, sometimes even on the weekends, but my job is crucial to my family's survival.

Cat is out of the house; she is visiting her shop to make sure everything's running smoothly. Her job has always demanded that she work on weekends. Her workload has temporarily doubled since her staff has suddenly shrunk.

I sigh and turn off the holo screen. I head downstairs to the living room and find the girls painting using their augreal glasses. They seem to be having fun.

In the past year, Manna has learned how to read and is slowly abandoning the augreal glasses. Lisa has recently turned more creative with her sketches. Both are growing up more quickly than I would like to admit. Their questions never cease to amaze me.

Manna has recently started to struggle with questions about extraterrestrial life, esoteric beliefs, and God, the same way Lisa did around her age. However, I no longer worry about the answers I give them now that I know the truth. God lives inside those who discover Him and who love Him; these people experience His miracles deep within their hearts.

It's a lovely day and I would have liked to take a walk outside if Catherine were here to take care of the girls. Because she isn't, I'll have to enjoy the view from inside. When I enter the kitchen, Manna quickly spots me. "Daddy, daddy! Look at what I've drawn," she shouts.

Lisa isn't so loud, but she runs to my side with her augreal glasses on. When they get close, they swipe their hands in the air to send their drawings to the holo screen on the counter. Manna's drawing befits her younger age. She has used bright, simple colors to draw me, Catherine, and her sister, all embracing her in a green meadow.

"Wow! That's really good," I tell her. "How did you think of that?"

"Well, you and Mommy are never home together anymore, and … and we haven't visited the park for months."

My brows arch upward in surprise; Manna is perceptive for her age. I have to reassure her or she'll think there's trouble between her mom and me.

"You're such a thoughtful girl, Manna. I didn't know you liked our visits to the park. Tell you what. I will call your mom and tell her to come home right away. Then we'll grab some doughnuts and head there immediately. Is that a deal?"

Her face brightens. "Yes! You're the best dad in the whole world," she says and hugs me tightly.

After her hug, there is no room left in my mind for failures and official responses issued by the department. I'm just happy I'm alive and healthy and able to enjoy being loved by my family.

Manna returns to the living room to continue her painting. That's when Lisa approaches me and tugs at my sleeve. Lisa is going through her shy phase, and she doesn't want to get loud or to attract attention in any away—except when she draws; that's when she shines.

"Dad, what about my painting? Do you like it?"

With a quick swipe of my hand, the pictures on the holo screen change. The difference in quality is apparent immediately. Lisa is a talented painter and a deeply emotional child. She picks her themes randomly, mostly from a pool of things troubling her.

This time she has outdone herself.

The drawing shows me hunched over my holo screen with my head on my hands. The holo screen lights up my face, but the rest of the picture is dark. Lisa perfectly portrays my worry on all those nights when I was using my holo screen to run the group and to compose letters to people around the world.

"Oh God, this is wonderful, Lisa. What made you draw this?" I ask.

She pulls back and cowers from her shyness. "I don't know. I just wanted to draw a picture of you to make you happy, and this is the first thing that popped into my head," she says.

I lean forward and hug her tightly. "Honey, why didn't you say something to me earlier? I didn't know it bothered you this much."

"I don't know. I didn't want to disturb you when you were working," she replies; this means she gave the picture deep thought.

"Well, from now on, you don't have to worry. I won't spend another night over the computer. We'll do whatever you want to do. Deal?" I say.

She nods and gives me a kiss on the cheek. Electricity passes through my body. I have grown too isolated over the last few months, trying my best to find a solution to the Mantle Project problem, and my family has suffered because I have been encased in a shell.

"Actually, you know what? Forget it. Let's go pick up mommy and head to the park. What do you say?"

The girls start cheering and quickly put away their glasses. This is their only day off, and they would rather spend it with their parents than stay home and play their games. Business and work can wait. There's always tomorrow.

\*\*\*

"Are you ready, girls? All buckled up?" I ask.

We're inside the car and they have already started singing their favorite kids' song. It's a catchy tune they were taught in school when learning about colors. They both love drawing, so it quickly became their favorite song. Catherine and I love hearing the song when we're in the car with the girls, because it means they're excited and happy.

I haven't called Cat to warn her about our sudden visit, but I'm sure she'll be happy to see us. She's always trying to persuade me to spend more time with the girls, but I always decline, citing work and the group. I'll spend the rest of the day with my family. Catherine and the girls deserve it after putting up with my inattention for so long.

Lisa helps her sister put on the seat belt, and after making sure it's tight enough, she turns to me and smiles. "We're ready, Daddy. Let's go!" she says and starts singing again.

I turn on the engine, and we're on our way to meet Catherine.

I decide to tune in my babies' favorite station so they don't have to scream at the top of their lungs all the way to the park. I shush them with a laugh and speak to Dorothy, our AI assistant.

"Dorothy, turn on the radio," I tell her.

"Of course, Tommy. Right on," she replies.

However, I've forgotten that I usually listen to a news channel on my way to work, so when Dorothy turns on the radio, it is tuned to that station.

"You're listening to the Live News Station. We just got a report about another victim of the vision flu. This time, a twenty-three-year-old woman was found lying on the road outside a grocery store, mumbling the usual end-of-time phrase.

"She's only the most recent victim of what some people call a mass hallucination. Online sources call this the Mantle omen wave, and it's considered by many to be a harbinger of the end of the world. Here we have Dr. Austin, an expert in mass psychology. Good morning, doctor."

"Good morning, Felix. I'm glad you invited me, because I think this scare-mongering has gone on for too long now."

Before I know it, I'm so lost in their discussion that I barely hear Manna speaking to me. "Daddy? Can you put on some music now?"

"One moment, honey. This is important to daddy," I reply.

"So, doctor, can you give us a logical explanation for what is going on with this vision epidemic? More reports arrive every day of people having weird visions of what they call the end of the world. What does an expert have to say about the coming apocalypse?"

Dr. Austin chuckles at the host's question. "It's easy to deduce that these events of mass hysteria have nothing to do with the end of the world. If I had to make a guess, I'd say these 'visions' are the products of lucid fantasies and of Mantle Project stress."

The host gasps to add drama to the conversation. "So, Dr. Austin, you're linking these incidents to the Mantle Project?"

Dr. Austin chuckles again but this time in a mirthless way. He sure sounds irritated. "Yes, of course. It would be foolish to deny the fact that these hallucinations—I beg your pardon, but I can't keep calling them visions—are the byproduct of the media coverage of this groundbreaking scientific method."

"Do you care to elaborate your views?" the host asks.

"Of course. That's why I'm here," the doctor replies. He then launches into a long, complicated explanation of what he calls the hallucinations.

I can't follow the rest of the conversation, not while driving. But despite his vaunted expertise, the doctor added nothing to the conversation about the vision phenomenon. He aimed to shatter the conspiracy theories about the Mantle Project, but from what I heard, he wound up bolstering them.

Because so many visions are occurring daily, the topic has long been exhausted by the media and internet sources, which have used it as the basis for their anti-tech propaganda.

With many people claiming that the visions are hallucinations or that the Mantle Project is a plan devised by Satan to turn Earth into his own personal hell, you can't have a conversation about the subject without falling into paranormal tropes. But having seen one of those vision victims, I admit the experience has a mystical feel.

After Darin's vision on the day of the announcement, I decided to keep my eyes open for more reports about people who experienced the same thing. For a month or so, nothing happened. But one day, out of nowhere, a small group of people claimed they had visions of Earth being shattered into countless pieces.

The reports started coming from a heretical forum, which had traded in dark conspiracy theories for years. That was more than enough for many people to challenge the validity of the reports. But more reports started surfacing, most of them from valid sources like media sites and longtime news bloggers. Shortly after the first wave of reports, the uproar grew to the point where holovision dedicated major blocks of time to explaining the visions.

Interested in the topic, I made it my mission to follow up every source. I sent emails and contacted people who experienced the visions. I was especially active while I was part of the group searching for answers about the Mantle Project. That's when I saw the many levels of the puzzle that was the vision epidemic.

Some people repeated the end-of-time phrase Darin uttered that night. Others saw Earth shattered in many pieces. More recently, a few heard screams of agony coming from Earth, but they were not of human origin. I sense someone or something is trying to communicate with us, to warn us that we're doing something wrong as a species and that if we don't stop, there's a strong chance the world will soon be destroyed.

The visions started the day the Mantle Project was announced. In the passing months, the intensity and frequency rose, and it seems the world is going through a new wave of visions.

"Daddy, we're almost there," Lisa says.

"What?" I reply, snapping out of my deep thought.

"We're almost at Mommy's place. Can you please put on some music before we arrive?" she asks, sounding disheartened.

I'm such a fool. Once again I've let down my girls while searching for answers. I stare at them in the car mirror. Lisa has crossed her hands over her tiny body, and Manna has almost fallen asleep from boredom. What began as a fun trip to the park is failing miserably due to my inability to abstain from the news.

God help me because I have a serious problem.

"Yes, of course. I'm so sorry, girls. I didn't mean to spoil your fun. Here, do you like this song?" I ask, changing stations and trying to find something worth listening to.

Manna's mood changes in seconds, but Lisa is a tougher nut to crack. "Yeah, sure. Whatever," she mumbles, starting out the rear window.

I feel a knot forming in my throat. I always considered myself a great father—funny, understanding, loving. Nowadays, though, I'm everything but that. I don't kiss them good night anymore, I don't share my happiness with them, and worst of all, I'm always busy trying to figure out what's happening to the world.

I slow down outside Cat's burger joint. It's still early in the day, so the place is empty, but Catherine is probably busy working on the expansion.

I get out of the car and the doors for the girls open. I take hold of their hands, and we cross the entrance to the shop. When Lisa and Manna see their mother, they pull free from me and rush to her.

"Mommy, mommy!" In the bustle of the shop, Catherine barely hears their voices and turns just in time to hug them.

"Oh my! What a nice surprise. What are you doing here?" she asks, her face filling with the joy of motherhood.

"It was Daddy's idea," Manna says. "He said we'd come and get you to go to the park. Please say yes, Mommy. Please!"

Lisa says nothing, but there's a burning desire in her eyes. I don't think she wants to be alone with me anymore.

"Well, sure. I don't mind taking a break," Cat finally replies. "But we can't stay too long. I have to be back in a few hours to take care of more things before we return home. Is that okay?" She pats the girls on the head. They nod in unison, agreeing to their mother's terms.

They look relieved, but I feel inadequate. My kids can't take my obsessive mood anymore. I have to change my behavior.

Catherine senses my distress. "Girls, go say hi to everyone in the back. They will be happy to see you," she says. Lisa and Manna's faces shine as they run to the kitchen. Catherine turns and looks me in the eye. "What's going on? What's with this nice dad act?"

It pains me that she of all people thinks being nice to my kids is just an act. "Lisa showed me one of her drawings. It was a picture of me sitting at my desk, glued to my computer screen."

"So what's wrong with that? The child drew what she sees. You've been a bit out of focus these past weeks."

"Well, it seems everyone in the house knew and none of you said anything. It was a wakeup call for me. I didn't know the girls felt this way toward me," I reply.

"For all your good traits, Tommy, you don't seem to be very perceptive," Catherine says with a smile. "Lisa was trying all week to show you this drawing you spoke of. And Manna kept talking in her sleep, repeating your name. I told you these things, but you shrugged them off and rushed to your computer to defend the world from the

Mantle Project. You have been on this path for a long time, but you didn't want to see it."

This day is getting worse by the minute. Even my wife has been unhappy with the way I've been acting, and I hadn't realized a thing. When did I become so distracted? When did my life stop being about my family and become about everything else?

Before I have the chance to reply to Catherine, the girls return. It's time to leave.

On our way out, Lisa stays behind and grabs my hand to stop me. She looks sad.

"What's wrong, Lisa?"

She lowers her head and braids her fingers into a tight knot. "I'm sorry, Dad. I didn't want to make you sad," she says.

I don't know if I'm going to cry tears of joy or regret. Either way, the crying part is inevitable. I pick up Lisa and carry her in my arms. For the first time in a long time, I feel like I'm once again graced by God's love and wisdom.

My family has an unmatched ability to make me a better person.

\*\*\*

# Chapter 15

# A Vision

*At the park, New York City*
*Narrator: Tommy Russell*

After half an hour's drive—and lots of singing and laughing—we arrive at the park. The sun is bright and the weather is still warm enough so that long-sleeved shirts aren't necessary. It's nearing noon. We get out of the car, and before Catherine and I can speak, the girls run off toward the playground in the center of the park.

A grin covers Cat's face. She's even more beautiful now that she seems determined to make me see the truth about the stressful life I've been leading this past year. It has been too long since the Mantle Project started, twelve months of ups and downs with many lonely moments.

I know it's late to make things right with them, but this doesn't mean I shouldn't try. The girls have lost their trust in me, and I have done nothing to keep that from happening. Taking them to the park seems like a good first step to earning back that trust.

Cat agrees. "You sure are stubborn, though. It took you months to realize the girls weren't speaking to you the way they used to. And no matter what I said, you brushed it off like it was nothing. We were all feeling neglected, Tommy."

"I know, Cat, and I'm sorry. It has been a rough year, but all this time I kept saying to myself that if I didn't do something, no one would. And when I saw that my words reached the ears of important people, I couldn't stop trying. It felt like I was so close."

"Why *was*? What happened?" Catherine asks.

"Oh yes. I forgot. You don't know about it yet. I got an email from the Department of Core and Earth Sciences today. They formally rejected our petition for full disclosure of the Mantle Project's files. Everything is over now. All I can do is wait for the year to come and go, hopefully without any major incidents."

"I don't know, Tommy. I'm on your side, but I think you're overreacting about the dangers. The department's scientists began implementing the project a year ago, and nothing has gone wrong. Isn't it time to stop being afraid and to return to your life? Our life?" Catherine says, staring into the distance, searching for the girls.

"I guess you're right. If something bad was going to happen, it would have happened already, right?"

She nods.

Catherine suddenly looks weary. She moves like she's walking on a hot summer afternoon, trying to preserve her strength for the way ahead. For a moment, I fall into the same trap. Exhausted and unable to speak without straining my already tenuous perception of reality, I feel like I'm walking in a giant bubble made of Jell-O. Only the movement of my eyes remains the same. I can see but not hear or speak.

I'm starting to panic. My mind seems trapped in my body. I can do nothing but keep walking toward the playground. I'm trying to scream for help, but the signals never reach my mouth.

As far away as my eyes can reach, I see a strange man. He must be enormous if I can discern any details of his figure from this distance. With his long hair and slim body, he seems like a shadow made up of life's darkest feelings gathered in one place.

The figure keeps getting bigger until only the feet of the giant are visible above me. I don't know what to think other than that this is a dream and I'll be waking up soon.

However, I don't.

I continue walking, and through the shadow, I see a sparkling light. It remains for a moment and then vanishes like a fleeting star. I don't know why, but I feel sad that the light is gone. I can do nothing about this, however. I just have to keep walking.

One of the figure's legs suddenly starts sinking in the ground, tearing the world apart. Lava and big chunks of land erupt, destroying everything around them. The rift tearing Earth in the middle expands, getting darker and deeper with every passing moment. Destruction and chaos spread, and after a short while, I'm one of the many victims falling into a pit of nothingness.

I close my eyes and wait to crash to the bottom, but this doesn't happen. I feel myself falling, but I'm not afraid.

A voice calls me to open my eyes. The voice whispers many words in my head at the same time—*the act of God, death, humans, fight*. At first, the voice speaks slowly, stressing the need to be heard. But as time goes by, and I keep my eyes closed for fear of what I might see, the voice repeats the words at a lighting-fast pace, becoming an inarticulate scream of fear and agony.

I feel the end approaching, the moment of the truth coming. An intense light engulfs my body. I float weightless, lacking gravity and any sense of human logic at work. There's only one thing left to do before everything ends.

I slowly open my eyes to discover something equally amazing and terrifying. I'm in space, floating around a shattered planet. My mouth feels dry and my hands shake. This can't be happening. This can't be the end. There must be something I can do, one last thing before I fall.

I squeeze my eyes shut and pray. The words come to my mind like a glass of water for a man lost in the desert. God with all His grace offers me a way out of this chaos, a door made of light. I think I see someone else in the distance, waving at me, but my eyes may be deceiving me.

Time stands still for a moment, and then I'm falling in the dark, but now the descent is fast and dangerous; if I hit the ground, I'm dead. But it doesn't matter, not if the things I saw about Earth's future are true.

Right now, it's more important to warn someone than to stay alive. I have to share the things I've experienced with someone I know will believe me.

Only Catherine will hear me and will tell me what to do. She is my guide and my teacher, my lighthouse on a stormy night. Without her light, I will crash on the rocky cliff.

I try to focus on the letters forming her name, the sound the word makes coming from my mouth, the vivid sentiments surrounding it. I close my eyes to make this easier, to make the feeling more intense. I think I see her in the distance, staring back at me. Maybe she is there.

Maybe she never left my side.

I move my head to the right and see her walking there. I gasp before starting to scream. Catherine, startled by my loud cries, jumps away from me. "What's wrong, Tommy? What happened?" she shouts.

But I can't stop screaming. My cry is long and chilling. Before I realize it, I'm on my knees, my head between my legs, holding it in my hands.

"Oh my God! Someone call an ambulance. Tommy, Tommy! What's wrong? Honey, tell me what's wrong?" she keeps saying.

But I can't speak or see her. I can only hear her. But her words have brought me back from a nightmarish world. Soon, my screams turn to growls, and Catherine feels confident enough to approach me. She places her cool hand on my back, and I'm quickly drawn back to reality.

It's only then that I realize everything I saw was a dream, a hallucination, a vision. The day I decided to give up on fighting the Mantle Project, God sent me a warning.

I still can't speak, but I can see and hear what's happening. A small crowd has gathered around me. Manna and Lisa stand next to Catherine, staring at me in fear. It takes me a moment to collect my thoughts and to come up with a way out of this mess without further concerning everyone.

"I ... I'm sorry. Er, I think I got stung by a bee. I'm really afraid of bees. I got scared and started screaming. I'm sorry," I say, putting on my best apologetic expression.

Some people leave without saying anything. Others snort and mumble in confusion. A couple of doctors make sure I'm okay before departing. When all four of us are alone, I try to get on my feet but it's impossible. My limbs feel heavy and wobbly, and I feel like I'm going to faint anytime now.

Catherine crouches down by my side. "What was that, Tommy? I know you're not afraid of bees. What happened?" she whispers.

"Cat, I think I had one of the visions everyone keeps talking about. Only mine … I think it was different. I think it was the right version of the vision God has been trying to send us."

"The right version of the vision? You know you're not making sense, right? Because if you don't know that, it wouldn't be a bad idea to visit a hospital, Tommy."

"No hospitals. I know what they're doing to people claiming they had visions. No, this is bigger than me and you. This is bigger than our whole family, Cat. I know what God is trying to say to us by sending these signs. It is a warning. He is trying to warn us to stop because Earth is in danger."

Adrenaline hits my bloodstream and I almost jump to my feet. Catherine is afraid for my sanity now, and so are Lisa and Manna. They don't speak, and they look at me like I'm a monster. I have to explain things to them.

I have to make them understand because we might be running out of time sooner than I thought.

"Please stop, Tommy," Catherine says. "You're scaring the girls. Can't you see you don't make any sense? You were just screaming like someone was trying to cut off your hand, and now you say God sent you a message no one else has received? This is it, Tommy. I'm calling an ambulance."

"No! Don't do that, Cat. Please don't do that," I shout as I take her hand in mine. I make sure I don't hurt her. This is not the proper way to make her see I'm right. I have to explain what I saw in my vision. But we have already drawn too much attention in this place.

Still holding Catherine's hand, I drag her away from the site. The girls watch silently as we get farther away.

Cat turns and tells them, "There's nothing to worry about, girls. Go have fun. We'll be back in a second."

Catherine insists we stay close enough to the playground to be able to see the girls. She's right. We're away from prying eyes now, and no one can hear us here.

"Can you please explain to me what's wrong, Tommy? For a moment I thought you were having a seizure. I was ready to call an ambulance," Catherine says.

"It's just as I told you, Cat. God sent me a message about the end of the world. He sent me the final piece to connect all the other visions together. I know what's going to happen if we don't stop the Mantle Project."

My words sound crazy to me as well as to her. I know I don't make any sense, but it's the best I can do right now until we return home and I consult my information. Still shaken to my core, I take a deep breath, trying to collect my thoughts.

Catherine is patient with me during this process. She keeps an eye on the girls in the distance while she holds my hand. Her warmth helps me recover. When I'm ready, I raise my head and face her.

"I don't know what you've heard about the visions, so I'll start from the beginning and try to explain everything to you. If you have any questions, stop me and I'll try my best to answer them, all right?" She nods. "Okay then, we both know what happened that night at the burger joint. Darin started repeating an end-of-time phrase."

"Yes, I remember. You told me what that phrase meant."

"I was deeply troubled by that phrase, but I thought it was pure chance. I started believing what the experts were saying at the time, that the Mantle Project induced a mass paranoia because of the stress an environmental change like that might have on our planet. However, that wasn't it."

Catherine looks at me in wonder; I'm not sure if she follows what I'm saying, but I must make her believe me.

"People started claiming they had visions about the destruction of Earth. Some saw our planet in many pieces, the land howling in pain, and a storm of thunder and white fire covering the sky. Individually, the signs pointed to the devastation of Earth because of our endless materialistic urges. We insist on taking the same path even though we know we're going the wrong way."

"Okay, but what does this have to do with your vision? And why did you say you have the key to unlocking the meaning of the other visions?" Catherine asks.

"Patience. I'm getting there. For the last three months, no one has had visions. Our online group believes there are two possibilities. One, this is pure chance and more visions are coming soon, or two, we're missing something, and God is done giving us more clues until we find out what it is. Some argue there is a third possibility, though."

"Which is?"

"Something big is coming. A vision to unite them all, a vision meant only for those who persevered through trials as the world tried to stop us. And there is no more fitting time than today for the third possibility to come true. In my vision, all the other visions happen at once under the banner 'the act of God.'"

Catherine stares deep into the eyes. "You know what you're saying, right? Earth will be destroyed as God's punishment of humanity."

I shake my head. "No, not at all. The world will be destroyed because it can't take any more of our abuse. It's God who's keeping the planet together. It's God's will for Earth to remain intact, but the land has become fragile. God is signaling us to stop now before it's too late. By ignoring them, we harm our planet irretrievably."

Catherine grows somber as she starts to understand what I'm saying. She opens her mouth to say something but does not speak. Instead, she lowers her head and starts walking back to the playground; I follow her. On our way there, she whispers to me, "We'll discuss this later when we're back home. Now go spend some time with the girls, Tommy. Show them you love them and set their young souls at ease. It might be a long time before we can be together like this again."

Cat is right. I can't get the vision out of my head, but this day is devoted to my family. I fear nothing now that I know the truth. God gave me my mission back, and it's clearer than ever. If I want to protect my family, I must make sure people stop exploiting the planet.

We near the playground. The moment they spot us, the girls run to our side. Manna is flushed, giggling from having too much fun, but Lisa seems a bit worried. I have to do something to calm her or this family outing will have been for naught.

"What's wrong, Lisa? Why are you so gloomy?" I ask.

"Are you okay, Daddy? You aren't mad, are you?" she asks.

I'm surprised by her question. "Why do you say that, honey? What made you think that?"

"I heard that lady over there telling her friends you're mad and shouldn't be allowed close to children," Lisa says. "You're not going to leave us, right?"

Her little eyes fill with tears. "What do you think, honey? Do you think your daddy is mad? Do you think I'm going to leave you?" I say in a soft voice. Lisa shakes her head slowly. "That's it then. Problem solved. You can't believe everything others say about your loved ones, honey. Only your heart can tell you the truth, and since your heart tells you I'm not mad, I'm not."

A smile cracks her face; she seems relieved. "Okay, Daddy. I won't listen to what others say about you again." She turns to leave only to stop after her first step. She lowers her head, a sign of shyness. "And I hope you weren't in much pain back there, Dad. I was really scared. Everything is going to be fine."

Lisa stretches to kiss my forehead, copying what I do every time she's upset about something. Her move brings tears to my eyes. My love of God and my family is my strongest weapon. I can't lose my girls, not when I have so many things to give to them.

Saving the world can wait for a day. I suddenly kiss my wife. She turns and looks at me in surprise. "What? What happened?" she asks.

"Nothing. I love you, Catherine. I love you so much it sometimes hurts." Cat smiles at my comment and puts her head on my shoulder. Her move gives me peace of mind. For a moment I feel like nothing can stop me from saving the world.

I'll keep the picture of this day closed tight in my heart, a safety net for the difficult days to follow.

God, please help my family get through this ordeal safe.

***

# Chapter 16

## The Rip

*Present day: November 15, 2074*
*One month before full implementation of the Mantle Project*
*New York City*
*Narrator: Tommy Russell*

The Mantle Project is almost completed. There's nothing we can do to stop it now. With only one month left before the Core and Earth Sciences Department places the injections in the last part of the planet that hasn't been treated, we're out of options.

We've expressed our concerns on holovision and on the radio. Our group started accepting money from organizations supporting our work, and we became even more vocal than we were at the start. However, the government constantly stopped us. The Mantle Project is a global undertaking approved by the United Nations. It can't be stopped because a group of people opposes it on religious grounds.

We said God didn't agree with this plan, and we produced evidence that the planet is suffering, but we were laughed at, mocked, and at times even cut off the air because our beliefs were thought to be radical. Loving God and Nature, once perfectly acceptable, is now considered an extreme option, and this pains me more than not being able to stop the Mantle Project.

As time passed and no major incident occurred, our credibility was challenged. Fewer people listened to what we had to say. In six months' time, our group dwindled, and no one invited us to appear on holovision. I am the only remaining member of the original online group. Catherine no longer discusses the visions, and I'm not searching for more incidents online.

I am keenly aware of God's warning and I know what's coming, but I must think about my family. I can't keep pushing or my daughters will be branded as the children of a fake prophet. I have stopped talking about the Mantle Project.

I spend my days tending to my children, helping my wife prepare food, and waiting for the event to happen. I'm on my way home from work when I stop at a grocery store to buy potatoes. Catherine forgot to buy them when she visited the store earlier today, and she asked me to do it before I return home tonight.

I park the car and get out. I search my pockets for my wallet and realize I've left it in the car. Thankfully, the car keys are in my pocket. I open the door, grab my wallet, and rush to the store. With winter approaching, it's getting cold, and I'm not dressed warmly enough.

The automated doors open to let me in. The temperature in here is more comfortable, but it takes me a moment to adjust. I rub my hands together to get rid of the chill while I'm searching for the potatoes.

Like every grocery store, this place offers holo access; using your phone or holo glasses, you can see the news, the food prices, and the weather forecast. Since I won't be here too long, I choose not to synchronize my phone with the shop's holo access.

I finally find the potatoes. The only other people in the store are two young men, an old woman, and the cashier. The other shoppers use the holo-access service; their glasses cast a ray of light on their eyes. Each person sees something different.

I grab a paper bag and throw in a handful of potatoes. I head to the cashier to pay. I hope I get back home before it starts to rain. The cashier is a young man who seems to be thinking the same thing. He looks out the window and sighs.

"The clouds seem heavy. I won't be able to leave before the storm arrives," he says.

"Nah, there won't be a storm. Maybe drizzle or a small shower. There are no storms in these parts," I reply, trying to make him feel better.

"You think? I hope so," he says. "Okay, that will be five dollars. Would you like me to use your credit number or do you carry one of the old credit cards with you?"

"No, go ahead. My credit number is—" I begin, only to be interrupted by a violent shaking that almost tosses me to the ground.

If the products didn't start falling from the shelves, I would have thought somebody staggered into me. The grocery store is a chaotic scene of broken eggs, spilled milk, and toppled boxes.

"Is everyone okay?" the cashier asks. Instead of replying, the old woman and the young men run from the store, shouting inarticulately. I look at the cashier. "This place is a mess," he says. "What was that?"

Before I have time to reply, the ground shakes again, only this time longer and with greater intensity. A loud humming makes me and the cashier cover our ears. I can't stay on my feet, but I know the building won't stand for long if the earthquake continues like this. I start for the exit when the cashier stops me.

"Are you out of your mind?" he shouts. "Get as far away from the windows as possible. You'll get killed if they break."

He's right. I crawl back close to the checkout counter and cover my head. The cashier is sitting on the floor and has covered his head as well. We can do nothing but wait for the earthquake to stop. Unlike any other natural disaster I've experienced, however, this one doesn't seem like it will ever stop. Five minutes pass before the shaking subsides.

Ten minutes later, the earthquake has stopped.

I carefully get on my feet to check the young man behind the counter. "Are you all right?" I ask.

The boy looks at me through a stream of blood flowing from his head. "I'm fine," he says. Adrenaline has probably numbed the pain from the injury.

"Okay. Can you stand? I'll help you get out of here," I say. He nods. Losing no more time, I grab his hand and slowly help him to his feet. He wobbles, dizzy from the hit, but we manage to get out of the store to the safety of the parking lot. The open space helps me feel safe again.

I help the young man sit before grabbing my phone. "You stay here. I'm calling for an ambulance."

"Okay," he replies, shocked by everything that has happened.

My mind starts working again only after I dial the emergency number. "Oh my God. Catherine and the kids," I mumble.

"Thank you for your help, dude," the cashier says. "Really, I'm fine. I have my phone with me. Go to your family. I'll call for an ambulance myself. Thank you. You saved my life."

The young man is smiling at me even in his time of need. "It's nothing," I tell him. "Be safe, son. And keep trying to call for an ambulance. Someone should look at that wound on your head." I rush to my car.

I turn it on and start driving. On my way home, I see all of the houses are damaged, but none of them has fallen. That's a relief. However, there's no light on the streets; the power must have been cut off. I have to be extra careful when driving. I don't want to have an accident now.

Red-and-blue light flashes in the distance. My guess is that more than one fire truck is producing the light. Somewhere in the distance, an orange flame lights up the dark sky. Some are not as lucky as we are.

I soon arrive home. Catherine and the girls are waiting for me outside. The moment I see them I realize I haven't been breathing all this time. Air rushes into my lungs, and the pain is strong enough to make me burst into tears. They are mostly tears of joy that everyone is safe.

I park the car myself; auto parking would have taken too long. I rush to their side. When they see me, they run to hug me as well. "Daddy!" my two girls shout.

"Oh my God. You're all fine. I thank God for protecting you. I don't know what I would have done if anything bad had happened to you," I say.

Catherine rushes to my side, crying. "Tommy. I've been calling you, but ... but ..."

I free one of my hands from hugging the girls and pass it over her shoulders. She needs my attention as well. "The lines must be busy, honey. The whole city has been hit by a crazy earthquake. I hope not many people died," I say.

Cat hides her face on my shoulder; my presence offers her a sense of safety. But I don't feel safe at all. I hate to admit it, but the longer I think about it, the more it makes sense to me. The end has started.

"Let's get into the car. It will be warmer in there," I propose. But as we move toward the car, the ground shakes again. This earthquake is shorter than the last one but of the same intensity. After a minute we can begin moving again. This time I rush my family inside the car and make sure I park away from the house. Nowhere is safe for us now, not before we understand what is going on.

My mind starts racing, trying to decide on a good place to spend the night. Our camping gear is inside the house along with blankets and food. It's too dangerous to go in there now, not before we have Dorothy check the integrity of the house. I bring out my phone and connect to my home's network.

"Dorothy, can you please do an integrity check on the house? Is it safe for us to enter?" I ask.

"Of course, Tommy. I'll initiate the checking sequence right away," she replies.

I feel like I'm forgetting something important. I take a look around me and see Catherine, Manna, and Lisa hugging in the back seat. Someone is missing.

"My mother," I suddenly say. "We have to check to see if Mom is all right."

Cat nods. "Try calling her first. It's too dangerous to drive through town now. Maybe the lines have cleared up a bit," she says.

I dial her number and wait for the call to connect. Thankfully, it does. "Tommy! My God, I was trying to call you for so long," my mother says.

"Mom, is everything all right? Are you hurt? Do you want me to come pick you up?" I say, the words leaving my mouth all at once.

"I'm okay, darling. Stay where you are. It's too dangerous to drive right now. I've met with some friends from around the neighborhood, and we'll stay together for the night. How are you? The girls? Catherine? Is everybody okay?" she asks.

"Yes, we're all okay. A bit shocked maybe, but we're good for the time being. What was that?"

"Haven't you heard the news?" my mom asks in awe.

"No. What about it?"

"You have to see it for yourself, Tommy. We'll talk again soon," she says and hangs up.

I turn and stare at Catherine. "We have to find out what's going on," I mutter. She simply nods. I place my phone on the car dock and speak to Dorothy. "Dorothy, bring up the news channel," I say.

"Of course, Tommy," she replies. In seconds, the windscreen turns to a giant holo screen. The newscaster seems shaken.

"We're here from Channel City to give you the latest details about the large-scale earthquakes ravaging planet Earth. Experts around the world speak about the planet breaking into two major pieces. I repeat, the planet will soon break into two big pieces. The situation is dire, and we expect a statement from the Core and Earth Sciences Department. Until then, we'll keep broadcasting as long as possible. We hope everyone is safe, and may God help us all."

There were signs. We didn't notice them at first, but they were always there, hovering over our heads, bad omens of what was to come—visions, lucid dreams, hallucinations, ripples of consciousness that started distorting our reality. Some of us tried to warn those who denied their existence, but they didn't hear us. They branded us false prophets and mocked and ostracized us. All the while, the project was underway.

It's human nature to doubt a threat until it's too late to act against the danger. Global warming was just a myth until several coasts were submerged under the sea; wars were always on the verge of happening, and when they did happen, people questioned why they had broken out. They didn't understand that the reasons were always there, lurking in the dark.

Maybe people weren't at fault. After all, isolated incidents didn't seem to portend war until we saw them as a whole. Even to us believers they were like stray letters in a message sent by the divine system. The message made sense only when we started piecing them together.

Nature was trying to warn us even in our last hour. It gave us a breath of hope just before we drowned in a sea of ignorance. But once again we didn't listen. I still look back and remember what we endured. It was a short but difficult time.

The signs started two years before the disaster took place. During those two years, everything changed so much that the world was not the same. Only humans remained the same, trading faith for mere science and the nameless monsters of our times.

We were never against progress, not in the least. All of us enjoyed having AI assistants, virtual reality glasses, and all the other perks of a machine-assisted way of life. But we didn't enjoy the release of untested technology into the markets. We didn't enjoy large-scale experiments that used nature as a guinea pig.

God is forgiving. God is loving. God is the One who gives us hope. But we forgot Him. We adopted our own ways of living, using His creation as we pleased. We turned our backs on Him to celebrate our last hours on Earth in supreme arrogance.

I look back and wish that I had done more, that I had yelled more loudly, that I had tried to convince more people about our right to protect the Earth through our faith. Now it's too late, and all we have left is a shadow of our own devise.

# Chapter 17

## Code Black

*Close to midnight, November 15, 2074*
*Planet Yahire*
*Narrator: Ambassador Judith Campbell*

"Amy? Can you please pass those papers to me?" I ask my sweet assistant.

She smiles at me from the other side of the conference room and gently rises to her feet to come to my side. She looks exhausted. I know I've been a slave driver for the last few months, but the Tri-Colony assembly is right around the corner and we have to be ready for it when it comes. It's our duty to make sure everything goes according to plan.

We don't want earthlings getting the best of us and further delaying Yahire's independence from Earth's government. Now that the Mantle Project has ensured them of more resources and they have a spirit of change, we have a chance to claim our own planet.

Amy arrives at my side, using her left hand to try to hide a yawn. The sound derails my train of thought. "So young and yet lacking the stamina for the job?" I mutter.

I return to reading my paper. She giggles before replying. "We're the last in the office, ma'am ... I mean Judith," she corrects herself. "You're the one with the unending energy. We just follow in your footsteps."

Her words make me sigh. "I guess you're right. People expect me to be a beacon of change. I can't remember how many times I considered stepping down. However, there's a trick to it. I wouldn't be here if someone didn't help me understand the importance of my job. Do you want to hear about it?" I ask.

She doesn't reply, so I raise my head to see what's going on; she's yawning again.

"I take that as a yes. This is as good a time as any for a break." I rise to my feet and ask her to follow me to my office.

I've asked my coworkers to make sure we keep a steady supply of snacks and coffee in the office in case we need an energy surge at midnight, like now. Amy gladly accepts the chocolate bar but passes on the coffee.

"I ... I try to go slow on the coffee, Judith. It makes me jumpy and doesn't help my elevated levels of stress," she mumbles.

"Suit yourself. I'll have a cup. I have to keep my mind functioning for another couple of hours. Tomorrow is Sunday. I'll have the whole day to recover," I say as I pour the dark, steamy liquid in a porcelain cup.

With the first sip, the fog that unbeknownst to me had covered my eyes is lifted. The colors of my office become bright and vivid like it's early in the afternoon rather than late at night. I relax while the warm coffee travels down my gullet.

I down another sip before I start my counseling. "Tell me, Amy. What is that you wanted to become when you were a girl?"

She's in the process of chewing a chunk of her chocolate bar when I pose the question. She gracefully swallows before replying. "Well, since our teacher taught us about democracy and the political system, I wanted to get involved in politics. Working here with you is actually my dream job," she says.

"Well, thank you. That's really nice of you. But isn't there something more to it? Anything you'd like to see changed in our line of work?"

"I ... I don't know. Maybe. What would this have to do with staying late at the office?"

She's shy about her thoughts. Oh, how much she reminds me of myself when I started.

"I was your age when I began my career in politics. I started out by doing volunteer work for the past president's campaign. Bennett was a slave driver, someone who could make you hate him and love him in the span of a minute. Back then, I was constantly tired, always catching up on my sleep with a nap or two on the office sofa. It was a tough time, one that taught me a great many things about how this machine works when the curtains are down.

"The greatest lesson I got from Bennett, though, was this: if you're chasing change, you never run out of things to chase. Either it's a constant effort for the betterment of a planet that is the home of outstanding people with red eyes or making sure you find new ways to protect your client, as your boyfriend does so well. People with a passion never get tired."

Amy is staring at me with the sparkling eyes of a student and the gawking expression of a child. I'm reaching to grab a cookie from a bowl in the middle of the coffee table in front of me when Amy recovers from her inertia.

"I ... I guess you're right, Judith. I haven't given too much thought to this before."

"Well, it's time you did, my child, because we have to return to our work soon. Time waits for no one, especially not for political people like us. The earthlings will want to make sure we don't vote for independence once the Mantle Project is finished, though I don't see what a scientific feat has to do with the political status of the Tri-Colony. But we'll have to play by their rules. See if you can find me the reports of—"

Owen barges into the room, interrupting our conversation. Amy's face brightens at once, only to be dimmed after seeing Owen's worried expression.

"Mrs. Campbell, please follow me. We're transferring you to the closest government shelter at once. We have a code black situation unfolding," he says.

I know he won't take no for an answer, but he can't drag me to that hole without first updating me on the situation. "What's going on, Owen? What happened?"

We stare at each other for a moment until Owen turns toward Amy, his significant other. "Honey, can you please move to the other room for a second? I have to discuss a classified situation with Mrs. Campbell," he says.

Amy nods and rushes outside, closing the door behind her. I get on my feet and approach Owen. Something must be very wrong for him to act like this.

"Mrs. Campbell, it's about the Mantle Project, the project you assigned to me ages ago." he asks.

"What's going on? Do you have news regarding the project?"

He nods. "Yes. It has failed, ma'am. It seems, the project has ripped planet Earth apart."

I can't believe what I'm hearing. The most ambitious human endeavor after the colonization of Yahire and of the moon has failed one month before being completed. "Give me more information, Owen. What happened? What is the death toll? What about the damage? Give me something, Owen," I say.

"I'd be glad to brief you, ma'am, but Lance Alexander asked for your presence in the shelter in ten minutes. We have already wasted five minutes discussing this. I think he's better suited to give you more information about the subject. He's the head of the secret services after all."

Owen is right. He probably knows more than he says, but I can't order him to tell me. He was assigned to protect me from Lance, the president's counselor and the head of secret services for Yahire. He's the man with all the answers and the one who can give me a clear picture of what's going on.

I rub the bridge between my eyes before nodding. "Take me to the shelter then. Lance has many things to answer for," I tell Owen and we head outside.

On our way out, Amy is waiting for us on the sofa, leg twitching up and down; thank God she didn't have that cup of coffee I offered her or she would have been doing jumping jacks. When she sees us, she heads our way only to have Owen stop her with a raised hand.

I can see Owen is worried about her safety, but there's nothing he can do for her, at least not directly.

"Owen, wait a second," I say.

He stops reluctantly. "Mrs. Campbell, you know the drill. It's code black, we can't stop for every little thing," he sputters.

I shush him. "Lance can wait another minute or so. We're fifteen minutes away from the shelter if we decide to walk there and three minutes using a car. Some things are more important than being punctual, Owen."

He snorts but doesn't continue arguing with me; he turns his back to us and heads toward the doorway in a loud trot. This is one of those rare occasions when I enjoy bossing him around.

Amy is shaking, not knowing what's going on. "Ma'am … I mean … what's going on?" she stutters.

I grab her by the shoulders and lean close to her to whisper, "Everything will be fine, my dear. Everything will be just fine. We're heading to a government shelter a few blocks from here. An emergency has arisen and it's procedure. But this isn't important for you right now. I want to ask you a favor."

"Y … yes, ma'am. Anything."

"I want you to come with us to the shelter, but to do that, we have to lie to my superiors, and we have to lie well. They won't allow a simple assistant in there, not unless we act like you're coming with me to make sure I'm safe. Do you remember where the first aid case is?"

"Yes. I do," she replies in a firm voice.

"Okay. Go get it. I trust you can come up with a convincing doctor act by the time we get there, right?"

She nods. "Yes, I can. But what about Owen?"

Amy whispers that last part. She's right to worry about him. Owen will try his best to stop us, even though it will be painful to him. "Leave Owen to me. Go, Amy. We'll wait for you here," I tell her.

The girl stops and stares at me for a second before leaving. She loves him, and he loves her in return. His feelings show the moment I turn my head to stare at him. His eyes follow her all the way to my office. When she's in there, he shakes his head twice before speaking to me.

"Are you ready now, ma'am? Your driver is waiting for you outside."

"No, we're waiting for Amy to come back. She's coming with us. I just promoted her to my health aide due to my recently discovered health problem. I can't go anywhere without her," I reply.

Owen's expression takes on a furious shade in seconds. If he could, he would storm out of the office alone. "This is illegal, ma'am. She's in danger of getting imprisoned for life if she lies in front of every major political figure in Yahire. You just put her life in danger," he complains.

"I don't know what you're talking about. She's a woman qualified by you to provide me with health advice in my time of need. She can pass the shelter check if we both assure the security people she's okay, right? There won't be time for them to do a background check regarding her credentials, not before this emergency is over. And even then, they won't deal with her if she stays low. It's the perfect ruse for us to bring her along," I reply.

Owen won't give up easily, though. "What about her dreams? What if she wants to become a politician herself one day? Staying low isn't exactly how you run a campaign for ambassador," Owen says.

Amy returns. We must have been loud because tears are running from her eyes. She looks disappointed. "I'm coming with you, Owen. Mrs. Campbell asked me to come and I'll come. Being with you is more important to me than running for office sometime in the future." Owen opens his mouth to interrupt her, but she isn't finished. "I'm not stupid! I know what code black is. I've read the security protocol. It's the highest code of emergency, right? It means the planet is in danger, right?"

Owen just nods.

"Then I want to make sure we spend these last moments together, even if that means lying to every person of importance. I love you, you fool, and I'm prepared to risk everything to prove that to you," she says.

Owen, dumbstruck by our joint assault on him, lowers his head in contemplation and says nothing for half a minute. I know that look; it's the same one Charles used to have when we were fighting and I was too stubborn to admit he was right.

Unable to say anything to change my mind, he would lower his head and muster the strength to forgive me. Owen seems ready to do the same thing, only his eyes are full of tears.

"Okay. You can come with us. But make sure you come up with a convincing lie or else all three of us will get in trouble."

With that, Owen wipes his eyes clean and signals us to move. Before following him, Amyy hugs me and whispers, "Thank you."

These stupid kids are going to make me cry now. God, what a fool I am for seeing my Charles in Owen's eyes. They are not the same and I'm not either.

***

We arrive at the shelter in the nick of time. Owen, Amy, and I are the last ones to enter the tall, sturdy building. The security people check our IDs, but when it's Amy's turn, they stop her. She doesn't have an ID with her.

"I'm sorry, but you can't continue past this checkpoint, ma'am. We urge you to turn back and leave this shelter immediately. You're trespassing on a military location," a handsome man wearing glasses informs her.

Owen comes to her rescue. "She's safe. She can continue under my clearance. Dr. Roberts is the ambassador's health expert. She's essential to Mrs. Campbell's health," he says.

The security officer doesn't seem convinced, though. "If she doesn't show up on my ID check, I'm not allowed—"

"Mrs. Campbell just hired her, and we are in the process of applying for high-grade security access. We couldn't have known code black would be declared, right?" Owen says.

The officer seems to change his attitude toward Amy. If a security chief like Owen Waters vouches for her, that's probably more than enough. Still, he seems reluctant to allow entry to this woman.

I soon decide it's time to jump in. "The head of secret services is waiting for me, officer. Please make up your mind. What will it be? Yes or no?"

Applying pressure at this moment seems to work in our favor. He nods and gives Amy a guest pass. "Carry this everywhere you go. If you lose it, the security officers inside the shelter have the authorization to shoot to kill. Regular laws don't apply in this building, lady. Remember that," he warns her and lets her pass.

Amy doesn't reply but does a great job of looking terrified. It helps that she probably feels that way after all the things she heard on our ride here. The three of us rush to the elevator that will take us to another elevator that will take us many floors underground.

But all this security won't help if Earth is indeed half-destroyed.

Our ride on the two elevators is short and uneventful. Owen warned Amy not to say a word, not even in the restroom. The shelter is monitored by an AI able to recognize human speaking patterns. If the AI picks up anything sounding weird, it will probably warn the security officers and get all three of us kicked out from the shelter.

And this is not the time to make mistakes, not before I consult Lance about the situation.

Luckily, he's waiting for us at the entrance to the shelter. He's the first person we see when we get off the elevator. "Judith! For God's sake, what took you so long? I thought something bad happened to you," Lance says.

"You know me, Lance. I wouldn't leave my office until my security chief informed me about the situation. But you've taught them well. I couldn't get a word out of him," I reply.

Lance's face darkens. He's the man with all the answers. Judging from his expression, things are not going well on planet Earth.

"You're relieved of your duties for now, Sergeant Waters. Escort Dr. Roberts to her room and make sure you report to your superiors. I'll call you when this meeting is over," he says.

"Sir, yes sir!" Owen barks and then leaves with Amy by his side.

I manage to sneak a tiny grin as they walk away together down the hall in the safest place on the planet. I don't know if we can save the planet, but I feel good about helping to save a couple.

I shake my head and turn to stare at Lance. He signals me to move into one of the information rooms; he has reserved it for us.

When we enter, he closes the door and pushes a button on the wall next to him. An automated voice says, "Security AI disabled."

Lance seems to be breaking some pretty important rules himself. "Judith, things aren't going great on Earth," he says.

"Brief me. What are we looking at? Thousands? Millions? Hundreds of millions?"

"I suppose you're talking about the death toll. Our first estimates are that 5 percent of the population died instantly in the first wave of earthquakes. They didn't stand a chance. The planet got ripped. If you look at the video, you'll be shocked. Some people in the control room started crying when they watched it. It's the worst devastation the human race has ever suffered," he says.

"Oh my God! Is the problem reversible?" I ask.

"I don't know. We've got some scientists from our department here, but they're not sure what resources earthlings have. There seems to be a solution in the works, but I don't know if it will be ready in time. What are we going to do, Judith? Even with the transportation channels we opened, we didn't expect this magnitude of destruction. There's no way we can transfer billions of people in such a short time," Lance says.

As soon as Lance finishes, I clap my hand to my mouth. "We're doomed. This isn't a simple disaster, Lance. This is biblical devastation. We ... we can't do anything," I mutter.

***

# Chapter 18

## A Perplexity

*November 16, 2074, a few hours after the earthquake*
*Mantle Project Laboratory,* Department of Core and Earth Sciences
*Narrator: Dr. Jonathan Bailey*

We didn't expect to get so far and to fail at the last minute. We have run the numbers countless times during the two years since we started working on the Mantle Project, and everything was going according to our plan. Adjustments to the procedure for the injections in Earth's mantle helped decrease the pressure exerted on it, which also helped us limit the risk of destruction to property to below 5 percent. The plan was a success.

I don't know what happened three hours ago. I don't know if this is a dream or a reality. We were able to survive only because the laboratory was built using cutting edge technology to ensure it isn't destroyed even in the worst conditions. The lab is located underground, and its ceiling can handle weight ten times that of the building above.

We knew if anything happened, we would be safer in the laboratory than anywhere else. But that doesn't change the fact that something did happen.

The team had assembled for late-night work when the first waves hit us. Natalie and Alvin were running last-minute tests of the warning system specifically devised to make us stop if anything went wrong with the project, but it never worked; nothing did.

When the seismic activity lessens, I'm able to stand on my feet and search for the other members of my team. I head straight for Alvin and Natalie, who are in the room with me.

"Natalie? Alvin? Guys, are you okay?" I yell. The lab is running on the emergency engines. The lights have dimmed to help preserve energy.

I can barely see the figure of a tall man in the distance; he's slowly getting on his feet. For a minute, I fear he's wounded.

"Alvin, man, are you okay?" I lurch toward him.

"Jonathan? Is that you?" he replies.

"Yes, it's me, pal. Are you okay? Are you hurt?"

He takes a moment to answer. "I'm okay. One of the hanging screens grazed my head, but I'm okay."

I sigh. By the time he has replied, I've arrived next to him. Natalie is lying on the floor next to him, but she's showing signs of moving. From what I can see, she's confused and probably hit her head while searching for cover, but it's nothing to worry about.

"Is this what I think it is?" Alvin asks.

I shrug. "I don't know. I hope not, but we were the only ones tampering with the planet's mantle. Maybe someone put a bomb in the building above. Either way, we have to get out of here as soon as possible."

Alvin nods and squats to help Natalie, who mumbles something. I lean closer to her. "Are you okay, Natalie? Are you in pain?"

"We … we're doomed. The end is near. They were right, damn it. They were right all along," she says.

"Who was right? What end is near? What are you talking about?" I bombard her with questions.

"The fanatics who asked us to stop the Mantle Project. We should have stopped, Jon. We shouldn't have started it in the first place," she says.

"I don't understand, Natalie. You're a scientist; you can't believe this nonsense. People use God to mask their fears and insecurities. He can't be responsible for this mess."

Two people enter the main laboratory where the rest of us are. "Guys?" Stewart yells.

"Over here," Alvin replies. "We're all okay."

"So are we," Dianna replies.

Natalie is now sitting on the floor, her back leaning against one of the desks where the holo screens are located. Our eyes are adjusting to the darkness; I can see Natalie face is full of tears.

"This isn't right, Jonathan. This can't be right. We sinned and God punished us."

All four members of my team have assembled now. The newcomers, Dianna and Stewart, don't know what's going on but don't dare interrupt us.

"Look, Natalie, I know you're shaken, but you can't believe God would punish us. Why now, so late down the road? We were getting there. The project was almost over," I tell her.

"I don't know, Jonathan. I don't know. But this is the truth. It's the only thing that makes sense. We double-checked every hole in the system, every thin layer of theory and concept, and it worked. The chances of anything going wrong had been reduced to below 5 percent. And even if something went wrong, it shouldn't cause destruction of this magnitude—not unless God intervened," she says.

I groan and turn my back to her. I can't talk sense into Natalie. Her firm belief that a deity or any such inexplicable nonsense pushed the planet over the edge defies logic. But convincing Natalie otherwise isn't important right now. We have to check the extent of the destruction; we have to come up with a solution.

The moment I turn to face the entrance, a familiar figure enters the devastated lab. It has been too long.

"Verna? What are you doing here?" I ask.

"Jonathan. Thank God you're okay. All of you are okay. Oh my," she says and collapses on the floor.

Before I know it, I'm standing above her and checking for injuries. Luckily, except for some bruises on her head and a broken arm, she's fine.

"What are you doing here, Verna?" I ask when she finally comes around.

"I was so worried about your safety. You won't believe what's going on out there. The planet is in pieces. We destroyed it, Jonathan; we destroyed everything."

\*\*\*

It takes us around several minutes to set up a connection to the global network and to check the facts. All six of us are still in the laboratory with no plans to leave anytime soon. The earthquakes stopped and we installed torches around the room. This will be our shelter for now.

Verna brought us news of the destruction around town. Her house collapsed; she is lucky to be alive and to have escaped with only the broken arm and some bruises. Using the expertise of the tech members on our team, we soon have a complete picture of the situation around the world.

And it isn't looking good. It was a magnitude of 12.8, the number ever recorded in the history.

"Guys, this is the worst-case scenario. Why didn't our system work to warn us?" Dianna wonders.

"I don't know," Stewart replies. "Maybe it wasn't complete, or maybe the surge of data was too sudden for the system to be able to pick up the problem. We have to sort through many factors to find out what went wrong."

"That isn't important now," I tell them, deriving calculation results at my screen. "Let's recap. Earth has been almost severed in two main chunks. Our biggest problem right now is the loss of gravity. At the current level of gravity, the core can hold the pieces together for the next six months. In the meantime, we have to figure out a way to reassemble the planet before the rest of the population dies."

"It's impossible," Natalie says. "Even if we had the resources, six months is too little time to save the planet. We have to come up with a concept, test it, then calculate the risks, and—"

"Resources aren't important," Verna interrupts. "The United Nations will probably grant us full access to anything we want. The problem is what could work? We're not talking about a broken vase here, guys. The planet is a living organism, a place where life exists. The solution can't be something radical, or else we'll reconnect the planet but kill off the rest of humanity in the process."

As we all fall silent, ideas start to form in my head. We made every sort of discovery when we first visited Yahire. I am thinking of anything available anywhere in the Tri-Colony that can act as a superglue agent. But no. I can't say anything yet. We first have to solve the problem of trust that has been created since the disaster occurred.

Natalie is still shaken, and the fact that Alvin doesn't talk makes things worse. They seem to agree that this disaster is God's punishment. To me, that sounds crazy, but we need all the ideas we can muster, and Alvin and Natalie are the team's problem solvers.

Verna is whispering something to Dianna when I clear my throat to stop her, drawing everyone's attention. "I ... I have something to say."

"What is it, Jonathan? Have you come up with a plan?" Verna asks.

I shake my head. "No, that's not it. I'm sure you all know the world is probably waiting for us to show everyone the way out of this mess. And I agree that only the six of us can solve this problem. But this won't be possible if half of us have lost trust in this project."

Natalie groans. "Just because I'm a scientist doesn't mean I can't believe in God, Jonathan," she says. "Have you ever asked about our lives? Have you ever wondered what we do when we aren't working like dogs in this hellhole?"

Her outburst takes me by surprise. Natalie has always been the first to arrive at the lab and the last to leave. She has never shown any sign of discontent.

I have to reply. "I'm sorry if I have disappointed you in any way, Natalie, but this is my opinion and I don't plan on changing it anytime soon. This doesn't mean we can't all work together to find a solution. After the planet is saved, I'll make sure we have a lengthy conversation about this subject, but this crisis demands our unity."

I somehow manage to get through to her, but Alvin, silent all this time, seems to be a more difficult nut to crack. "And why should we believe you, Jonathan? After all, it's your fault that everything took this turn for the worse. If it wasn't for your decision two years ago, the Mantle Project wouldn't have come to life. It was your idea that we conceal the real data from the council. So why should we listen to you of all people? If someone has to lead the team, Verna is the one."

Again, this isn't what I expected. "Come on, guys. This is bullshit! You're missing the point. I don't care if you want me or Verna to lead you. We have to stop arguing and do something to save our planet. If you think I'm the problem, then after this crisis is over, I promise to turn myself in. But until then, we have to work together," I tell them.

"It's too late, professor," a voice from behind me says.

I jump, not expecting another person to arrive in the laboratory. I turn and see a team of ten police officers rushing into the room. All six of us raise our hands. "What is the meaning of this?" I ask the chief officer.

"You're the lead designer of the Mantle Project, right? And I assume the men and women with you are members of your lab staff, right?" he says.

"Excuse me, officer, but what's going on?" Verna asks.

"All six of you are under arrest for crimes against the planet and against humanity. You have the right to remain silent. Anything you say can and will be used against you," he says while his men put electronic handcuffs on us.

Natalie and Alvin don't speak, lowering their heads and submitting to the officers. Verna is spared the harsh treatment due to her broken arm, but she's still led outside.

I don't know what has gotten into me, but I'm trying my best to resist arrest. It's not like I'll be able to do anything to help the planet if the police are chasing me.

In a rage, I focus on the person I suspect is responsible for this treason. "You have made a mistake, Alvin," I shout. "If we get locked in a prison cell, the world is doomed. God can't help you, Alvin. If God is the one who did this, what makes you think He'll fix the problem if we get punished?"

Alvin doesn't answer to me. Instead, he willingly leaves the lab. I'm the last team member remaining. The chief officer addresses me. "Professor, you might not want to admit it, but your coworkers did the right thing in calling us. God might have had nothing to do with the destruction of our planet, but the one who did must be captured and imprisoned," he says.

"The laws of man are created for times of peace, officer," I reply. "This is the worst disaster humanity has ever faced, and you're more invested in finding out whose fault it is. If this doesn't seem wrong to you, I pray your God can help you in your time of need." The police push me out of the laboratory.

We're doomed.

***

# Chapter 19

## Times Of Distress

*Early morning next day*
*New York City*
*Narrator: Tommy Russell*

We barely had three hours of sleep in the car. The girls were freezing all night, and I had to keep the engine running to help them stay warm. But that was the least of our worries. The aftershocks from the earthquake continued for some time, and some of the houses in our neighborhood collapsed.

Lisa and Manna were scared that the world was ending; they didn't understand what was going on, and they were doing their best to stay calm. But to them, it felt like the shaking would never stop.

The truth is that the planet is on the brink of destruction. This is the first wave of the apocalypse, and according to reports on the internet, the planet is ready to burst into many pieces. But I'm sure the core and earth scientists will do something to stop this from happening. They have to since they were the ones responsible for the problem.

Cat is hovering between sleep and wakefulness. I'm too stressed for my exhaustion to catch up with me. I'm checking the websites, hoping for any favorable news, but the only official announcements I see are the death tolls.

The figures are constantly rising, with some sources estimating 5 percent of the world's population perished in the first wave. With no visible way out of this mess, people are living in constant fear.

The only different news that arrives is the report that the Mantle Project's development team has been arrested.

"This is nonsense," I mutter.

Slipping in and out of slumber, Cat seizes the chance to make conversation so she can clear her foggy mind. "What is nonsense?" she whispers.

"Oh. Are you still awake, my love?"

"Yeah. I've been trying to sleep for some time, but I can't. I'm afraid another earthquake will come and wake me up. How about you? Still checking the news online?" she asks.

"Yes. Everyone is talking about the death toll. No announcements have been made by the Core and Earth Sciences Department, no help from Yahire as of now. All we know is that our planet will be destroyed in the coming months unless somebody does something."

"Wait a minute. Didn't you say the planet had been ripped apart? What more can happen?" she asks after making herself comfortable in her seat.

"A rip that has already occurred in the Atlantic will gradually cause the loss of gravity. Although, it's still too early for us to notice it now, but in about six months, gravity will be reduced by 20 percent, and pieces of the planet will be severed from each other, destroying the core that allows gravity to exist. The atmosphere will disappear and all life on planet Earth will perish."

"The planet's core has started to spin at decelerated pace, making the mantle around it spin slowly as well. Our days will gradually grow longer. The experts say we might have up to twenty-seven hours in a day in the next few months. That's because Earth will spin more slowly. Up to now, that's the only thing they've announced on the news. All that remains now it's to tell us what went wrong and what they're planning to do about it."

My short narration of what happened seems to get through to Catherine. She appears shocked and scared. Her hand covers her mouth and her eyes are wide open.

"I can't believe this. Everything is over. How will they be able to fix this, Tommy? How will they be able to reverse the damage they've done? Millions of people have died, the world is severed in pieces, and our children—oh my God, our children won't have a place to live if this continues. We have destroyed our planet in our pursuit of greatness, Tommy. I didn't believe you and now ... now this happens. If only I had helped you—"

"Hey, hey. Take a breath," I say as I lean closer to her. I cross my arm over her shoulders and hold her in a tight hug. When she calms down, I continue. "Nothing is over, honey. Everything broken can be fixed. God hasn't abandoned us, or else He wouldn't have sent all those visions to warn us. He wanted us to stop this, so I'm sure He is with us if we want to fix it."

"All we have to do is have faith and make sure we survive until a solution is found. That's all," I say.

My words make her feel better. "You're right, honey. If it wasn't for you, I don't know if I'd be able to go on. She says, holding my hand.

"We have to stay strong for Lisa and Manna, Catherine. They're the best thing in our lives." I say.

Catherine musters a grin. "You're right. Yes, you're right, Tommy. We have to remain strong for the girls." She clears her throat. "Now you didn't tell me; what's nonsense?"

"Oh, yes. They arrested Bailey and his team. As we speak, the six of them are headed to a precinct for questioning."

She seems puzzled. "And why is that bad? If they're responsible for this disaster, they have to pay, right?"

"Of course they have to pay. But at the same time, they're probably the only people in the world who know how to fix this. We can't waste our time pointing fingers now. We have to make sure the world is safe before we do that."

Catherine nods, trying to suppress a yawn. "Again, you're right, Tommy." She gives a short giggle. "You must think we're stupid for not picking up on the signs in the first place. It must have been a lonely road to here," she says.

"Are you out of your mind, Cat? What are you talking about? If it wasn't for you and the girls, I would have done many stupid things. You're my brakes, my safety valve. If not for you, my life would have been empty, and I wouldn't have been the man I am today. Stop talking like that, please. You're worrying me," I reply.

"I'm sorry. I didn't mean to upset you," Cat says. "I just feel so bad that I couldn't see this coming while you were right in the first place. I allowed the safety of nothingness to sweep me away."

"Don't start this again, Cat. You're a different person than I am. Don't continue blaming yourself for that."

We continue discussing our relationship over the last two years. Cat admits that she could have been more supportive, that she could have used her connections and her shop to help me further my goal but didn't. All I can do now is make her feel safe and strong, as she has done for me so many times. We have always been a tight couple, discussing our problems and finding ways to solve them together. But this ordeal goes beyond the two of us.

This is an ordeal born of humanity's overreach.

By the time the sun's first rays appear in the sky, Cat has fallen asleep and I'm staring into the distance, considering our next move. I could try to head into the house to see if it's safe, but I doubt this is a good idea. Earthquakes are unpredictable, and I can't risk being inside if or when another one hits.

The girls will be hungry when they wake up, so the best plan is to try to find something to eat. The news reports haven't mentioned any emergency spots, so this is not an option. All that remains is to visit my mother to make sure she's okay. She said everything was fine, but that was last night. The planet has had a rough half-day since then.

The rumbling of car engines awakens Catherine and the girls. Manna, the youngest member of our family, is ready to burst into tears when Lisa, her big sister, leans close to her and hugs her.

"It's the cars, Manna. Don't cry," she says, assuring her everything will be fine.

"Mommy, Daddy? Are you awake?" Manna asks.

"Yes, honey. What is it?" Catherine replies.

"I had a bad dream. I'm scared," she says.

Catherine unbuckles her safety belt and gets out of the car. Another earthquake suddenly occurs. Cat quickly gets back inside the car and closes the door. Shocked by the intensity of the quake, she covers Manna and Lisa with her body.

I check for cracks in the road or any pillar ready to fall, but fortunately, we're still safe here. People get out of their cars and run away from their houses. For a moment, I think it would be best if we followed them.

However, when I turn to look at my family, I see their eyes filled with fear and I change my mind. It's better for all of us to stay together in here than to risk losing each other on the road.

The quake is soon over and everything returns to normal. But the new normal is a world filled with chaos and danger, a world I don't want for my children. I have to do something, even if it means I must save the planet with my own two hands.

I look at my family once again before starting out for my mother's house. I hope she's in better condition than we are.

***

The roads to the other side of the city are filled with rubble; the situation here doesn't look too good. Many buildings have collapsed. People lie on the ground injured or dead. My eyes drift toward Cat and the girls; she makes sure they don't look outside.

The sights are gruesome, but what's worse is that it has been half a day since the first earthquake hit and we still don't have an official update from the government. This strikes me as weird. Shouldn't officials tell us something to stop us from worrying? Most of the news comes from blogs and websites.

It's like the whole system has collapsed and only a few people continue to think of their fellow men.

Our drive is slow and steady. There are other cars on the roads. I'm not sure where people are going; they're probably heading to check on their loved ones. The way I see it, there's no safe place left on planet Earth.

Catherine yawns and the girls start asking questions. "Mom? Are the earthquakes over?" Manna asks.

"I don't know, honey. I hope so," Cat replies.

"Really? I'm so scared of the earthquakes, Mommy. I want to go home," Manna says.

"I'm sorry, my love, but home isn't safe now. But I promise we'll get there as soon as possible. All right?" Cat pats Manna's head. She sulks over the bad news but says nothing else.

However, now that Manna has broken the silence, Lisa seems to have more to say. "Mom, are we visiting grandma?" she asks.

"Yes. We're going there to make sure she's okay."

"But what if another earthquake happens while we're on the road? Isn't this dangerous?" Lisa asks. "Our teacher told us we should stay in one place and wait for the shaking to be over. But the shaking isn't over yet, Mom."

"I know, darling. But you have your sister and me and your father, and grandma is all alone. We have to go there and make sure she's fine, all right? Don't worry. We'll be back home soon."

Lisa grunts but doesn't say a thing. Both girls are afraid and don't like being on the road when they don't know what's going on. I want to do something to help them calm down, but I have no idea what. Maybe my mother will know; in fact, I hope she'll be able to keep the girls occupied while Cat rests for a while.

I take a right turn; we're close to Mom's house now. The traffic noise and the sparse buildings make our cruise outside the city seem surprisingly easy. I pull down the window to let in the fresh air. As soon as I do, a chill runs down my neck.

We haven't gotten out of the car for some time now, so I hadn't realized I'm sweaty. However, I don't want to close the window yet. I feel refreshed and surprisingly confident. The last time I felt like that was during the summer when we visited the beach with Cat and the girls.

It was a day I won't forget. We spent the day swimming, having a picnic, and playing in the sand. Cat caught up on her reading, I bonded with Lisa and Manna, and we met some funny people in the process. On the way back home, the girls were exhausted and fell asleep in the back seat. It was a hot day and I didn't want to wake them up, so I opened the window. When the cool breeze entered the car, I experienced one of those picture-perfect moments when life stops and you hope nothing changes.

Now, even though things are vastly different, I feel like I'm back in that moment, happy we're safe and alive, a frail reality ready to burst at any moment.

The district where my mother lives is no different from the rest of the city. Buildings have been reduced to rubble, and I see protruding iron bars, broken glass, and bloody rocks. Even though there are no bodies on the road as in the other neighborhoods, the signs of last night's disaster can be clearly seen everywhere.

Cat holds the girls tightly in her arms while we pass the remnants of the old church we used to visit with Mom every Sunday. Like every other building in the vicinity, it's been destroyed and isn't easily recognized. If God did this, He didn't spare His home in the process.

If this is His doing, things are worse than I expected.

Arriving at Mom's house, I'm see the true extent of the misfortune; her house, where she and Dad spent their last years together, lies in shambles. I place my hand on my mouth in shock. I thought that if our house was lucky enough to withstand the disaster, my mother's house would also have survived.

I was searching for a sign of hope but I found despair.

"Is Debbie here?" Cat asks.

Her voice helps me escape my gloomy thoughts. "No, I don't think so," I reply. "She probably is somewhere close."

"She would never leave the house, not even if it's destroyed," Cat says.

I sigh and pull away from the parking slot. Last night Mom said she and some neighbors were getting together to spend the night. At least she isn't alone.

As I drive around the neighborhood, I notice a makeshift camp in the distance. People walk from one tent to another, still afraid another earthquake will take their last ray of hope. I let the car's automated system handle the parking while I talk to Catherine.

"Honey, I'm going to check if Mom is in that camp ahead. Move into the driver's seat and make sure you're ready to leave at a moment's notice," I tell her.

She nods but looks troubled. "Okay. But why is that, Tommy? Are you afraid something might happen there?" she asks.

"You can never be too sure. People tend to behave strangely in times of distress. Mom might trust these people with her life, but you can never be too certain about anything. Also, if an earthquake hits again, drive away with the girls. I'll call you on your phone and find you as soon as possible."

My last sentence seems to hit a nerve. "No! I can't do that," Catherine says. "I can't drive away and leave you behind, Tommy. And that wouldn't help us either. If an earthquake happens, we'll wait here for you patiently, like we did last night. So make sure you come back quickly, and bring Debbie with you. The kids miss her." She leans forward to kiss me on the cheek.

I say nothing. It's one of these times when Catherine won't take no for an answer. She sounds too scared to leave me behind and to take the responsibility of caring for Lisa and Manna by herself. She's right. I can't ask her to do something so awful to herself and the girls.

"Okay, then. I'm heading for the camp. I'll be back in a moment," I tell her and open the door to get out.

As I approach the camp, I notice it's bigger than I expected. People of all ages walk around the grounds, some wounded and others tending to the wounded. Even amid the worst crisis humanity has ever faced, we manage to find a way to adapt and to survive.

Strangely, all the tents in the camp are the same color and size, with only a few having different shapes and textures. From what I gather, many shop owners in the area are distributing resources for free: blankets, tents, food, water—everything people need to survive.

It's an organic effort to make sure everyone continues to live comfortably even out in the open. For a moment, I'm enamored by this tiny miracle happening in the middle of the road. I forget my main goal in visiting this place is to find my mom.

Sweeping the area for familiar figures, I almost fail to see a woman looking like my mother. White hair, frail body, confident composure— I'm sure it's my mother until I see a man helping her walk. Her foot is wrapped in bloody gauze that needs changing.

Last night Mom said she was fine; she said she wasn't wounded.

However, when the woman turns toward me, my worst fear comes to pass; the wounded woman *is* my mother.

I rush to her side. "Excuse me, mister. Excuse me. Can you please slow down a bit?" I yell.

When they finally hear me, my mother's face is painted with a shock that rivals mine. "Tommy! What are you doing here, son? I told you everything is fine."

"Apparently, you lied to me. You're hurt badly. You have to visit a hospital. Why didn't you say anything to me last night? I would have come here to help you," I say, my voice trembling from worry.

"No! Your priority should be your family. Last night, no one knew for sure what was going on. Also, most of the buildings fell during the first wave, so if you drove through the city at that moment, it was highly possible you'd end up getting crushed by the rubble." Her voice is firm, but I can see she's trying to hold back a moan of pain.

That she appears so weak makes me even more upset. "What if something bad happened to you? I drove outside the house and saw the aftermath of last night's earthquake. What if you had no one to help you, Mom? What then?"

I suddenly vent all the stress I've accumulated since yesterday on her. My mother won't go down that easily, though. If she thinks she's right, she won't allow anyone to say otherwise.

"Then so be it, Tommy," Mom says. "It would have been God's will. You should worry about your family, my son. I've lived enough years to leave this world in peace and dignity. Lisa and Manna, though, are too young to lose their father to a stupid act of heroism. I know you love me, sweetheart, but you have to make sure you stay safe for your family."

Tears appear in my eyes. Suddenly, I'm the one who can't handle this situation. "You're right, Mom, but I'm here now. We should get going. The girls are expecting you," I say, my voice breaking.

I turn to lead the way when I hear the same firm voice utter one word: "no."

"No? What has gotten into you, Mom?" I say in a strict voice. "Are you out of your mind? It isn't safe here, not anymore."

"Nowhere is safe, Tommy. At least here I'm close to my house."

"So? The building is destroyed, Mom. It will be a long time before you can return there. Why do you want to stay here so much? There's nothing for you except danger and ruins."

"You're wrong, son. This place holds the memories of the life I led. Just because the house doesn't exist anymore doesn't mean the memories your father and I built aren't still alive. I can't leave this place, Tommy, not now, not ever."

The man helping her stand on her feet whispers something in her ear before leading her to a chair around the corner. He helps her sit and leaves to tend to the other injured. Like everyone else in this camp, he seems tired and weak. These people keep moving due to the strength of habit and of false hope. They keep their minds occupied while they make sure others are okay.

Mom doesn't speak. She seems determined to stay here, a guardian of the memories of a lifetime. I have to say something to persuade her; I won't be able to live with myself if I leave her behind. I kneel next to her to put my head on her lap.

With a mother's intuitive sense, she caresses my head. I make my plea again. "I know you can't leave your memories behind, Mom, but the kids need you. Catherine needs you. I need you. I can't leave this place without you. If I do, I won't be able to focus on my family. Maybe I'm asking too much of you, but please come with me. When we fix Earth, I'll make sure we return here to fix your house and your memories as well."

My words may have been different, but the meaning was the same. What changed was the distress in my voice.

A mother can be many things, but above all else, she remains a mother. And like every woman who has brought a new life into the world, she can't stand seeing her child in pain.

"All right, my love. All right. I'll come with you but only because you need me. My heart belongs to this place and now lies in ruins like the cracked cement and broken windows you saw. Lead me to my grandchildren now. I want to see them," my mother says.

With a wide grin on my face, I help her walk all the way to the car. On our way there, my mind is racing. I made a promise to my mother to bring her back safe and sound; I made a promise to my wife to fix the world so Lisa and Manna can have a life.

With those promises to fulfill, I forgot the most important thing: how can I help fix a planet that lies in pieces?

# Chapter 20

# A Moment Of Epiphany

*Early morning, November 20, 2074*
*Mantle Project Laboratory,* Department of Core and Earth Sciences
*Narrator: Dr. Jonathan Bailey*

The planet is hanging by a thread. Our intentions to terraforming Earth's crust pushed nature to the breaking point. I never expected the Mantle Project to end up the way it did. I didn't expect my vision for the future to destroy the world. And yet here we are, humanity on the brink of extinction because we were too hasty, too ambitious, too materialistic.

But I can't be haunted by regret. What's done is done. Now I have to get the team back together and start working on a way to save the planet and all the lives at stake here. And the five other people I know are capable of finding a solution should be waiting for me in the lab.

I hope our little adventure with the police hasn't intimidated them. I know it hasn't fazed me, even though I'm accused of withholding data from the government and causing this mess. But that's my sin to bear, not theirs. And if we don't produce a plan to survive, then even if I am convicted, I will be a guilty corpse floating in space.

That last thought brings me back to reality. The prospect of death, not only for me but for the billions of people living on this planet, makes my heart pound in agony. What will happen if we don't come up with a good plan? Or if my team doesn't show up at the lab? Natalie and Alvin certainly made their intentions known by calling the police. And Verna was against this endeavor from the night we were discussing how to salvage the project.

I won't blame them if they ignore my plea for help, but I can't do this thing in time if I'm alone. And right now, the only reason I'm free is because the world needs me.

On the drive through the city I saw the debris of a destroyed world. Things I never even imagined now haunt my memory—huge cracks in the ground, collapsed buildings, dead bodies piled along every road. But I can't think about that now, not when the most crucial place—the laboratory where we can work on a solution—is still up and running.

Other people weren't as lucky as we were. Many of the leading institutes in the core and earth sciences field didn't escape the disaster, and most of our colleagues have stopped working with us.

Last night, after returning home from the police station, I contacted everyone I know to double-check what has happened around the globe. The first thing I learned is that only 20 percent of the esteemed scientists on my extensive list are interested in working with me on a solution. It seems that their egos are bigger than their will to survive or that they have already fled to Yahire.

I have discovered that gravity has gotten weaker since the mantle was shattered. The change is barely noticeable now, but after the estimates we got from at our previous meeting, the one police officers interrupted, I decided to check the gravity level with a simple rule-of-thumb experiment.

I tossed a coin and calculated the time it took for the coin to hit the ground. When I checked the global constant for gravity, I noticed the speed was slower than I expected. I'm not sure what has leaked to the media yet, but if this comes out, people will start panicking sooner rather than later.

Using my AI assistant, Ruby, I logged into my personal account and checked satellite pictures of the planet. The change is obvious;

once round and egg-like, Earth is now divided into two chunks that are about to split completely.

It might take some time before the chunks separate, but the process is underway. Gravity from nearby planets in our solar system will start pulling these pieces their way. And that is if we're lucky.

The scenario with the highest probability is that the bigger chunk will be pulled by the sun and burn long before nearing it. But that won't matter since all life on Earth would vanish much earlier. That's because the atmosphere will be destroyed the moment the chunks diverge from each other.

I calculated the threshold we'll have to pass for that to happen, and it seems we have around six months before the damage will be irreversible. In these six months, gravity will grow substantially weaker, and people on the moon will probably start noticing problems with their gravity as well.

If we pass the six-month threshold, we're probably dead no matter what we do. And that is the argument I will make to my colleagues. Either we work together or we die the moment the atmosphere dissipates around us. We have no choice except to work out this problem.

I'm lost in thought, moving from one room of the lab to another, checking which pieces of equipment are still operational and which not. Our mainframe—a custom-built monster of processing power and mechanical enterprise—is intact. No damage, not even a scratch.

You would think someone wanted us to be able to work on a solution. But for a fatalist, thinking like that makes little difference. I have to stick to the events that have transpired and not indulge in guesswork that will distract me from the facts.

The lights in the laboratory aren't all operational, but they will do for now. It's still early in the morning, and the sun offers plenty of light. Also, while the government is working on ways to provide millions of people with basic needs like food, water, and shelter, energy isn't a priority.

Luckily, the Core and Earth Sciences Department's HQ runs on green energy, so we can probably work out an arrangement. That's if the others arrive soon.

I check my holographic skin-clock. "It's nine-thirty. Where is everyone?" I mumble.

A holographic skin-clock is a pretty simple technology that uses human skin as the canvas for quick depictions of vital information like the time and date, messages, and the weather. A small screen is created on the wrist by the earphone transmitters we all use.

With a simple shake of the wrist, I change the interface to one that allows me to check my email account. There are no replies from team members, which can mean only two things: either they ignored me or they are on their way.

All of them live close to the lab, so the longer it takes them to arrive, the greater the chance they ignored me. Come on, guys. I'm sure you know only we six can fix this problem. I have only so many days to work and no other experts to work with. It's like I'm a brain without the rest of the body, and right now, I think I'm drowning.

I was hoping all five of them would race back here if they discovered I'm out and free to protect the planet I love. But they are not here, which means they probably have decided to live the rest of their lives ignoring me and the responsibility they have to save the world.

I'm holding a metal section of a destroyed monitor in my hand the moment rage overtakes me; I toss it to the opposite wall, using my whole strength. The metal hits the wall and makes a loud thump when it rebounds. But that isn't enough, not by a long margin.

I want to scream, to let out a long howl of fear mixed with agony. I know it isn't my fault. I know we made the right calculations even after the Mantle Project started. It isn't our fault. I can feel it. The numbers seemed to work after we tightened the security measures; not only that, but the Mantle Project was implemented in every part of the planet for nearly a year without incident; the disaster happened in the last month.

That must mean something.

Wandering around the lab, I end up at a chair with a clear view of the entrance. I don't dare check the time.

Maybe the traffic was too much. Or they want to surprise me by arriving all together.

*It's not your birthday, stupid,* I tell myself. *Two of these six people are responsible for putting you in prison, for exposing your mistakes. You might say you have forgiven them now, but what will happen when you see them? If you manage to save the world, what will happen next? Will you be able to live the rest of your life in a prison cell for a mistake you didn't make?*

"Dammit, there's no breakthrough without risk," I say out loud and rest my face in my hands, hiding it from the world.

"Well, I know only a handful of people who would dare say that at this time."

I sit bolt upright and stare at the entrance. It's Verna. Without thinking, I jump off my seat and run to her. When I draw near, I slow down and examine her face. She looks stern.

"Verna, you are here," I mutter even though I want to hug her.

"Yes, I am. I've been here before and during the Mantle Project; now I want to be after it," she says with a cheerless smile.

I respond in kind. But after our awkward greeting, it's time to discuss the important things.

"Of everyone on the team, I thought you were the one who wouldn't show up. And here you are—the first. What changed your mind?" I ask. I desperately need a good reason to keep fighting for our planet.

"I love this planet, Jonathan. We don't have another place to go. Even if we could travel to Yahire, it's this planet where I'd prefer to stay. It's our planet and if we don't fight for it, no one else will," she says.

Thankfully, that part of Verna hasn't changed in the least. She knows how to motivate me, though the prospect of a planet in pieces is motivation enough.

We catch up on the four days it took the police to learn the truth from me. There is nothing else we can do for now except wait for the others to show up. But the waiting becomes easier with Verna here.

She was the first person to support me and the first to make sure everything worked perfectly so I could assemble a team and create the science project of a lifetime. She's my professional double, and I'm sure she thinks of me that way.

At least I know she used to think of me that way. Now I'm not so sure.

"And that's about it," Verna says. "After I gave a statement to the police saying I hadn't been involved in the current interpretation of the Mantle Project, they decided to let me go. I'm not off the hook, but I don't think I will go to prison."

When she says that, I gasp. "What do you mean you're not off the hook? You of all six of us should be left alone. You walked away the moment the discussion started. There's no reason for you to end up in jail for us," I say, trying my best not to run all the way to the police station to give the officers a piece of my mind.

"Well, it's not that simple, Jonathan. I might have left, but I didn't say anything about the inconsistencies of the project even though I knew about them. I've been withholding information as much as you have. But we'll see. For now, they just asked me to stay put and not to try to move to Yahire."

I simply nod. Almost two years have passed since that time, and I'm still haunted by a decision it wasn't up to me to make. I know I shouldn't regret what has come to pass, but when the world keeps reminding you of your faults, it's difficult not to feel accountable for them.

I take a deep breath and place my arms around Verna's shoulders; I don't care if she decides to push me away or to kick me out of the lab. I need to know I still have a chance to redeem myself for my mistakes, even if that happens behind prison bars.

Fortunately, Verna doesn't pull back.

"So, just the three of us?" Stewart suddenly pops in.

Verna and I turn and see him smiling at us. Stewart always was the optimistic one in our group. He would smile even after sixteen hours of working on a failed formula and say, "Well, now we know what doesn't work," and grin at every one of us.

Today his smile is slight, tense, and forced. It's his way of telling us he isn't happy to be here.

"Yeah, for now no one else has come. It's just the three of us," I reply.

I want to add that it's better than none appearing, but with just the three of us, we still have no chance to make things right. All the members of the group were handpicked because they were the best in their areas. If Verna was missing from the group, we wouldn't have a core specialist who could tell us more about the behavior of that strange mechanism.

Stewart is our computer magician. He and Dianna tested the models before we put them to work. Natalie and Alvin are the team's math geniuses, some of the best model developers I've ever met. Every person on this team is irreplaceable, and as the clock ticks, the chances the other three will arrive grow slimmer.

"Have you talked to Dianna? Is she coming?" I ask Stewart.

Stewart shrugs. "To be honest, after the other day, I haven't talked to anyone. It's a miracle I'm here, especially since the police kept telling me I'm facing treason and other criminal charges. But I had to come and help you. The planet will not survive without our help."

The moment he finishes speaking, Dianna appears at the entrance. "I agree. I'm not happy I'm here, Jonathan. I want you to remember that. But this is not about you or your ambition; it's about Earth and humanity surviving. And I couldn't live with myself if I evacuated the planet and didn't do everything in my power to help."

I know what Dianna said wasn't meant to encourage me, but I get a warm feeling inside. It's that feeling you get when your favorite person in the world pops up in the bar where you're having a drink with friends and you can't help but stare at her.

That's exactly it; my favorite people in the world keep arriving one after the other to help me save the world. Though I know I'm not the reason they are here, that doesn't change a thing.

Dianna, unlike Stewart and Verna, is always strict and logical. I expected her to appear first since, in the email I sent the team members, I mentioned saving the world from my mistake. The logical thing, especially for scientists like us, is to set aside our personal feuds. And I'm happy Dianna did that.

"Now the only two missing are Natalie and Alvin," Verna says.

"Are they coming?" Dianna asks as she moves toward her workstation near the mainframe computer.

"I don't know," I reply. "They haven't said a thing, but I don't think they will appear. They were the ones who decided to call the police, making their allegiance known. We can't do this without them, but I'm not sure if they will put their personal feelings aside for us."

"Then you're wrong again, Jonathan," a woman says from the entrance.

I turn quickly and spot Natalie and Alvin staring at me. They're holding hands and look stiff and anxious, like being here is physically painful for them.

Still, I'm happy to see they are okay. For a while, I was afraid they had left the planet.

"I'm sorry I didn't believe you, but after everything that happened the last time we were here, it was only natural," I say, trying to explain myself.

"It's too bad you assumed our personal opinions would get the better of our scientific duty. We're here to save the world, Jonathan, not to listen to your foolish apologies. Whether you believe it or not, we're here because our faith has made us stronger in this time of need," Alvin says.

I can see Natalie's hand tensing in approval.

"I never doubted your right to believe in a greater force, but in our field, faith is many times a barrier. And if you want to continue moving the boundaries of what's possible, barriers aren't your best friends."

Natalie sighs. "There it is again," she says, "the exact same thing that made us call the police and tell the truth about our mistakes. You treat faith and everything else as a hindrance, measuring the ideas of those around you like lumps of coal. If they don't advance your goals, you toss them in the fire to make yourself warmer, to feed your ego.

"But you know better than anyone that all five of us have put our lives in danger just so your project could work, just so you could become the greatest scientist who ever lived."

Her words are like flaming daggers piercing my chest. She is absolutely right. All my life, I've treated the world like a big canvas that I can draw on. I never considered the feelings of those around me, their thoughts and opinions. If it wasn't Dianna or Alvin or Stewart or Natalie, I would have found someone else to help me fulfill my dreams.

And that's what hurts now. The main reason this is happening is because I couldn't stop to think about what I was doing or where I was wrong. I chased my dream with such fervor that when I turned around to see what I'd left behind me, I saw only destruction and pain.

The realizations keep coming one after the other, and finally I start crying. I fall on my knees and let the tears flow, unable to hold back my feelings anymore. "It's my fault. I know it's my fault the world is facing its worst crisis. But that's why I need you so much. I need you to … make everything right again. I have to make everything right again."

Natalie runs to my side and kneels next to me. "It's not your fault the planet was destroyed, Jonathan. The problem started hundreds of years ago. Your mistake was that you failed to notice it even though you're one of the most brilliant people we have ever met," she says, giving me a hug.

At that moment, I'm out of breath and out of things to say. I'm a total wreck, shaking from the shock and from the bottled-up feelings I've just released, but all my friends surround me and hug me. And for the first time in my life, I feel it. It's not discernable at first, but the more tears I shed, the clearer it gets.

I have a feeling of purpose, something I never knew existed inside me—a light so bright I'm afraid I'll explode in a million pieces. I can't name it. I can't put a label on that light, and yet one word keeps coming again and again into my head. One word I never thought I'd say.

That light inside of me makes me feel like God has shared His holy grace with me.

And it's beautiful.

\*\*\*

# Chapter 21

# A Climb Out Of A Ditch

*November 25, 2074, a week after the earthquake*
*Mantle Project Laboratory,* Department of Core and Earth Sciences
*Narrator: Dr. Jonathan Bailey*

"And that's it for the day," I suddenly say after I check my holo-skin clock. "We have been working nonstop for ten hours now. We have to rest or tomorrow we won't be able to present our plan to the government officials."

Verna is the first to reply. "You're right. There are only so many things we can do before tomorrow, and one of them is to rest. If we go there with dark circles below our eyes, I'm not sure we'll inspire trust. And the plan is too bold to allow for any mistakes."

A yawn comes from the back; it's Stewart stretching his arms. "I think I'm starting to hate numbers."

For him to say that means it's time for all of us to head to our homes or whatever is left of them. My apartment building was destroyed, so I'm staying in the lab, but the others still have their homes. Verna has repeatedly offered to let me stay with her until this mess is sorted out, but knowing the chances of success are slim, I wouldn't enjoy hanging out at her house and talking about the plan all day.

I value my personal space as much I value working with these people, so I've decided to stay in the lab. That way I can work on the project to my heart's content until early in the morning. That's what I've been doing recently.

Natalie and Alvin look up from behind a giant screen in the back, rubbing their eyes. "My head feels like it's made of checks and loops, guys. If you get no response from me, it will probably mean I'm checking to see if an answer is valid," Alvin says half-jokingly.

Natalie is the only one to laugh. The rest of us nod and smile, unable to keep our eyes open.

Today it's the last day before the deadline we got to present our work to the Council of Directors of the Core and Earth Sciences Department. Many politicians and army operatives will attend the event. The eyes of the world will be on us because we have finally found a viable solution that could potentially be implemented within the six-month threshold.

This was the only plan all six of us supported, and we believe it has a good chance of stitching the planet again.

We decided to spend the day double-checking every parameter, searching for problems in the code, and running multiple scenarios. Unfortunately, we didn't have time to delve into the deeper waters of our theory, but if we're right, which I'm sure we are, we're looking at the only way our planet can be saved.

We still have to correct elements of the plan, but if we get the first okay from the council, we'll have a few weeks to work out the details. Those of us with families have checked with them and have made sure they are okay. We will practically be living together for the duration of the project.

Natalie and Alvin gather their things and head our way for a quick recap of the plan. Stewart puts on his glasses and makes sure he has his holo screen with him. Dianna seems focused on something behind her monitor, but I'm sure she will pay attention at our last meeting.

When we're together in a circle, I get on my feet and say, "So the work has been tough, almost impossible I'd say, but it's now over. We have completed the first draft of the plan that might save Earth from its imminent doom."

Verna can't help but smile with me; she was a key player in producing this plan but lets me do the presentation. She says I'm the most charismatic person on the team, but I don't share her opinion. Nevertheless, my colleagues have all agreed that since I have experience at presenting high-profile plans to the council, I should be the team's spokesman.

"Skip the introduction, Jonathan. I'm hungry," Alvin says.

We all laugh; our spirits are high. "Yeah, yeah. You're right. So let's review the plan one last time before heading home, ladies and gentlemen. The science behind this plan is simple. The core is a mass of metals and other materials moving at great speed because of the high temperature. If the temperature of the core were reduced even slightly, the spinning would decelerate, creating the effect we now face: the crust getting torn to pieces."

I pause and take a breath. I have to nail this, and to do that, I must have the encouragement of the people who worked so hard to make this plan a reality. One look in their eyes tells me that I'm doing fine and that I should go on with the same energy.

"Now we think the core is still spinning in Earth's center but at a slightly reduced speed than it has been since Earth was formed. That's why we are going to experience longer days. And the spinning will keep getting slower, reducing gravity. In about six months, if we do nothing, the core will have slowed enough for the atmosphere to be destroyed by the distance between the pieces of Earth.

"But there is a way to prevent that. The solid form of the AX chemical from Yahire, we all know, works exactly like our magnets do. The effect is natural and easily enhanced by adding electricity to the equation. The best chance we have of repairing the planet is to install AX plates deep in Earth's mantle and to ionize them so the chunks start moving back together."

"The pieces will connect with a speed and a force guaranteed to close the tears that created the problem, and this will work as glue until the core regains its original temperature, making it spin faster and allowing Earth to become whole once again."

They all nod at me while trying to suppress their excitement. I'm trying to do the same thing, but I'm failing miserably.

"I think it's a great presentation," Verna says. "You're wisely leaving out the complicated parts and introducing a simple idea they can comprehend. I'm sure they will love the plan and will do everything they can to help us implement it in time."

"Yeah, I know. It's the only plan among those we considered that can fix the planet and not potentially make things worse. Other magnetic solutions could work as well, but AX is the only one that can blend with Earth's mantle and work on such a big scale. And it can do that without destroying the rest of the world in the process. The only challenge is to import a sufficient quantity of AX from Yahire."

When I mention that, most of the faces in the room lose their smiles.

"How much are we talking about?" Natalie asks.

"Sixty-eight million kilos; eighty million including the margin of safety," I reply. "There is no time to work on another solution, and even if the pieces move closer, the next biggest problem—the loss of gravity—could be our demise. The atmosphere will dissipate one way or another after that, and everything will be lost."

"We can't think like that before a meeting like this," Natalie says. "We have done everything we can; maybe the scientists from other departments will find a better solution. Right now, though, we are the only chance Earth has to survive. So until we know for sure whether our plan will work, no one should give up on it. Okay?"

After a short silence, everyone nods in agreement. It's all or nothing.

\*\*\*

# Chapter 22

# An Unfair Bargain

*Early morning, December 13, 2074*
*Government shelter, Yahire*
*Narrator: Ambassador Judith Campbell*

"So Earth has a plan?" I say as I barge into Lance's office.

He nods behind me and greets Amy, posing as my personal doctor in the shelter. Lance is the only official who knows the truth about her and what we had to do so she would be safe.

"Good morning to you, too, Judith," Lance replies. "I would prefer to discuss matters of national security over coffee if you don't mind."

I step farther into the office, undeterred by his refusal to share the news with me. "Lance, it's common knowledge now. They say Earth has started working on a new plan to rectify the mistakes of the old one. Is that true? Do we have a trustworthy source who can confirm it?"

He sighs and shrugs his shoulders. "I haven't even told my wife about the Earth plan, and you barge in here knowing the details. Maybe I should be the one asking you, Judith. Do you have a trustworthy source who can confirm it?"

He's mocking me and trying to confuse me. I don't know what Lance hopes to achieve by withholding his intel about the crisis, but I know it can't be good. For him to act around me like that, it must have something to do with the treaty.

"You have your ways, and I have mine. Now tell me everything you know about this plan, Lance, and don't spare the details. Earthlings don't back away from their original positions. Even worse, they now claim that in a time of crisis like the one Earth is experiencing, they consider Yahire Earth's territory and will treat it that way. Is that what you're hearing?"

Amy is still standing behind me, her head lowered, listening to my conversation with one of the most influential men in Yahire politics. I hope she can learn a thing or two about negotiation, even among people in the same government.

"Judith, you're an ambassador and I'm the minister of intelligence. We might be good friends, but don't push your way into unknown territory. You might find yourself lost, or even worse, you might fall off a cliff."

I'm sure he doesn't mean that as a threat, but Amy perceives it as such. I can hear her muffled gasp. She's nothing like the fearless woman we sneaked into the shelter by telling everyone she was a doctor. She now seems more like a young girl who found her way into Lance's office by accident.

"Lance, I won't say it again. I know there is a plan and I know it has something to do with AX material, which is our property. Why can't you let me know what is going on? Why hide things from me? What reason do I have for being here if even the people I support don't trust me?"

With a deep sigh, Lance gestures to a chair in front of him and signals me to sit down. He does the same for Amy. "You always drive a hard bargain, Judith. I don't know how you always manage to stay one step ahead of all the others, but you would have made a great minister of intelligence."

I give him a kind smile, but I have another question on my mind. Do earthlings have the resources needed on their planet without Yahire getting involved? One of our main concerns in negotiating a treaty with Earth was the AX trade between the two planets.

"To answer your questions: yes, earthlings do have a plan, and yes, the main element of their plan is AX material. They are going to dig giant holes in canyons down to Earth's core and to install AX plates inside the holes. They will ionize the plates, and the rocks will create a strong gravity well that will pull the pieces together."

"Is that it?" I ask. "Just that? And it's going to work?"

He shrugs. "They don't have time to try something else. And you have to admit the plan is ingenious. AX is the one material that can do what they want concerning gravity and not destroy the chunks of Earth in the process. I think the plan worth a try if it's going to save billions of lives."

I lie back in my chair. Lance is right, but I suspect he's hiding something important.

"Lance, how did humans get enough of this material?"

He doesn't look me; his eyes travel around the room and fall on Amy, who remains silent. "Your protégé is smarter than you, Judith. She doesn't ask questions and knows when to stay quiet and wait for the crisis to pass."

"If I were smart, Lance, I wouldn't be a politician but a doctor. Tell me the president didn't give the okay for an under-the-table deal without talking to me first. Please, just give me that and I swear I won't ever buy you one of those ugly sweaters for Christmas."

Seeing his eyes, I realize I'm right. The president has made a secret deal with Earth's ambassadors regarding Yahire's independence, and I'm sure it wasn't favorable.

"Goddammit, Lance," I say, springing up from my chair. "It's always like that. I spent two years traveling back and forth to Earth to make sure the treaty we were negotiating would protect our interests, and the president has just destroyed everything in one day. Shit."

Lance tenses up behind his desk. "We didn't have a choice, Judith. Billions of people are going to die if we don't help them. Billions. Do you understand the urgency of the situation?"

"Yes, of course I do. I also understand the president has probably promised to make Yahire earthlings' new playground if their planet is destroyed."

Lance looks shocked. "How do you know that? Only five people in this building have been told about that, and I'm certain you weren't one of them. And don't tell me you also know we agreed to transport ninety-four million kilos of AX to Earth!"

"Ninety-four million kilos! Oh, my God. I shouldn't be surprised. When they first started manipulating our AX ten years ago for their so-called Mantle Project, I knew why they always had their eyes on us. I know earthlings, Lance. I know the way they think and act. Their politicians are relentless and will stop at nothing to get what they want. And now, in their time of need, they have taken advantage of us."

"Do you hear yourself talking, Judith? Billions have already died, and more are expected to die by the end of this ordeal. What should the president have done differently? What would you have done?"

At that point I stop. My rage has gotten the best of me and I am not thinking clearly. For once, Lance is right. Earthlings have suffered billions of casualties and are in dire need. Giving them access to our AX material is the least we can do for them. And Yahire cities were originally Earth colonies. Earth will retain a measure of control over our planet even if we gain our independence one day.

But the moment I found out about the deal, I was angry. The president has undone my life's work and has let it go to waste. At the very least, he should have let me know about his decision. The deal should have included some terms favorable to Yahire, but I am sure they weren't even considered.

I take my seat in front of Lance's desk again. Amy looks at me in bafflement. I must have been quite a sight. "I'm sorry, Lance. You're right. It was inappropriate of me to put personal aspirations over the good of the human race. But I feel like I've been betrayed by my own people. I'm confused. That's all."

His expression eases. That's the reason Lance and I are such good friends. We might be fighting at one moment, but at the next moment we are laughing like children. That's mostly due to his cool demeanor and his strong, analytical mind.

Rarely, if ever, will Lance say something that he hasn't given good thought. That makes him perfect for his job. If I were in his position,

I would be spilling all the important secrets. I'm not good at keeping them. But that's another matter entirely.

I have to calm down and to make sure I leave Lance's office with my head held high and not like someone who doesn't believe in her skills.

"It's all right, Judith. I understand your confusion. But you have to remember we are just politicians, elected by the people, and we put the interests of the people above all else. If Earth is destroyed, and the rest of the solar system stops moving in its usual way, that's a problem all of us will have to face sooner or later."

I'm not exactly sure how he does it, but as always, Lance is right. What I must do now is apologize and get out of here. Still, I'm angry with our leaders, with myself, with Amy, with everyone. Even after years of trying to anticipate the moves others will make, I don't understand how people think.

It's not our fault earthlings didn't take good take of their planet, and it's not our fault they were here today. We are humans as well, but at this point there are adults on Yahire who have never been to Earth. How do you explain to people like them that they will have to live in crowded cities because their new neighbors didn't take good care of their previous home?

There will be upheaval, especially after they realize the treaty is probably off the table by now. Yahire won't be independent, not until earthlings are 100 percent sure their planet will hold together for another three thousand years. And that's what ticks me off the most—that I agree with them. I understand their need and want to help them but not on their terms and not without our president first consulting me.

After five minutes of awkward silence, I decide it's time to surrender. It's not like I can do anything, not without opposing my friend and colleague Lance Alexander, head of Yahire's secret services. "Thank you, Lance, for sharing the truth with me. I understand it must have been hard for you, but I had to hear it from you."

"It's okay, Judith. But next time, don't push your luck. I won't say anything, but no matter how much you trust your colleagues, meetings like ours should remain exclusively for government-approved personnel."

Now that's a threat. But he isn't wrong, and after the scene I made, I can do nothing but smile at him and shrug. "Amy is my personal doctor, Lance. What if I had an allergic reaction to something while I was in here? Would you be able to save me?"

I get on my feet and head for the door. I won't admit I've made a mistake in taking Amy with me. She is the girlfriend of my head of security, who is almost like a son to me. It was the least I could do for him after everything he has done for me.

Still, for Lance to be so aggressive means only one thing; things aren't going well on Earth or on our planet. The world has gone mental, and the only thing we can do is wait for the storm to pass inside a shelter that probably won't provide much security in the end. Yes, this shelter is also a crisis management center, but there's nothing we can do except comply with Earth's conditions now that the president has agreed to help its inhabitants without discussing the proper course with us.

We had already opened the migration routes and had prepared spots around the planet to welcome Earth's survivors in less than two weeks. We were ready, but now it will seem like the president did all the work when in fact he just reaped what we sowed.

And that's exactly why I'm so pissed.

When we leave Lance's office, Amy walks by my side but doesn't speak. We're heading for my room where I plan to take a shower and to get ready for the afternoon briefing. Officials will probably announce the deal the president struck with Earth.

Amy seems to want to say something, but she's afraid I'll retaliate after losing my argument with Lance. Depending on what comes out of her mouth, I just might.

"What's on your mind?" I suddenly ask her.

She turns to face me, but I keep walking, staring into the distance. "Did you really get so angry because the president didn't consult you about the secret treaty?" she asks.

I'm a bit surprised at her question, but I don't slow down. I reply, "My dear, if you one day decide to follow my path, you'll understand why I had to make a scene in there. I have been working on this treaty for most of my political career. If the president had consulted me, I would have told him the proper way of dealing with this crisis without becoming human punching bag. They think of us as an extension of their planet, and they have to realize we are not. By agreeing to their demands so easily, we showed them that we're still not ready to carve out our own future and that we are run by their politics."

Amy has to walk more quickly to keep up with me. I'm trying my best not to sound furious, but I'm starting to believe the other side should have taken my feelings into account and not the other way around.

Amy seems to be doing her best to understand my thinking. She's struggling, but she's close. "Okay, but what if we didn't agree to the terms? What if the earthlings decided to take their chances with the resources they have and after the crisis went to war against us for not helping them?"

Now Amy sounds panicked. Living in the shelter with politicians and analysts and every kind of expert has made her think like them. She's trying to make sense of the information Lance provided, but she's hung up on a technicality.

Maybe she doesn't have what it takes to become a politician after all. Taking risks is part of life, and the moment she realizes that, she can drop the innocent facade and become the girl who would lie to government officials to be with her boyfriend.

"We are not inhumane, Amy. Earthlings would have gotten our help one way or another. Lance and I and other political leaders opened a line of communication between Earth and Yahire to make sure that in crisis like this there would be no hindrances. However, we did it in a way that wouldn't interfere with the talks on the treaty. Earthlings would have gotten their help, and we would have gotten our way on the treaty. Everyone would have been happy."

"Everyone except the people in need, Mrs. Campbell. Who would have protected them when the treaty talks ended? And what if the path you opened wasn't enough? Maybe an open-borders policy like the one the president adopted is the best way to make sure the planet is safe."

We arrive outside my room and we stop. I usually invite Amy inside for a cup of coffee and to discuss the details of the latest briefings. But today I'm in no mood to babysit her. If she wants to question my tactics, she will have to do it somewhere else.

"Fast and faster are two different words, but they have the same outcome. Earthlings have enough resources to kickstart their plan, so the fast route would have gotten them resources in time to complete it. The faster route indicates a willingness we shouldn't have to show them. What if the same had happened to the moon colonies? Do you think Earth would run to help them?"

My last question seems to be the answer Amy wanted to hear but wasn't ready for. Preserving life is the top priority in situations like this, but if Earth's ambassadors weren't afraid to bargain over the conditions of their immigration to our planet, why should we have backed off? Why should we feel guilty when they came ready to bargain?

"I understand," Amy finally says, unwilling to look me in the eye. Seeing the system up close has changed her opinion of politics. "Still, this doesn't seem right to me. Fast might be as good as faster in politics, but if it would save one more life, I would go with the latter without thinking about it. Good day."

And just like that, she turns and walks away.

***

# Chapter 23

## A Neighbor In Need

*Same setting*
*Narrator: Ambassador Judith Campbell*

The shower helps me clear my head a bit. Maybe I was overreacting a bit before. I don't know what has gotten into me. When I found out they destroyed my life's work, I blacked out and went into full-throttle mode. I never meant for my work to harm anyone, but in their eyes, I had become the bad guy, even though my life is based on good will.

"I don't know," I mutter as I head to the main area of my room.

A holo screen there constantly plays a feed from local news channels. This is an important day. The first migrants are arriving from Earth. They are the first to evacuate, so their future is important to both planets.

Yahire's citizens are watching them closely. The atmosphere between Yahire and Earth is tense. The crisis that began a month ago has divided Yahire. Some people believe earthlings shouldn't be allowed on our planet, and others believe we should help them wholeheartedly.

The first group claims earthlings are to blame for their planet's destruction and for every other evil in the universe and says they should deal with their problems by themselves. The other group says human life matters more than anything, so we should put survival at the forefront and not argue over what is right.

My opinion lies somewhere in the middle. I agree earthlings are to blame for destroying their planet, but I don't believe we should punish them for their weakness. Their demise started many years ago when they were introduced to materialism and the relentless pursuit of wealth and material goods.

Their obsession with following their dreams instead of caring for their souls led them to this chapter in their history. In their ruthless quest for power, they were struck down by their weakness. And that's why I think they should face repercussions just as they made the moon colonies do after their uprising.

Lost in thought, I sit down on the sofa in the middle of the room and continue drying my hair. My focus drifts from this morning's events to an interview on the holo screen. A reporter from a news channel is interviewing a man from Earth.

They are in a spaceport waiting room amid thousands of people. Most of them are scientists, teachers, and other people of importance who will be easier to integrate into our system. If the worst comes to pass, these people will be able to offer their services to Yahire and won't be a burden.

Earth's political leaders haven't evacuated yet, but if the plan doesn't work, they will quickly abandon the ship that is their destroyed planet.

The man from Earth looks absolutely destroyed. He must not have slept in many days, and his mind seems to be off in the distance. Nevertheless, he has agreed to be interviewed, so he must have something important to say.

"Good afternoon, everyone," the reporter says. "We're here from the first emergency migration center that has been set up on our planet for the people from Earth. After the failure of the Mantle Project and the devastating earthquakes that followed, the first wave of survivors has arrived in Yahire.

"Today we have with us, Adam Huntington, a chemistry professor, with his family. Good afternoon, Mr. Huntingtan." The reporter uses a small gadget on his wrist so the man can be heard.

"Hello," the man says, sounding as weak as he looks.

"I hope you had a good trip to our planet," the reporter says, trying to break the ice with pleasantries.

"Um, yes. It was as good a trip as any could be if you were leaving your past life behind."

Seeing an opportunity in this grim reply, the reporter asks, "What do you mean by that? Would you like to describe your feelings?"

The man stops for a moment and stares into the camera lens. I don't know what he sees there, but he looks terrified. "I ... I'm not sure I'm ready to talk about that."

The reporter isn't pleased with his reply. "There must be something you can share with us to give us a picture of how things are back on Earth. Maybe you can describe the moment of separation."

A fire is kindled in the man's eyes. It's deeper than fear and stronger than anger; it's desperation mixed with hopelessness.

"The earthquake came out of nowhere. It was the last month of the implementation of the Mantle Project, and we were already celebrating humanity's victory when the first wave hit us and hit us hard. Buildings collapsed everywhere, and people lay dead in the middle of the road. The earthquake struck early in the evening, so everything was dark and scary. The only light came from the burning buildings and from the moon. It was hell and I still can't believe we came out of it alive."

Tears fall from his eyes as he speaks. The disaster must have been much harder than we suppose. One tenth of the human population was wiped out in minutes, with more projected to die before the plan to save the planet can be put into operation.

For us here on Yahire, the casualties were just numbers, nameless people who were unimportant to us. I don't know in what part of my career I lost my empathy, but seeing the man struggle to hide his tears, I'm getting a glimpse of the person I used to be.

I can barely hold back my tears.

"That must have been ... awful," the reporter says, his discomfort showing. Still, he has a job to do and continues questioning the man. "What did the Earth government tell you after the first wave? Did you already know it was the Mantle Project's fault, or was there an official announcement?"

"Most of us had to find shelter for ourselves and our children during the night. We didn't have time to wonder what caused the earthquake. However, when we managed to get inside a government building and asked officials, we were told the Mantle Project had gone awry and they were still trying to assess the situation.

"It wasn't until the next morning that official help arrived. For one night, the people helped each other cope in their neighborhoods. It was the only ray of light in the darkest night humanity has ever lived," he says.

Shaken by what he has heard, the reporter has lost his focus. "Um, uh, I understand. God, it must have been awful. One last thing and I'll let you return to your family, Mr. Huntington. Can you tell us what you'll miss most about your life on Earth?"

I can't believe he has asked that question. He's searching for material to move viewers and to fuel the turmoil spawned by the tragedy. I hope this man is smarter than the reporter and gives him a fitting answer.

"What I will miss the most? Did you really ask me that question?" he says.

"I'm sorry if I offended you, but I'm trying to help our viewers understand your feelings better," the reporter says.

With a deep sigh, the man gathers his strength to continue the interview. "Home. Home is what I'll miss most. Planet Earth, all the aromas, the streets, the roads, the flowers, the trees, my family, my friends, the foods, and the life we led back there. It might not have been a pretty life many times, but it was ours. And due to our mistakes, we managed to lose it. Thank you," he says and heads back to his family.

I can't help but smile. Without knowing it, the man gave the best reply for a damaged community. If the news channel doesn't downplay the importance of that reply, we might have a way to rebuild trust between government officials and people.

But to do that, we first have to help solve the crisis. It has taken me a long time to understand this, but my foolish dreams of grandeur were as materialistic as the pursuit of material goods. Caught up in my political aspirations, I forgot human lives were hanging by a thread.

I immediately push a small button on my earphones and call Amy and Owen. I have to get out of this shelter; as one of the ambassadors of our planet, I have to help the survivors. If we can't be kind to our neighbors in this time of need, how we can aspire to be kind to our own people when the time arises?

And with that thought in my head, I prepare for a new battle unfolding in front of me, one that will make the previous battles seem puny and unimportant.

It's time to take back our humanity.

# Chapter 24

## Christmas Lights

*December 24, 2074, about a month after the earthquake*
*New York City*
*Narrator: Tommy Russell*

It has been a month since the first earthquake. The Tri-Colony Union was in awe the day our planet was ripped apart. Our government failed to take full control of the situation, allowing many areas to be overtaken by criminals and by utter chaos.

For many, the world ended that day. I believe the tragedy resulted from the way we were living for many years.

I'm not feeling proud to have been among the handful of people who tried to warn the world of the imminent catastrophe; I'm feeling inadequate. We were unable to stop the Mantle Project when we had time. The project was the embodiment of our fears of materialism taking over our lives, and we let it take control of us in the end.

But I'm coping better than I expected; the world is coping better than I expected. Manna and Lisa aren't so afraid now that the earthquakes have stopped. They still ask us why they had to stop going to school, but I think that after a long conversation we had with them, they figured out for themselves that the planet isn't doing well and that it's better if they don't ask for more details.

It's Christmas Eve. We and some other families around the neighborhood decided to put up Christmas decorations and to make sure our children have fun. Most of us aren't in the mood for anything grand, but since it's the holiday season, I guess we can all find it in ourselves to believe a bit harder and to make things festive, even for a day.

Some are still wishing for a white Christmas, but I'm not sure that will happen this year. I asked my AI assistant, Dorothy, to forecast the weather, but she couldn't give me a definite reply. Most things aren't working as they're supposed to, and the things that do work aren't able to give our kids much hope for the future.

The Planet Mending Plan is humanity's last hope. However, I can't explain to the girls that their present this year will be the hope of surviving till next year. I'm not sure there is still a way to survive. I want to believe in Jonathan and his team, but aren't they the ones who brought us to the brink of destruction?

He and his team are brilliant people, and I'm sure they have found a way to piece together the planet, but I'm afraid it's far too late to do anything.

Not if they ask God for His help.

Now that I spend all my time at home, I often look back on the last two years. I'm trying to think what I could have done better, how I could have influenced the world to change its opinion, or at least to listen to me. I don't know if I could have saved the world, but at least I wouldn't feel so useless now.

When I discuss this with Catherine, she always tells me I'm thinking it too much. I wasn't the one who should have tried harder, she says, but the rest of the world. We went out of our way to warn everyone. Many people around the world had visions of destruction that no one believed; some governments warned the Mantle Project might be too much to handle given humanity's current expertise.

And yet no one did anything to stop it. In the end, everyone was so consumed by the desire to have more that we ripped apart our home.

My head is filled with such thoughts, today more than other days. I've covered myself in a blanket, and I'm having my coffee in front of the fireplace. It's cold outside, and it's still too early in the morning for the kids or my mother to be up. Cat is taking care of some last-minute preparations for the Christmas Eve dinner tonight.

I'll take care of decorating the Christmas tree with the girls when they wake up. It's the least I can do after everything Cat has done for me since this ordeal started.

I want things to be the way they were before. I want to return to the bank and to start working on new projects. I want the girls to feel safe again and to laugh their hearts out during the holidays. But I don't know how to make all that happen.

Lately I've been trying to interpret the vision God sent me so long ago. Earth has obviously suffered because it couldn't any longer contain our materialism, as the vision showed, but I have never understood the part in which I saw the shadow of a man approaching me and an intense light that quickly vanished.

I do not know who this man was or why he was so important that God would send me his image, but I never seriously considered this question until recently. I'm out of ideas, and the people in my internet group who might have helped me either died in the earthquake or are trying to survive.

I have to find a way out of this mess; I promised that to my mother and to my children.

I used the internet to try to identify the mysterious man or at least to get a hint about his location, but I didn't know how to search for him. What parameters to use? "Holy man who can save the world with his faith"? I don't think this man would use the internet, and even if he did, I doubt he would go by the nickname Holy Man.

Still, I've been spending an hour or so every day trying to understand my vision.

That's when I am not watching the news. Nowadays, the only thing we hear is that more people are fleeing the planet and that the Planet Mending Plan is on the fast track and will be ready in the nick of time. That's worrisome because if it fails there will be no time for the scientists to find another solution.

And because I have been unable to figure out that mysterious part of my vision, the world is running out of ideas.

I sigh and turn around in time to glimpse Manna trying to sneak up on me. When she realizes I've spotted her, she frowns. "Come on, Daddy! How did you find me?" she asks.

I smile and point to my ear. "Did you forget Daddy has super strong hearing?" I reply.

Manna stares back at me in awe. "Oh, yeah. I totally forgot about that," she says. A second later, she's running around the sofa, straight for the empty spot next to me. "Dad, it's Christmas Eve! Santa is coming tonight," she says.

"Yeah! Santa Claus is getting ready to start his journey." I don't like lying to her about Santa, but she's too young to hear the truth.

Besides, hope is quite sparse around this place. It wouldn't be wise to take that away from the kids as well.

"So are you ready to set up the Christmas tree?" I ask.

She nods enthusiastically. "Yeah! We're still waiting for Lisa to wake up, right?"

"Yes. But if she doesn't get up soon, you can go upstairs and wake her up. I'm sure she won't mind."

Catherine hears Manna's voice and comes our way. "Good morning, sweetheart. Did you sleep well?" she asks, giving her a kiss on the top of her head.

"Yes! I couldn't wait for today to come to put up our Christmas tree and then eat cookies and wait for Santa."

Manna is obsessed with Santa Claus this year. That's unusual for her. "What did you wish for this year, Manna?" I ask.

An impish smile pops on her face. "You'll see. I hope he doesn't take too long to bring my present this year."

I stare at Catherine and she stares me back; we have no idea what she wished for this year, unlike in previous ones. The girls won't be getting toys this year. Instead, the gifts will be on the symbolic side. That's not only because Earth may be facing its demise but because we want them to learn that material things are good only when they are necessary.

We have no idea what Manna wished for, but chances are she will be disappointed tonight.

"Okay. I hope it isn't too heavy on Santa's back, though," Cat says and returns to her chores.

I take a sip of my coffee and place an arm around Manna. She giggles and hugs me back. Lisa, Manna, and I have gotten way closer since the crisis started. They come to me to talk about their insecurities and fears, and they seem to take my advice to heart.

Manna is too young to be too concerned about her future, but Lisa is turning into quite a considerate little lady. Seeing them grow, even amid this catastrophe, makes me proud to be their father. Still, if I don't find a solution to that vision, our life on this planet will end in the next four months. Just thinking about that makes my stomach clench.

I decide it's time to assemble the tree and then to wake up Lisa and to decorate it. I want to spend time with the girls before dinner tonight, and then we're thinking of going to the city to get provisions for the next month. The government is providing food and other goods for free. Now that officials are working on the plan to save the planet, they have gotten a bit too strict, but we have enough resources to last for a month without their help if need be.

Unlike with the Mantle Project, the government has provided the world with the full details of the plan to fix the planet. Scientists will install AX plates in big holes in the ground and will ionize them to create a gravity field strong enough to put the pieces back together at optimal speed. And by optimal, they mean they hope not to kill the rest of the population by producing too high a speed or by failing to connect the pieces at too slow a speed. The transportation of AX from Yahire has started.

I'm certain the plan will help the situation but won't solve it. God has showed us many times in the last two years that we will end this crisis only with His help. But even though Earth has been divided into two chunks, I haven't noticed a difference in the way people think. They still trust the scientists, the same ones who brought us to this position in the first place, and hope they find a way to save all of us.

If I knew where to find the man in my vision, I would ask him for another solution to this problem, one showing everyone that God still cares for humanity and that we should spend more time praising Him and stop trying to destroy our planet.

"Good morning, everyone. Happy Christmas Eve," my mother suddenly says.

"Grandma!" Manna yells and runs to hug her. "Happy Christmas Eve, Grandma!"

"Oh, my dear Manna. Thank you so much. I see you haven't started with the tree yet."

"Yeah. We're waiting for Lisa to wake up. Do you want to help?" Manna asks.

For a moment, my mother looks at me, her eyes full of despair. Her house, the one where she and my father spent their last years together, was destroyed in the first wave of earthquakes. Since the day she moved in, Mom has been struggling to get used to living with us. It's not that she doesn't love being with us, or that she doesn't prefer a house over the camps that have been assembled for the homeless, but she misses the memories of my father that were everywhere in their house.

Still, a warm smile appears on her face. "Of course, my dear, I'll help you. We don't want Santa Claus to think we don't love him anymore." Giving Manna a pat on her head, she says, "Go on then. Wake up your sister. I'm going to have a short talk with your father."

Manna rushes to the top floor, leaving me and my mother alone by the lit fireplace. "Thank you for that," I tell her the moment Manna is too far away to hear us.

"Don't. It's almost Christmas. The kids deserve to retain their hope." She sits next to me. "How have you been? Are you holding up okay?"

She asks me the same thing every day. The answer gets more difficult every time. "Yeah, I think. I'm trying to be strong for the girls, but I'm running out of things to say to myself. How about you?"

She nods. "About the same. Everything feels so surreal. Living in this house with you, celebrating Christmas … it's like nothing is wrong with the world, but inside me I feel the difference."

"Yeah, I understand. You're right. But we have to be strong for them," I say as Lisa and Manna run down the stairs to the living room.

The air in the room immediately becomes lighter and the colors brighter. Maybe we won't admit it, but our love for those kids is stronger than our desperation over the world's situation. I'm conflicted about what I should do. For the last few nights, I have been talking with Cat about what will happen if the plan to save the planet doesn't work.

I don't think Mother would want to move to Yahire, but Cat and the girls should. I want to go with them, of course, but a strong feeling keeps me here. I haven't said that to Cat, but I feel if I leave now, I'm abandoning Earth. And after the vision God sent me, I think doing that would mean ignoring Him.

Emergency spaceports have been set up all around the world. Many ships are leaving every other week with thousands of people on board. Officials say that by the time we find out whether the plan has succeeded, only 0.32 percent of the population will have been evacuated to Yahire. That amounts to nineteen million people, but New York City and its suburbs have a greater population than that.

I am not sure whether Yahire will take us. Still, it's the best chance we have to save our children. Cat and the girls stand a better chance of getting on a spaceship to Yahire if I'm not traveling with them. That's how I persuaded Cat to wait until the last minute before heading to a spaceport.

After we came to an agreement on that, I was able to relax a bit. Making sure Manna and Lisa survive is my main concern. Now I'm thinking only about how to find that man in my vision.

"When you're spacing out like that, you look exactly like your father," my mother suddenly says.

I snap out of my thoughts. "You have told me that before, but I don't remember him spacing out a lot when I was young. He always looked so certain of himself, like he knew the purpose of his life and how to achieve what he wanted. He seemed sure the path of his life was laid out before him as clear as day."

"Well, that was before he met that man."

"What man? What are you talking about?" I ask.

"Haven't I told you about Izan?"

The name means nothing to me. I have never heard mother speak about him. "No, you haven't. Who is he? And what did he have to do with Dad?"

As soon as I ask that question, Manna and Lisa surge into the room with the force of a typhoon. "Daddy! Grandma! Good morning," Lisa shouts, unusually happy today.

"Good morning to you too, Lisa," Mom says with a warm smile. "Why so happy today, darling? Did you have a good dream?"

Lisa looks at me and then at her grandma in awe, thinking that I must have said something to my mother or that Mom was able to read her thoughts. "Yes! How did you know?"

"Well, grandmothers know all about good dreams. Now tell us about your dream."

Lisa opens her mouth but then closes it. "I'm sorry," she says, "but I can't tell you. It's a secret."

And just like that, she rushes off to find Catherine to give her a hug. Mother turns and looks at me. "So the girls love to play games with you, don't they?"

I feel like a lecture is coming, but she adds a funny frown at the end that makes me relax. "Yeah, they do like playing games with us. But they have grown to trust us, and that's worth it."

I want to ask Mom about the strange man named Izan, but we get swept away by the Christmas spirit. Before we know it, we're neck deep in Christmas ornaments and Christmas lights. The day goes by quickly but pleasantly.

\*\*\*

# Chapter 25

# An Old Friend

*Later that evening*
*Narrator: Tommy Russell*

"It's time for bed," Cat tells the two half-sleeping angels on the sofa.

"But I want to meet Santa Claus," Manna says, more persistent this year than in other years.

"We have talked about this before, Manna. Santa is pretty shy and doesn't like meeting young children when they're awake. Also, it's never too late to be put on the bad children list and not to get your present this year. Do you want Santa to cancel his visit to us?" Cat asks.

Mother and I are enjoying a glass of wine and are smiling at this exchange. I would love to allow Manna to stay up all night to wait for Santa Claus, but she has to go asleep. She looks tired but she's trying her best to keep awake for Santa.

The moment Cat mentions that Santa might not bring her the gift she asked for, Manna calms down and starts off for her bed. Before leaving, though, she tells us, "I really hoped I could meet Santa this year. Maybe next year we won't have the chance."

And with that, she walks away.

Lisa, two years older but still an avid believer in Santa Claus and in the Christmas spirit, follows her, half-asleep. She isn't one to complain, especially if sleep is included in the deal.

When the two of them are gone, I whisper to Cat, "It's time to bring them their gifts," and I head for my car where I've kept the gifts hidden.

Cat makes sure the girls aren't peaking from upstairs, and my mother comes out to help me. It's pretty late, and the sky is covered by dark clouds. Some people hope it snows; others hope the weather gets better. No one wants to know what's going to happen in about four months, so people are focusing on the weather and the holidays.

I open the trunk and bring out two small bags full of the girls' favorite candies, a doll for each, and a new software chip for painting. These are the only things we could find that they would love and that they didn't have. Also, since they both love reading, we made sure to include a book for each.

These may be the last books the girls read before leaving Earth, so we wanted them to be special. Maybe they will make the girls happier.

While we're outside grabbing the bags, I take the opportunity to bring up an earlier subject. "So, Mom, can you please tell me more about the man who helped Dad change? Um, what was his name?"

"Do you mean Izan?" she asks.

"Yes, him. Can you please tell me more about him?"

Her face instantly darkens and she stops moving. This morning, she looked comfortable talking about him. But since I went out of my way to ask, she must suspect I'm thinking of leaving my family to find him.

If I hadn't seen that vision, or if I had agreed with Cat to move with the girls to Yahire, I wouldn't have thought about doing this. But now I'm free to pursue my intuition.

"Why do you want to know more about Izan?" my mother asks curtly.

I don't understand why she sounds so hostile. It's not like I want to make the same mistakes my father did. I'm just a desperate man searching for solutions.

"Because I think he can help us," I reply.

"The only way to save this planet is for people to leave right now. That and to make sure God is in our hearts. Izan is a hermit who won't help anyone even if you go out of your way to ask him. Hermits live in a world of their own. They have found ecstasy inside their hearts. They are different people, disconnected from the rest of the world."

We enter the house and tiptoe toward the living room where the Christmas tree stands. The gifts are wrapped up in colorful paper and look flashy and new, as they're supposed to. We place them beneath the tree and return to our seats in the living room in case one of the girls wakes up during the night.

I pick up the conversation again. "Why do you say that, Mother? If he is a holy man who helped Father find his true path in life, why won't he help humanity as well? You say they are disconnected from the world. But I believe they are connected to the Creator of the universe, and that is what matters now!"

With a short sigh, my mother grabs her glass and lies back in her seat. I can see in her eyes that she is searching for the right words. "Izan is ... well he is a hermit. The last time I remember your father talking to him, he was in Australia. Originally from a beautiful valley in the Himalayas, Izan was a deeply spiritual man, one who guided many people to their proper paths. One of them was your father.

"So disgusted was Izan with the world, so dispirited about humanity's lack of faith, that he decided to walk away from civilization and from earthly goods. He dedicated himself to praying and to cultivating his soul rather than to helping others."

After Mom has described the man, I start to dredge up memories from the past—my father calling someone but never talking, my mother mentioning the name in the background, Father always looking in the distance, lost in thought. He might have considered returning to Australia to find Izan, but because of me and my mother, he never did.

Still, something strikes me as weird. Mom said she knew nothing of what Dad had done during his trip to Australia, only that he went there to discover himself and that for two years, he didn't return, making her worry he might have abandoned us to follow his spiritual path.

"How do you know all these things, Mom? You told me before that Father never talked about what he had found out there or about what he had to go through. I thought Dad never discussed that experience."

Mother looks at me with the wisdom of a woman who has been through bad times. "Your father started talking to me about Izan a few months before dying. Jacob knew he wouldn't live much longer, and he asked me to try to track down Izan. He said that he had little hope of finding him but that he wanted to hear his guide one last time before passing away.

"I tried to find the man. I called every number your father gave me, but no one ever picked up, not a single soul. When I told him that, he asked me to keep trying because one day Izan might answer. In the meantime, your father wanted to remember his years in Australia, so he started talking."

The crackling of burning wood gives the room a cozy feeling. So Dad knew a holy man, one so pure and unblemished that he might be the man I'm looking for. That someone would walk away from the modern way of living to follow his faith sounds almost unbelievable to me.

A bell began ringing inside my head the moment I heard my mother speak his name. I have to know more about this man. I have to find him.

"You know, Mom, I had a vision a while ago, way before this ordeal started. I saw the world crumbling around me and, in the distance, the shadow of a man. He might be the key to this problem, the solution we have been waiting for. I want you to tell me everything you know about Izan. I want to know how I can find him if I go to Australia."

I hadn't expected to say that last line; I hadn't thought of leaving my family in the middle of this crisis, but the longer I talk about this Izan and the more I hear about him, the more I believe that great teacher might be the one I've been searching for.

"What are you talking about, Tommy? It's impossible to travel to Australia now. The borders have been closed, and services have been shut down in many nations. How will you be able to get there and to find Izan? Besides, I'm not sure Izan will want to help you."

"Why? You have said he's a holy man. Why wouldn't he help me save my family and the rest of humanity?"

"If God has abandoned us at this time of need, do you think His followers will help us?"

That question sparks something in me. My insecurities were holding me back. I wanted to take action, but I was afraid I might fail. But after hearing my mother's words, I know my time is running out. God chose me to find Izan, and I'll do it even if I have to give my life.

"I understand what you're saying, Mom, but your objection sounds a bit implausible. There is every reason to believe a person like Izan would make a plea to God if all of humanity is involved."

The passion in my words rekindles my mother's hope; she's starting to see my point, and I'm sure she knows humanity is in dire need of a miracle right now.

She puts down her glass and faces me. "Someone has to convince him to intervene. These mystics love their Lord so much they forget about everything else and stay in a meditative state."

Hearing more about Izan, I'm starting to understand what an extraordinary man he must be. Still, I myself have objections to his insular faith. "He seems to be a selfish man, doesn't he?"

My mother shares a soft smile with me. "That's what I thought when your father told me about him. But it's not that simple. Mystics get so deep into their souls that they forget themselves as well as others. I don't know what you have in mind, my child, but Izan should be the last solution to our problem, not the first."

But who said saving humanity would be easy? Who said traveling to the other side of the planet just to meet one man—a person I might never find if he doesn't want to be found—would be easy?

Miracles are hard to come by, especially life-changing, cosmos-bending ones.

A wide smile forms on my face. I'm starting to understand the kind of faith this man has in our Lord. And in a sense I feel like him.

Mother is expecting a reply. "I can't wait until the nick of time for the government to see the merit of our way, Mom. I have to find Izan and ask him to pray to God for humanity to be saved. I will be more than happy to see such a man. We are as good as dead. Why not take one last honest step?"

The light of the fireplace gives my mother's face a warm and calm look. She isn't smiling, though, not after seeing my determination. I'm not sure how our conversation went in this direction, but it's too late for me to turn back. For the first time in my life, I can clearly see the road I must follow, and I am in awe. Mom seems to get that.

"Go, my dear son. Go and may God be with you."

"And with all of us," I say.

"And with all of us," she whispers after me.

\*\*\*

# Chapter 26

## Going To Space

*Early morning, January 15, 2075*
*New York City*
*Narrator: Tommy Russell*

I've been staring at my suitcase for more than an hour. Catherine is scurrying about the house, taking care of last-minute chores. After long discussions during the past few weeks, we have decided that Cat, my mother, and the girls will head to Yahire and will stay there until it's safe to return and that I will go to Australia to try to find Izan.

Now I can travel without the fear that another massive earthquake will hit the planet and my family will die while I'm away. At first, Cat didn't like the idea of traveling to another planet with the kids, but my mother talked her into it.

The original plan was for me to stay here and for Catherine to take the girls to Yahire sooner or later, but after the revelation on Christmas Eve, I couldn't stay put. Knowing there might be a man who can save the planet makes me anxious to get underway. I have to meet him and to persuade him to help us.

I'm flying to Germany today, and even though I feel this is the right thing to do, gazing at the suitcase in front of me makes everything all too real.

Today might be the last time I see my wife and my children. It might be the last time I see mother. I'm scared that if I fail, it will be my fault, and the thought of carrying humanity on my shoulders is starting to take a toll on me. I have barely slept for the last five days, and every time I have managed to squeeze in an hour of sleep, I have seen the figure of the man I first saw in my vision. I'm not sure if it's Izan or someone else, but ever since I decided to make this trip, a presence has been calling me. My head is a ball of confusion. I have to do something to take my mind off the details of the trip.

I leave my bedroom and head downstairs. Mother is outside talking to the girls, keeping them busy until it's time to leave. Seeing them laugh, play, and have fun makes me feel happy. I am content and unafraid now that Cat has agreed to take them to Yahire. I couldn't forgive myself if my children paid the price for the sins of their ancestors. It's all our fault for failing to stop this disaster from happening, and they shouldn't have to live in a world destroyed by greed.

I head to the kitchen, searching for Catherine. She's the only one who can calm my nerves now. I'm not sure I can take this journey without her, but I'll have to manage. This is my path in life, and Catherine shouldn't have to put her life in danger so I can succeed.

When I enter the room, she is leaning over the table, hiding her face. "God, Catherine. Are you okay?" I ask and rush to her side.

She raises her hand to stop me. "I'm fine! Don't come near me."

For the first time I see she is crying. I'm standing close to her but decide it's best to give her some space. "Catherine, please talk to me. What's wrong? Why are you crying?"

She doesn't face me while speaking. "This is way too much for me to handle, Tommy. I know you expect me to be strong and supportive, but you are my husband and the father of our children. Leaving you in this shattered land makes me afraid for your life, today more than ever before. It isn't easy for me to keep up the image of a strong woman when I'm leaving behind my whole life."

Her outburst gives me a clear insight into her thoughts; I knew she didn't like this plan, but I never thought she had so much fear inside her. I have to help her, to give her something to hold on to while we're apart.

"I'm sorry for making you feel like this, my love, but this is something I have to do. Maybe it won't be necessary. Maybe the scientists will find a way to make everything right without the help of our faith. But I can't stay here and wait to die while I have the chance to find this Izan and to ask him to pray for us all."

Catherine looks straight at me. Her face is full of tears; she must have been crying for some time now. "I know it's important, and I know you have to do it. But is it any surprise I'm worried about you? I'm your wife, after all. I have every right to shed tears for you. I might never see you again."

I lean closer to her and kiss her. It's a sweet kiss, a peck on the lips, but it's enough to calm her down a bit. I place my hands on her shoulders and draw her close to me. I can feel her heart beating on my chest. She must have been holding her feelings inside for a long time.

"I love you so much, Catherine, but you have to do this for me. This plan is best for everyone. I want your support more than anything. I have to know the girls are safe with you or I won't make it to Australia and I won't have a chance of finding this Izan person."

I feel so selfish and for moment wonder why I can't listen to my wife and head with her to Yahire. However, I have no choice. God has given me a mission and I have to see it through.

With a deep sigh, Catherine takes a step back from me and wipes away her tears. At this moment, she is the most beautiful woman in the universe. Her mellow beauty breaks my heart; like her, I realize this might be the final good-bye for our family, but I can't think like that. My quest to save humanity is just starting, and if this first hurdle is so hard, the rest of the journey will be even more difficult.

But I am not making this trip to discover myself. This trip is about saving humanity and about making contact with God, the Lord of life and of the universe. The scientists can do their best, but I'm confident this ordeal won't end until we seek God's help.

Catherine seems more collected now. Her fear of abandonment gone, she now has the strength to journey to Yahire. That's what I had to see to restore my own calm.

"You are right, Tommy. I have to be strong for our kids. Just return to me when you're done saving humanity, darling. I know you can do it, but we are only humans. Our job is to love each other."

Cat passes by my side without turning to face me. Her eyes are firmly set on the girls; they are her one and only purpose right now, and she will do everything in her power to protect them.

Now I'm alone in the kitchen. We have made so many great memories in this house—the day Manna said her first word; the day Lisa showed us her first painting; the day Cat and I moved in. There are so many memories to choose from, and yet it feels like they were only the beginning.

"This is God's will, Tommy. Don't get lost in your sentiments. You have a mission," I whisper to myself.

With one last look at the kitchen, I head to the bedroom to pick up my traveling bag. The small suitcase contains shirts, pants, and other things I'll need for my journey. I'm not sure how the weather is in Australia right now, but I have made sure I'm ready for anything.

We head to the Pennsylvania space station, the first one built specifically for Yahire space travel. The moment is tense. Many thoughts rush into my mind. Manna and Lisa are playing, teasing each other, excited they are going to space. They dreamed of traveling to the stars one day, so the moment my mother told them what they were going to do, the girls couldn't stop talking about it.

I'm happy they are excited. I couldn't let them go if they were crying or calling for me, but now that I see their wide smiles, I somehow feel everything will be okay. It has been so long since I've heard their laughter that the sound makes me smile. It does the same to Catherine.

We reach the station after a two-hour drive, and my mother gives me a look of pure love. "Are you ready to do what you believe in?" she asks.

I say nothing. Just a nod and a look filled with love are enough for my mother to understand me. If a person cannot find God in this life, he should stare into his mother's eyes, and there he will find the glimpse of bliss he is looking for. This is an emotional moment for me, but I have to get on with my mission, and it's time to say good-bye.

The girls cheer. "Yeah! We are going to space! We are going to space!"

"Great. Now say good-bye to your dad because it's going to be some time before you see him again," my mother tells them.

Their cheerful expressions change to unhappy ones; they don't want to say good-bye to me. I'm not sure if they have overheard any of our conversations since I decided to search for Izan, but they seem sad to leave me.

They are my children after all. It's only natural for them to feel sad about leaving me here. They seem to know what I'm risking by staying behind; they seem to have figured out everything in their young minds. Still, they don't lose time; they rush toward me and hug me as tightly as they can. Even together they are not big enough to wrap their arms around my body, but they try.

I open my mouth to say something to them, a word of advice or an important clue about life, but nothing comes out. For the first time in my life, I'm out of things to say. I have reached that point as a parent when I can do nothing else but love my children and make sure they don't stray too far away from their paths.

I lean down and lift Manna in my arms; she has started crying.

With a kiss on her forehead and a tight hug I say good-bye. Before setting her down, I whisper in her ear, "I love you, little pumpkin. Make sure that you eat all your food and that you brush your teeth in the morning. When we meet again, I want to see that beautiful smile of yours shining."

She nods and uses her hands to wipe away her tears. My voice calmed her down a bit.

However, Lisa is now in tears. Because she's older than Manna, it's possible she has figured out something about my plan. If that's true, she does a great job of hiding it. Now it's time to bid her good-bye as well. I pick her up in my arms and give her a kiss and a hug.

This time, though, she is the one who whispers in my ear. "Pray as hard as you can, Daddy," Lisa tells me. "It's the only way to save us all. We'll be praying for your safety from Yahire, too."

I set her down and nod at her as calmly as possible even though deep inside I'm in shock. What is she talking about? Why should I be the one to pray? The plan is to make Izan do everything in his power to protect Earth. I'm just a humble servant of God, certainly not a holy man able to save the humanity with my prayers.

She must have misunderstood—except if she had a vision as well.

Lisa said that she had a dream but that she couldn't say anything about it because then it wouldn't come true. Maybe God sent her a sign as well, a hint that I'm headed in the right direction.

I want to ask her; I'm sure she'll tell me now. She might even know the outcome of my journey to Australia. But no. I can't do that. I shouldn't do that. Lisa and Manna will be safe in Yahire; Mother and Catherine will be safe with them. That's all I need to know right now. Everything else is just noise that is calling me to drop everything and to go with them.

I can't listen to it. I have to make this journey. It's God's will.

"Okay. It's time for me to go or I'll lose my flight and so will you. Cat, make sure that the girls listen to the flight attendants and that they make many friends on Yahire. Mother, I promise you one day we'll return here and you'll see your house and get back your memories. I'll do everything in my power to make it happen."

Cat and Mother hug me one after the other. They are both in tears but are crying silently. They are confident that I will find the solution to this problem and that when I do, they will return to this planet and we'll all live together again.

We part our ways, and wave good-bye to each other. I manage to hold back my tears for a moment. I'm alone now, with my family off to a new start on a different planet. If I don't make it, their new start will be my salvation. I'll die but at least they will have lived on.

And that will have saved my soul.

***

# Chapter 27

## Internal Compass

*Flight to Germany*
*Narrator: Tommy Russell*

I fly to Germany in space over the Atlantic, and I'm not in an ordinary airplane flying at forty-five thousand feet. That's because the big rip in the Atlantic would pull an airplane inside of it. My plan is to first reach Germany and to take another airplane for Victoria, Australia. Most of the direct space flights to destinations on Earth were halted after the earthquake, and the carriers have been busier transporting people to Yahire. That's why I didn't have the stress-free option of traveling directly to Victoria.

I have left my family behind to start a journey to the unknown, searching for a man who might not want to be found—Izan, the mysterious holy man, a modern-day hermit, someone who might hold the solution to the crisis threatening planet Earth.

I have mixed feelings as I head to my destination. I'm excited but also afraid. I want to meet Izan and to talk with him, but I also want to take the first spaceship to Yahire. I hope my family will have no trouble getting accustomed to a new way of living, but I'm worried that moving to another planet might not be enough to save them.

The latest reports from the Core and Earth Sciences Department indicate that Earth's disaster triggered a domino effect that might cause the destruction of our solar system. Earth's gravity kept the system stable, but now that its gravity is diminishing, the system is threatened. The duration of the moon's orbit around the torn earth has increased to thirty-five days, and it's projected we'll see even more changes as the final threshold draws closer.

Gravity is already 10 percent lower, and the rifts that divide the world can be seen when flying over them from space. We're close to Germany now, where I'll have to book the next flight to Victoria. If everything goes as planned, I'll be there in two days at most.

Seeing the rift over the Atlantic made me and the other passengers shake with fear. The ocean was suddenly interrupted by a dark scar that extended all the way to the other side of the planet. While we were flying over the rift, I couldn't breathe properly. I worried that if our plane's altitude fell too low, that would be the end of us.

However, the primal fear of extinction has been a wakeup call for me. For the first time since my vision, I'm determined to see this mission through to an end. I have to save my family and humanity, and to do that, I have to clear my mind and take appropriate actions.

The closer I get to Australia, the clearer his voice becomes in my head. Pigeons use an internal compass to know if they are traveling south or north, and I have a similar sense. I have a general idea of where Izan is and how to find him, but I know the trip will be long and I'm running out of time. I don't know what people are doing in Australia since it's one of the countries that fell into utter chaos after the first wave of earthquakes.

Though the government had an excellent handle of the situation, the aftershocks caused even more damage than the main event, destroying the country's infrastructure and cutting off communication with the rest of the world. For all I know, Australia might be in flames or all its people might have died. Either way, I'm fairly certain I will have to talk to a government official before I can travel there. And knowing the core and earth scientists, citing religion as the main reason for my trip won't be enough.

Still, my faith is all I have right now. I have to trust myself and to make sure it's enough to get me to the other side of the world.

A sudden turbulence makes me snap out of my thoughts. I look around me in panic, staring outside the cabin for the cause. I have to wait for the pilot's explanation.

"Ladies and gentlemen, we will be entering Earth's atmosphere in about one minute from now and will reach the space station in about four minutes. You will be facing extreme turbulence while entering Earth's atmosphere, so please stay calm and buckle your seat belts. And don't worry; we will be just fine."

The pilot's explanation makes me feel a little better, though I hadn't noticed the fact that I wasn't breathing. When I manage to get some air in my lungs, I look around me, checking the faces of the other passengers. They are all desperate and depressed; they're all flying to Germany, hoping the waiting times and the baggage system will be better than in America.

Most of them are with their families, holding hands and praying to God for their safety. I'm not sure, but I get the feeling that most of them are praying for the first time in their lives, that they're turning to faith out of fear. I know that God is merciful and that He will forgive us of our sins, but praying out of fear feels wrong. These people have an unnatural look on their faces; their prayers appear disingenuous, and that makes me angry.

If they had prayed all their lives, if they had listened to the voice of reason before it was too late, we might have been spared the pain of losing our planet. However, it's too late for them to walk back their mistakes. The honest thing to do would be to accept their faults and to try to redeem themselves by loving each other, but praying for their lives when they are the ones who have endangered them feels twisted.

It makes me want to puke.

I unbuckle my belt and try to head to the toilet, but a stewardess stops me on my way.

"Excuse me, sir, but the pilot just informed us of the extreme turbulence, so it would be much safer for you to remain buckled in your seat."

"I really need to head to the toilet," I tell her. "I'm not feeling well."

"I understand, sir, but this is an important time. We're close to landing. I'm sure if you try to hold back for a few more minutes, you'll be fine by the time we arrive."

I want to scream at her that it's the other passengers, the injustice of this world, and the materialistic nonsense that are making me sick, but I restrain myself. I must do that because I'm fighting for these people. I'm trying to save their lives, the lives of their children, and their future children. I have to put up with their foulness to endure this trip, and that means I have to accept that we humans are faulty beings.

The biblical story of our creation, of Adam and Eve, shows the flaws in us. It's an indication of human nature. We don't want to fall from God's grace, but the world is calling us and we listen. Then perhaps we lose our spiritual paths and our souls. Maybe fighting to make God hear us is a good thing. That way, we have a reason to live, and making God listen to us sounds like the best reason right now.

Deep in thought, I'm barely aware of any turbulence. The only thing I feel is the pressure on my chest due to extreme gravitational pull; the sweat on my forehead results from an involuntary adrenaline rush.

"Ladies and gentlemen, thank you for your patience and for your trust. We have arrived at the German space station. My crew and I hope you have a great rest of your journey, and we wish the core and earth scientists success in carrying out their plan. And may the God of every religion help us all."

I feel a tear running down my face. I quickly wipe it away, surprised by the man's show of sympathy and by his heartfelt wish.

I lie back, looking at the land extending below us. The man's wish twists and turns in my head.

May God help us all.

* * *

Picking up my suitcase feels impossible. The station is stuffed to the gills with people wanting to travel to Yahire. Flights from all over the world land in Germany where Europe's main airport is located. An emergency airport is being built in the United Kingdom, but those with the means to travel here have chosen to do so.

The world is holding its breath while the scientists of the Core and Earth Sciences Department set up their plan. They announced it about two months ago, and three of the six vantage points are ready. They are trying to keep everyone in the loop, but it has been too long since their last report. They were trying to contact their branch in Asia and the Russian government the last time they made a public announcement, but since then, they have gone dark.

I don't think the American and European governments will abandon their plan to reunite the ripped chunks of the planet, but they may have to go to great lengths to make sure everything is ready in time.

When I finally get my suitcase, I head toward the exit. The passageway is nearly empty and my trip is short. I see only two other people. They appear stressed; they probably want tickets to another country.

When I pass through the automated doors, I stop and look around me in awe. "I can't believe this is happening," I mumble. Thousands upon thousands of people are crowded around the airline booths; the lines extend all the way outside.

They all want tickets for the next flight to Yahire, and they can't seem to remain calm while they wait. The space station staff is overwhelmed, and everyone who can help is manning a booth. Many people argue over priority, making the noise in the waiting area unbearable.

I'm not sure if I'm walking in the right direction since my request is pretty particular, but returning to the baggage retrieval area doesn't seem like the right move.

I put down my suitcase and comb my hair with my fingers; I have no idea what to do now that I'm here. I thought there would be order or at least a sense of cooperation here since all of us are in the same boat. People fighting over tickets but can't find it in themselves to save what's most important: humanity's future.

"I can't believe it," a man says behind me. "Tommy, is that you?"

I turn around and see Jonathan, the creator of the Mantle Project and the man leading the salvation plan.

"Jonathan, it's nice to see you," I say and extend my hand to greet him.

"What are you doing here, Tommy? Why haven't you gotten on a spaceship to Yahire?"

It's funny he's asking me that. Isn't he the one with the plan to save the planet? "My family is heading there now, hopefully. How about you? Are you here as part of the Planet Mending Plan?"

"Yes. I'm flying to Russia from a military base close to here. Where are you headed? Maybe I can help you move through this madness," he says, gesturing toward the people getting squashed outside.

However, at that moment, I have an idea. "Well, I was hoping I could get a flight to Australia. Specifically to Victoria."

The moment he hears my reply, his eyes almost pop out of their sockets. "You want to do what?"

I knew I would probably have to persuade a government official, but Jonathan is the last person I expected to find here.

Now I'm starting to see the difficulty of the rest of my journey.

# Chapter 28

## The Power Of Forgiveness

*Late at night, January 15, 2075*
*Germany's spaceport*
*Narrator: Dr. Jonathan Bailey*

Meeting Tommy in the exit at Germany's spaceport surprised me but not that much. He is a man who follows his faith, and surely his faith brought him to the center of the action, the last battle for survival. He was one of the many people who tried to warn me that pursuing the Mantle Project would mean the end of our planet. Still, his will to stop me wasn't enough.

And in a way, I didn't do anything to make him think I'm the one responsible for this mess. The numbers were only a bit off, and by the time the Mantle Project's first anniversary neared, we had lowered the probability of something going wrong down to almost zero. There was always a chance Earth's mantle wouldn't be able to withstand the chemicals we poured in, but it was so small that it was close to impossible.

I won't feel guilty over something I can fix, and this plan is the product of six desperate people trying to do right by their own books. I'm sure it will work. It has to work. And to make certain of that, I am meeting with the Russian government and with the Asian branch of the Core and Earth Sciences Department. Together we can make this work, and I'm doing everything in my power to proceed with the plan.

I have a few hours before taking off for Russia. Maybe I can talk with Tommy and find out why he's heading to Australia.

"You want to go to Australia? Why is that, Tommy?" I ask as we stand behind the spaceport's main exit.

The crowd is too tense for us to proceed. Taking a moment in this quiet spot is advisable.

Tommy looks at me with eyes full of fire. He doesn't like the fact that I'm here, but he sees it as an opportunity to get where he wants.

"I ... I'm searching for a man, someone important. I think he can help with the shattered planet, Jonathan."

Again, I'm surprised, but not that much. "Is he a scientist? Someone I should know?"

He shakes his head twice. "No. No.... He is a hermit, a holy man who might be able to summon God's help."

I don't know if I should cry or burst into laughter. Poor Tommy must have gone mental after everything that has happened to the planet, especially since he was part of those groups trying to warn the rest of the world.

No, I won't turn him down. I have to prove to him he is wrong so he can return to his family safe. Knowing Tommy and his mulish ways, turning him down without showing him the error of his ways will only increase his desire to get to Australia.

Seeing him, I'm reminded of the old days when we used to talk about the differences between religion and science. I can hear his opinions about materialism in my head. Still, that will make it easier to beat him at his own game.

I have seen God now, and I know how it feels to have a purpose. Only my God is hiding in the faces of my loved ones while his is an idea belonging to an ancient era.

"Okay then. I will help you find him but only if you prove to me that sending you to Australia, one of the most dangerous continents, would be worth the resources. How is that? I have to leave for the military airport in two hours. That is your deadline. If you can't prove to me in two hours that you are right, I'll leave this place and take off."

His eyes get all flashy, but he doesn't reply. Instead, Tommy takes a step back and leans against the wall. "This isn't a game to me, Jonathan. Either you help me or you don't. Don't try to measure my faith with silly mind games."

So Tommy is off to a good start. He is trying to counter my argument by using passive-aggressive psychology. He is trying to prove I am the one at fault here, even though we both know the problem started hundreds of years ago.

"Either way, Tommy, I'm the one with the means to get you where you want to go. I can help you, but I have to know the pilot taking you to Australia won't risk his life for Christian nonsense. I'm not trying to measure your faith, my friend; I want you to persuade me that God, your God, exists and that He can help our cause."

And with that, the fire in his eyes is extinguished; I have managed to draw his attention. That's good. I want Tommy to use all his weapons to get me to understand his point. After all, for once, I won't hold back. I'll show him his radical thought and make him stop chasing false prophets.

"Okay. Now I understand. You want me to persuade you about the existence of God. You want to see a purpose to my mission, the same one I see. Well, that's difficult, Jonathan, since you aren't a religious person yourself. There are many differences between a scientist and a believer, and you have dedicated your life to science. How can I change your mind when you have spent all your life believing that my faith is nonsense?"

He has a point. But if I'm going to entrust the planet's future to a miracle born of faith, Tommy will have to work his miracle here first. I know he can do it, but he is just like me and not above me. We are both passionate about what we love, and we both will do everything in our power to get what we want. Tommy wants me to believe in him, and I want him to prove the truth of what he believes.

I have glimpsed God, but now I want to see the whole thing, to feel the warmth of believing in a power bigger than life itself. And here in the eye of the hurricane is the best place for Tommy to show me that. We won't have another chance like this to talk, and after I leave him, I'll probably spend the rest of my days traveling from country to country, making sure the plan is working.

I put down my suitcase. The spaceport's electric lights are a strain on my eyes. I desperately need to light a smoke, but I don't want to have any trouble with the staff.

Nevertheless, I take out my pack and pull out a cigarette. "I never said your faith is nonsense, Tommy. I haven't ever believed it was, not even for a minute. You like thinking of yourself as the underdog, the one people blame for their problems even though you are the nicest guy I've ever met. And yet here you are, trying to do something for the billions of human beings who will cease to exist if we don't save the planet. But I'm not asking you to prove your faith is important to you. If you want to pass these doors and head to Australia, you must make me feel like I have to take you with me."

I keep the cigarette in my mouth and lower my head. I'm eager to hear what he'll come up with in reply.

He seems to be struggling to find the right words, and yet his whole body seems brighter than the spaceport lights. I can't keep my eyes off of him while he's shining like this.

Tommy takes a deep breath before speaking. "God is light, Jonathan. Believing in Him is a way of living, not just a way of proving you are right or wrong. If it weren't for my father, I probably would have ended up a materialistic person, always struggling for the next big thing, not caring for the well-being of my family or cultivating my soul and giving my all to amass more wealth, more earthly goods. However, when I saw the light for the first time, I figured nothing was more important than loving my family and the people around me, and to do that, I had to leave behind every selfish thought. That's religion for me, and it pains me that you don't seem to understand that."

Is this his best case for religion? Is this what believing in God means to him? If so, it's nothing like the feeling I had that night.

I decide to talk to him about it. Maybe if I share my experience, he'll do the same. "I don't know, Tommy. Even though your words seem right, it feels like you're talking through your head and not your heart. You gave me a textbook answer to the question I asked you, but there was no hint of your God in there, just big words like *family* and *love* and everything lying in between. It's like you are afraid you aren't good enough to prove to me you are right, like you are holding something back."

Tommy seems in shock; he thought his answer would be enough. Seeing him like that makes me feel awful, but faith isn't all that different from science. He doesn't reply, so I decide to go on.

"A couple of months ago, some nights after the first wave of the earthquakes, I was released from the police station so I could gather my team of scientists and find a solution to this problem. That night, almost all of them turned on me and tried to prove to me that I was at fault and that I should be kept in prison for my crimes against humanity. They poured out their feelings. We had never been more honest with each other, and even though when everything is over I'll probably spend the rest of my life in jail, that night I got a glimpse of God and of His workings in their tears." I take a pause.

"You tell me God is loving everyone around you, and I tell you this is common sense. You tell me the Mantle Project was my part of my selfishness, and I accept that and choose to deal with it. However, you don't speak about love but preach about it. And to someone who has never been in a church, you sound monotonous. How could you expect me to ask someone to risk his life for a guy who doesn't even know how to speak about his faith?"

Tommy wants to retaliate but seems depressed. He has made it this far, but now a scientist is preaching to him about the basics of religion. I can see him talking to himself, putting his thoughts in order, trying to pump feelings of love and spirituality from his head, but it doesn't work.

It has been half an hour since we started talking, and instead of getting better, our relationship gets worse. I would accept even a simple answer if he gave it to me wholeheartedly, but trying to explain God using broad terms doesn't feel like the right strategy.

Still, he won't give up. "How can someone like you speak about religion when he hasn't even visited a church? How can someone talk like that about God when he himself doesn't pray? This is a sin, and this kind of sin led us to where we are. You *think* you know everything about religion because you read about it in a book, but guess again; having God in your life isn't as easy as you might think."

"Tommy, do you even hear yourself? Your words seem to come from someone who hates those who don't believe in the same God he does. This isn't you. No, if you want to have a chance at saving this planet, you have to get back to who you were before this disaster happened. Do I have to visit a church every Sunday to be religious? Do I have to pray every night? Aren't those technicalities? Loving God and helping those in need aren't enough to be called religious?"

I have delivered another blow below the belt—this coming from a person who until recently would hear the words *religion* and *science* spoken in the same sentence and would burst into laughter. However, the words pop into my head when talking to Tommy, like someone is speaking through me to him. Maybe meeting at this place wasn't a coincidence; I must be the person preparing him for what lies ahead.

Suddenly I get scared. I have never felt like this before. Is God speaking through me to Tommy?

Gosh, I must be going mad. In the back of my mind I suspected everything I was saying sounded like it came from another person, but it never crossed my mind that those words might have been sent from God to Tommy.

That is proof enough for me to let him go on with his journey, but something still feels wrong. I have to lead him to the right path, and to do that, I have to push him even harder.

"Well, aren't you going to try harder? The clock is ticking, Tommy."

"What do you want me to say? I had to abandon my family to get this far. I had to send them off to another planet to make sure they were safe before I went on my journey to find Izan, the only man I know who might be able to help make things right on this planet. But other than a distant feeling, I have no idea how to find him, and it might be too late when I do. And now you are preaching to me about God and about how to believe in Him? How much harder must I try if I'm to save the world?"

And with that, he sits down on the floor.

For several minutes, Tommy doesn't speak. He is lost in his thoughts, unable to move or to do anything. He is breathing heavily, like he is sleeping, but I can see that his eyes are wide open. He has given up and won't even try to convince me anymore. Maybe I was wrong and my words weren't a trial from God to give him more power. It could be the other way, right?

But it didn't feel like that. It was the first time I felt compassion over jealousy, love over greed. For that short moment I was speaking to Tommy, I didn't want the world to recognize me as the greatest scientist who ever lived but for Tommy to say that I was his friend and that he forgave me. Then I would have been convinced he was on a mission to save humanity, and I would have taken him to the airport.

Throughout his difficult journey, though, Tommy seems to have confused passion with religious fervor. He doesn't understand that God is protecting him or that God wants him to succeed. He is so focused on his future hardships that he has lost himself. And being far away from his family hasn't helped.

But that's also the main reason I can't give up on him. Breaking him was the first step; now it's probably time to put him back together.

"Hey, Tommy. Are you okay?" I ask him after an hour of silence.

"I don't know. I feel … lost."

"It's okay to feel lost now and again. Even when I'm working on a new theory, I feel lost most of the time. It's not easy to walk a path no one else has ever walked before. It's like walking on a road without a light; it's easy to stumble and fall. But all you have to do is get up and keep walking."

He raises his head and stares at me; that's good. I have caught his attention. "You are right. But if I am like this now, how on earth will I be able to keep moving forward until I find Izan? I don't even know if he's alive. How will I find a man who doesn't want to be found in the middle of this chaos?"

Tommy's questions are logical, but it seems he has forgotten everything about his faith. He shouldn't think like that, not when the problem he is facing is of a different nature. I have to help him see the light.

"Look, Tommy, this might not be great advice coming from me, but you are approaching this situation the wrong way. If this was a mathematical problem, you would have to break it in pieces and analyze each part with a different mind-set. But this is different. You don't lack faith; in fact, you radiate a sense of purpose more than any person I've ever met. I know you are stressed over leaving your family, and I know it's almost impossible to find a man in a place as big as Australia, but this isn't a question of logic; rather, it's a question of how much you entrust your faith to your God."

He lowers his head and thinks; Tommy is doing everything in his power to see the light by using his mind when he knows perfectly well this isn't the way to go. Of all the firm believers I've met, Tommy is the last one I thought would need someone to remind him about his faith.

I cross the distance separating us and squat in front of him. I grab him by his jaw and push his head back to make him look at me. When I do that, he appears angry with me.

"What's wrong with you?" Tommy asks. "How did you manage to find this light of faith inside you? I don't understand. I'm the one who's supposed to save the world; God has given me, not you, that mission. I'm the one who's supposed to save my family. But I have no idea how to do that, not when I can't feel God's grace inside me. It's hard and I feel like I'm ready to break into a thousand pieces."

Right then I understand. I get a distinct image in my head of how to make him see where he is wrong. Tommy doesn't need me to be his teacher; he needs me to be his enemy.

I pull back and turn on a holo tablet I'm carrying with me. It takes me a moment to search for the files in the system, but after I find them, I push some buttons and compile them into a presentation. I use a holocaster to show Tommy the results.

The flashing lights of the hologram make Tommy turn his attention to me. "What is this?" he asks.

A spherical object is floating in front of him; I'm sure he knows quite well what he is looking at, but he doesn't want to admit it.

"This is Earth before the tear. This is our planet before my masterpiece, the Mantle Project, split it into two chunks." I say this deliberately to agitate Tommy, although the whole world now knows it wasn't my masterpiece that went wrong.

Hearing the word *masterpiece*, Tommy suddenly gets twitchy. "You mean before your work destroyed our home."

"That's your opinion. Nevertheless, look now."

With the press of a button, the planet is ripped to the core, exactly like it happened that fateful day. The Americas are one piece, and the rest of the world is the other.

"This is Earth now?" he mumbles in awe. I nod.

"And getting to Australia will require a multi-day journey from here to the one spaceport in Asia that handles transport there. However, there are no flights at the moment, and the only way to get there is by persuading me to give the command."

I see a spark in his eyes. But I'm not done yet. To show him the possibilities, I press another button and the image of the shattered planet expands to encompass the solar system. The hologram now shows a loop of the chunks moving in different directions.

One of them heads straight to the sun and the other possibly to the sun or to Jupiter due to its heavy gravitational pull.

The moon is destroyed, resulting in even more debris roaming the solar system. In what seems like moments, Earth and the moon are destroyed. Mars is possibly next in line, but it is spared by the flying debris, which heads straight for Yahire.

What I'm showing Tommy is but a simple estimation of how much damage the two chunks of our planet might cause. Essentially, this is what I'll be showing my Russian and Japanese counterparts to convince them to help us save the world.

Tommy stares at me awestruck, unable to do anything but cup his mouth with his hand. He now understands that his family won't be safe, quite possibly not even on Yahire.

"Is this true?" he asks.

"This is the predominant projection of the aftermath. If we don't manage to save our planet, the damage it will cause to the rest of the cosmos will be massive. Something has gone terribly wrong, Tommy, and we are standing here arguing about who has greater knowledge of faith and religion."

That last line must have triggered something inside of him because he reacts differently than usual. Tommy clutches his hands and shows the first sign of tension in a long time.

"It's your fault. God forgive me, but it's your fault. All this wouldn't have happened if you weren't so arrogant. You have to solve this problem before it gets even worse."

"Even if it were my fault, which I can assure it isn't, you have to find it in yourself to let it go, my friend. You have to find it in yourself to forgive me if you want to keep moving forward."

The words again rush out of my mouth, and I am unable to hold them back. Even for me, these words are a revelation.

My watch suddenly starts beeping. It takes me a moment to realize twenty minutes have passed since we started talking again. By now, soldiers from the nearby camp will have arrived to pick me up. I can't stall any longer. If Tommy doesn't give me an answer worthy of his cause, I'll leave without turning back.

"I'm sorry, Tommy. I pushed you too hard. Maybe you are right. My plan may be the only one that might save us all. Nevertheless, I'll send someone to pick you up and to get you to the base. From there, you can head to Yahire by skipping the long lines at the civilian spaceports. I can also arrange for you to meet your family there. I have to go now. Best of luck, Tommy. It was a pleasure seeing you one last time."

I turn my back on him and head toward the automated doors. Not too long after, I hear a weak voice saying, "Stop. Please stop."

I turn and look at Tommy; he has risen to his feet. "I have to go, Tommy. I'm in a hurry."

"This will take only a second," he says and starts walking toward me.

For a moment, I have no idea what to think. Is he going to slap me in the face? To murder me? To do something violent and inexplicable? I don't understand. I'm staring into his eyes, trying to figure out what he is feeling only to see the bliss of nothingness.

Tommy almost smiles at me the closer he gets. His sudden change of attitude gives me the chills. Did I break him to this degree? Is this the end? I have no idea. Still, I stand firm as he draws closer. In the seconds before he is a breath's width from me, I get the feeling Tommy has the power to do anything.

He can bend the sky in half or move a mountain. Instead of feeling hopeless, though, I suddenly feel the exact opposite.

Unbeknown to me, I've closed my eyes at his arrival and don't see him anymore. I feel his aura caressing my skin, his thoughts taking form in front of me and pulsating all around me; is he a human being?

Suddenly, I feel a pair of hands around my neck pulling me closer in a tight hug. Surprisingly, I feel safe, believing that if I stay here with Tommy, everything will turn out fine. I have never felt like this with anyone before. It's a feeling stronger than love or friendship. It's the feeling of believing in the acts of God and in His will.

And right now, the will of God is the will of Tommy, the banker from New York City.

"I forgive you, Jonathan. I forgive you and ask for your forgiveness as well. You are right. After I solved the riddle of the vision God sent my way, I felt the weight of duty crushing my shoulders. If the answer to saving our planet is a man, I thought maybe everything would be all right. But that belief led me to stray from my road. And if it wasn't for you, I would have failed to find the hermit, because I wouldn't be able to forgive the rest of humanity for its sins. But now things are different. After letting go of my anger, I finally feel free to continue with my mission. So please go on with your mission, and I hope our paths meet again in the future, my friend."

And just like that, he releases me from his hug and heads outside to the never-ending crowd of people waiting to be saved with a ticket to Yahire.

I have to breathe; why did I stop breathing? Tommy and his words stole my breath. I never expected him to radiate such light. Now that he has rediscovered himself, he has nothing to fear, and I can go on with my plan.

But first I have to make sure Tommy can continue with his plan.

I rush after him and barely catch up after fighting my way through the crowds. I stretch and grab his hand to stop him. When I do so, he turns around and smiles at me. "Is everything okay, Jonathan?" he asks.

"Yes. More than great. I have good news for you, Tommy. But first I want you to come with me to the military camp. We have to get you to Australia in time."

I pull him toward the spaceport's exit. The people around us sound irritated as we push them aside in a desperate bid to get outside. When we're finally out, the soldiers responsible for transferring me to the military camp find us in seconds.

They stand at attention before me. "Dr. Bailey? Jibe and Stefan at your service. Are you ready for your transfer to the camp, sir?"

They haven't lowered their hands while speaking. They are both too young to have to deal with an almost destroyed planet and to risk their lives to get me to Russia.

Still, at this moment, this is of no importance. "My friend Tommy Russell and I are ready to head to the camp. Also, I need to speak to your lieutenant. Can you call him on your communicatons device?"

Even with their military discipline, they can't hide their surprised expressions. "Excuse me for asking, sir, but we didn't receive any orders to transfer Mr. Russell to the camp. Is there some sort of emergency?"

I turn to look at my friend. Then I say, "This man, soldier, is playing integral part in the survival of planet Earth. We have to help him get to the Victoria province in Australia as quickly as possible. Do you understand?"

And that's how my time with Tommy ended and how our paths separated for the time being.

***

# Chapter 29

## A Stranger Aboard A Flight

*January 23, 2075*
*Landing at Victoria*
*Narrator: Tommy Russell*

It has been some time since I met Jonathan at Germany. Before seeing him, I didn't know I had lost myself and had deviated so far from the path of true belief. I was nursing a grudge at the world for not seeing the point of view of the people who looked to God for support and guidance.

My behavior reminded me of when I was a teenager and wouldn't listen to the things my father and mother told me. All I cared about was doing everything in my power to acquire material goods, things that would add nothing to my soul.

This time I got so lost in my desire to follow God's instructions that I forgot what believing means. The darkest shadows come when you are close to the sun, and I ended up falling into a trap I laid for myself. Jonathan helped me get past this moment of weakness.

I thought he was to blame for everything, but the way he spoke to me, the way he treated my insecurities and my fears, showed me he has found his path. And for that, I'm extremely happy. Now it's time for me to find Izan, the holy man who can help me save our planet.

I still have no idea where he is or what he is doing. A slight clench inside me tells me that I'm on the right track, that Victoria can be a starting point for this journey, but I'm running out of time. If what Jonathan told me is true—and he has no reason to lie to me at this crucial moment—I have about three months before the planet has reached a point of no return.

Still, I can't lose hope. I'm the only one who has solved the riddle, the only one who knows the importance of finding Izan, and I must give my all to that quest, even if it costs me my life.

The airplane's pilot interrupts my thoughts. "Our ETA to Victoria airport is ten minutes," he announces. "You'll have five minutes to disembark and to head to the person appointed to guide and train you. Everyone except Mr. Russell will have to go through training before ..." and he continues for some time.

So I'm the only one on the plane treated with such respect. Thank you, Jonathan. I never expected him to be so understanding and effective. For a man accused of crimes against humanity, he has amassed quite a bit of power. People trust him, even after everything that went wrong.

I trust him as well. I couldn't have gotten here in time if not for Jonathan. But humans find it much easier to forgive others in a time of need, even after tossing rocks at them the previous day.

Waiting for the plane to land, I check outside the window. A glimpse is more than enough to strike fear in my heart. It's early in the evening, and the sun should still be in the sky. Instead, I see a half-dark, half-gray sky with holes in the middle.

The atmosphere over Australia has thinned more quickly because the continent is surrounded by oceans. In the next two months there is a great chance that the sky in this part of the world will turn completely dark and that the atmosphere will thin so much that living here will be dangerous. I have no idea what will happen then, but the government is doing everything in its power to evacuate people and to transfer them further west.

And I'm chasing a man who doesn't want to be found. That's a pretty strange situation.

I sigh, and a woman on the other side of the plane notices me. "Family?" she asks.

I'm a bit surprised by her reaction, but it's heartwarming. She is looking to connect with someone in a situation like hers. Maybe it would be better to ignore her. I'll probably never see her again.

But then I remember everything that happened just a week ago with Jonathan. God is sending me all the help I need in the form of people.

"No. I'm searching for a man."

She nods again. "Oh. I understand. I'm here to help my parents evacuate. They are too old to do it by themselves, and since Australia went gray earlier this month, the spaceports don't work. Who got you on this plane?"

"A friend of mine. He is a lead scientist with the Core and Earth Sciences Department. You?"

"My husband is a commanding officer." We stare at each other awkwardly for a moment before the woman extends her hand. "Grace."

"Tommy. Nice to meet you," I say.

"Likewise!"

In the time it takes for us to introduce ourselves, a bump signals our landing. A whole spectrum of feelings passes over the woman's face—agony, anxiety, happiness, relief, and then fear.

The story about helping her parents suddenly doesn't sound quite right to me. Maybe Grace lied to me, or maybe she underplayed her explanation. Either way, I feel like I must say something to her. I feel like I should do what she did for me when she heard me sigh.

Maybe I should show compassion, just as people have shown it for me.

"Sorry for intruding, Grace, but I couldn't help noticing you are a bit stressed. Can I help you with something?"

My question puts her off a bit. She didn't expect me to ask it or maybe didn't want me to. No, that's not it.

"You are a sweetheart, Tommy, but unfortunately there is nothing you can do to help me. This is something I have to deal with all by myself. Maybe this time I'll be able to convince them to listen to me."

The stewardess opens the cockpit door and the exit and shouts over the roaring engines, "You have five minutes! Five minutes and then we will take off."

Grace and I quickly get on our feet and hurry to the exit. People are already rushing outside. Glancing back, I spot two people with eyes shut, half-risen from their seats, unable to take another step. This picture of utter helplessness is imprinted on my mind.

Only after I'm out do I realize I'm the last one to disembark. The pilot closes the door behind me. Until the next flight to one of Earth's two chunks arrives, we are trapped in the land of the dotted sky.

Grace has vanished. That's resolved. She really wants to save her parents. But why do feel bad for those people left behind? They made their choice and will have to live with it.

I stare into the distance until the plane is nothing but a dot in the sky. The two people left on board haunt me; I can still see the dread in their eyes, the way their muscles locked and they couldn't move. I don't know what made them take the trip to Victoria and then freeze in fear, but whatever it was, I feel the impact deep in my bones.

If I hadn't met Jonathan in Germany, I could have been one of them. I am shocked at how things have turned out. The man who envisioned the Mantle Project is the one who helped me move on with my trip and arrive here in Australia.

Now I have to push forward. I must learn Izan's whereabouts, and fast. It's the only thing that will keep me sane.

A man suddenly appears at my side.

"Oh! Hello. I'm sorry I didn't notice you," I tell him.

The man is in military attire; he is around my age and height, but his eyes have a certain edge to them that makes him look older than he is. He doesn't salute me like the soldiers did at the camp in Germany. The man doesn't seem to enjoy being here with me. I can't blame him.

"You must be Mr. Russell. I'm Travis Hall. I'll be at your service for the duration of your stay in our country, sir. I have orders from my superiors to help you succeed in your mission here in Victoria."

I thought he would offer his hand in greeting, but the man stands perfectly still and stares at me without blinking. The way he acts makes him look like a perfectly built android.

A moment passes while I consider how to respond to him. "Thank you, Travis, but you don't have to risk your life for me. I think I can find the man I'm looking for without your help. I don't want you to carry my weight."

Travis frowns and takes a step closer to me. "You won't be able to navigate in the wilds of the Australian desert, sir. If I let you go by yourself, you'll die even before arriving deep in the wild. I might not totally agree with the orders of my superiors, but if the man you are searching for is indeed the key to saving this planet, I don't mind risking my life to succeed."

With that, he turns on his heels and starts off for a warehouse straight ahead. His step is quick and decisive, allowing no time for second thoughts or fear. He doesn't want to be here with me, but Travis is looking at the bigger picture: he might not like me, but he likes his home—this planet. And together we might be able to save it if we find Izan in time.

I follow him to the warehouse. We enter by a door on the side. The warehouse is dark and the air smells moldy. No one has been inside this place in a very long time, making me wonder what we are doing here. Travis seems to know his way around. Using a military-grade flashlight, he picks up several items and moves them out of the way.

I stand close to the door and the light of the sun. If I move deeper into the warehouse I'll get in his way. On the other hand, I'm curious about what he is searching for. The warehouse is full of old cars, models that were off the road years ago. Some of them seem in better condition than others, and others are only half the size they should be.

I can't help it anymore; I have to ask. "Excuse me, Travis. Is this a garage of some sort?"

The man stops what he's doing and points the flashlight at me. "Yes. I'm searching for something in here."

He lowers the light and continues. I don't feel satisfied with his answer, so I ask, "What are you searching for?"

"A device that can help us communicate using radio waves. My superior briefed me on your mission, sir. It might take us as long as three weeks to find this Izan, and that's assuming we know his whereabouts. Australia has gone black because our power system couldn't hold. Without the device I'm looking for, we won't be able to communicate in time with the rest of the world."

He is right. I never thought about the details of this mission—where to live, how to find Izan, who would show me the way. The only thing I thought to prepare was a small pack of provisions that would probably have lasted me a week. After that, I would have starved.

The more I think about it, the better I feel that Travis is with me. Jonathan has made sure my mission will be successful.

I don't like being dependent on the help of other people. But this isn't about me or about what I want. It's about the future of the planet. And if not for all the people I have met, that future would have looked bleak.

***

# Chapter 30

# Compassion

*Searching for Izan in the deserts of Australia*
*Narrator: Tommy Russell*

I'm not sure how many days it's been since we started this journey. The endless sand and the unbroken rigidity of the land have made me lose a sense of time. Travis says it's around the end of the month, but it feels like more than a week has passed since we began our trek.

We spent half a day at the airport making sure we didn't forget anything important. Travis soon found the device he was searching for, but that was only the beginning. We used a car to head to a town in the west and got provisions, a tent, and other things essential to our trip. Unlike me, Travis made sure to get a physical copy of a map instead of a digital one. He used it to create an optimal route between towns to make our trip easier. He also did this to make sure we'll have many places to recover our provisions if problems arise.

There is a strong chance people in some of these towns will have information about Izan's whereabouts. Logically speaking, we have a better chance of finding him this way than by searching blindly.

Today has been a long day. Our sojourn in the wasteland of Australia is exhausting, to say the least, but we manage to cover quite a distance every day. We still have no idea where Izan is or how to find him, but

I have a distinct feeling we are getting closer. I haven't said anything to Travis yet, but that isn't because I don't want to.

It's mostly because I can't.

Something inside me is stopping me from talking to him about Izan and his whereabouts. It's like I'm allowed to know where he is but Travis isn't. Either way, taking the route he has mapped out, we travel west through the wildly beautiful Australian landscape.

It has gotten late and it's time for us to stop to set up camp. Travis is doing all the driving and is in charge of our daily schedule. His leadership has gotten me this far. Still, during our journey, I have noticed certain things about him. He never talks if I don't speak to him, he never mentions his family, and his expression is always rigid and restless, like he is trying his best to hide something from the rest of the world.

I haven't found the courage to reach out to him, but I can't help remembering that lady on the airplane, Grace. She reached out to me when I was in need, and in doing so she allowed me to snap out of my vicious circle of fear and doubt. In her own little way, she helped me, and I feel I should do the same for Travis.

Tonight, Travis somehow seems different. His face is no longer a taut canvas of agony, and he keeps looking up in the dark sky, especially since we got out of the car and started setting up our tents. When everything is ready, I realize there is no better time to talk to him than now.

"Hey, Travis. Can I speak to you?"

Astonished, he turns to face me. "What about?"

For a moment, I think maybe it's better not to meddle in his personal affairs. After all, how will that help our mission? But a certain feeling keeps coming back to me. It's the feeling I had when Grace spoke to me. I felt better even though she was a stranger.

I muster my strength before asking, "Is there something troubling you?"

He looks fairly surprised by my insight. "What are you talking about? How did you …?"

"I don't know. I had a feeling. Your sadness is apparent all over your face. I can't help but ask you."

Travis stands still. He can't believe I was able to read through his expression. "I thought I was hiding it well. I still have no idea how you figured it out, but I guess you are right. My sorrow is deep."

He takes a step forward and sits on one of the small stools we picked up at the start of our desert adventure. Travis is suddenly lost in his memories, but before I can say something to bring him back, he begins to share his tale with me.

"I guess you are around my age, maybe a year younger. The info I got from headquarters said you have a family that has fled to Yahire to survive this mess. Before reading the details of your life, I had decided not to help you. My superiors came to me because they know I'm one of the best in the country at tracking people who don't want to be found, but I had decided not to take up any mission." He takes a pause.

"You might wonder why I started with that. Well, the truth is my wife and son died during the first wave of earthquakes. I was out here in the wild when the first one hit, so I was relatively safe. But we had no warning. Everything happened so fast they couldn't run to safety, and they both died in the debris of the ruined house.

"I returned as quickly as I could, hoping that they would be okay, that Emma managed to keep Jimmy safe. I found our house destroyed, but I didn't know they had died until I identified their bodies at the local shelter. I thought that my life was over, that even if the planet got pieced together again, I wouldn't be able to survive the shock of losing them. And in a sense, I can't."

He stops there, unable to hold back his tears any longer. I want to say something to him, but I'm not sure any words can heal the wound inside him.

I don't know what I would have done if Catherine, Manna, and Lisa had died in that earthquake. I might not be able to undertake this mission if I was alone. Seeing this man disregard his own feelings, his own pain, makes me admire the beauty of humanity.

The day I left New York I believed that the only people who have God inside them are those who are religious and faithful and who follow my path. However, after meeting Travis and Grace, and after stumbling on my good friend Jonathan and learning he has discovered his own spiritual path, I'm starting to understand human nature better.

We are not perfect; we get angry and we always seem to focus on the wrong things. We follow the same path even if we know it's the wrong one, and we hurt people with our words even though we don't mean to do it. But that's part of being human. Our greater attributes have helped civilization thrive, and our lesser attributes have led our God and savior to help us in our times of need.

Without stopping to think, I embrace Travis in a tight hug. His silent tears become sobs of anger and sorrow as he pours out all of his suppressed love for his family.

***

After three hours of discussion, Travis finally falls asleep. His face looks strangely serene. I have never seen anyone sleep with that much peace of mind. He looks like a reborn man, and for some reason I feel like a proud parent. I pat his head before leaving his tent for one last stroll around the camp before falling asleep.

I have to make sure that the campfire is out and that we haven't left any food out in the open that could draw wild animals. During my walk, I think about the power of words and of simple compassion. For the last few weeks, people I barely knew or trusted have showed me the kind of compassion I never thought possible.

A simple question, a hint of love, some encouraging words—all of these things are their own kind of miracles. Before tonight, I never thought a simple God-given tool like *words* could work miracles. I thought faith came from the will of people to believe in a power bigger than themselves and more important than their dreams.

But this trip has given me so much more than the prospect of meeting Izan. Now I know a way to help others without resorting to arguments with everyone who disagrees with me. Now I know how to be a better servant of my God. It's impossible for gifts so grand as language, technology, and life to be random. They are powerful. To unlock that power, we must rediscover what we have lost in our lives.

And that prospect gives me peace.

A strange light flashes in front of me. It's like those laser dots that make cats go haywire, but it's brighter and has a warmer feel. I have no idea what I am doing, but my heart and my body want to follow that light to find its source. It's impossible that something so beautiful is dangerous, and I have more than enough time to return before Travis wakes up and we have to continue our journey.

I walk till my feet start hurting me. Still, I press forward, getting closer to the source of the light by the minute. What is it? Why do I feel like I've seen this light before? Why is it impossible to stop following it?

I keep wondering until I see a small house at the foot of a boulder in the wasteland. When I get close enough, I notice a garden of vegetables and flowers in full bloom. I look around me, making sure I'm still in the middle of the desert. When I see that the house is the only oasis within miles, I realize this is a miracle, one only a holy person could achieve.

And then it hits me.

Though I'm exhausted, I find renewed strength and run toward the house. The distance becomes smaller and smaller until I'm standing in front of a fence, panting. I'm only a few steps away from meeting Izan and finally finding a way to solve this mess.

The light that guided me here has vanished, but I can still feel its warmth. I want to move past the fence and to knock on the door, but I don't know if it's polite to bother Izan. He doesn't expect me and probably doesn't want to see me at this time. But if I turn around now, I might never be able to find this place again. It's practically in the middle of nowhere, too far away from all the towns we have passed.

Still, I can't do it. I can't walk past the fence. What I've learned makes it impossible to take the next step; compassion can work miracles, and if Izan has chosen to be a loner, I must let him lead his life the way he wants.

That's why I decide to turn around and walk away. Izan is a holy man, but if he doesn't want to help humanity, bothering him will turn into a nuisance for both of us.

"Well done, Tommy. You have passed the test," a voice says from behind me.

I turn around to see a man with a lined face, short white hair, and striking blue eyes. Was he here the whole time?

"Are you ... Izan?" I ask.

The man nods at me with a smile. "Yes, my child. I'm the man you've been searching for this whole time. I'm your father's friend, Izan. Please come in. I'm sure you are tired."

The bony man passes around me to enter his property. He leaves the fence door open.

I still have no idea what is going on. Izan mentioned something about a test. I passed a test I didn't know I had been given. It takes me a moment to piece out what's happened; meeting Jonathan, talking to Grace on the plane, and helping Travis were all part of an elaborate test.

This wasn't a test of faith but a test of compassion. I didn't know I had lost the ability to feel the pain of others and to help them alleviate it. But now I have regained this ability, and it's stronger than ever.

I am speechless over how I finally came to the doorstep of the person I have been waiting to see this whole year. I never felt this way when I met people like Jonathan, Grace, and Travis. There is something different here that I have yet to figure out. It's time to say good-bye to Travis. And this is how we part ways.

# Chapter 31

# Time For Breakfast

*At Izan's house*
*Narrator: Tommy Russell*

My first reaction on seeing Izan was that this man couldn't be the real thing, that I had been tricked by another one of life's weird coincidences. I had imagined him as a man out of this world, wearing shabby clothes and living in a cave.

Hermits, in my mind, were people who give up all worldly goods and devote themselves to their purpose. It may be meditation and a quest for philosophical answers, or it may be religion and faith. I didn't think a hermit needed a house or regular clothes to get by. But Izan has proved me wrong.

His small house in the middle of nowhere is equipped with all the amenities. He has an oven and a refrigerator, heating and air conditioning, even a television and a phone. Izan certainly doesn't look the part of a hermit who has devoted himself exclusively to God.

"Would you like me to get you a glass of water or carrot juice?" he asked as we entered his home. "Breakfast will be ready soon if you want that."

He had the voice of a simple man, the appearance of a normal human being, and the personality one of the next-door neighbor. My first thought was that I had been deceived, and I considered heading straight back to my camp to continue my journey with Travis to find the real hermit.

However, as always, a light deep inside my soul kept calling to me, telling me the man standing in front of me was the real thing, my father's mentor, Izan the hermit.

When his question finally reached my ears, I realized I had to reply. "Thank you, sir, but I'm okay for now. The only thing I ask of you is that you answer my questions. I have come a long way just for that."

With his deep blue eyes, Izan stared at me with the patience of a thousand saints. For a moment, I feared my presence disturbed him, but his compassion quickly dispelled that feeling. Maybe he was glad I arrived the moment I did; maybe he wished I never arrived. I didn't know and I didn't think I had any way of finding out.

The man nodded at me and showed me the way to his humble study. Two armchairs were waiting for us, turned to face one another. Bookcases lined the walls, filled with every kind of masterpiece. I did not doubt Izan's all-around knowledge, but I wondered how the man found the time to read all these books if he meditated all day. How could Izan consider himself a hermit if he spent his time doing things other than thinking about God?

I didn't understand. This made no sense to me. If God had chosen Izan to help humanity, why didn't the man look like he was devoting himself entirely to God?

I waited by the door for Izan to make his next move. Though I didn't realize it at first, our meeting turned into an elaborate game of chess. Izan looked at me and through me, analyzing my every move, still testing me and my mettle; I stared at him, trying to understand where the wise mystic was hiding behind the worldly man.

In the end, I decided the best way to get to know the man was to follow his example and to sit opposite him in the study.

Every step I took was heavier than the last one. I sensed his eyes weighing on my shoulders, the guilt of my doubts shattering my mind. Was I so shallow a man that I judged someone by his appearance, or were my instincts warning me about the man standing in front of me?

When I finally sat down, I quickly realized the armchairs were positioned in such a way that we couldn't miss even a twitch on each other's faces. No matter how hard I tried, I couldn't ignore Izan's presence in the room.

I'm sure he didn't mean to make me feel this way, but for a moment I felt like I was being judged for my thoughts, like I was being read thoroughly by a master.

Izan, in his wholeness, was calm and contained. His muscles were relaxed and he had a slanted smile on his face. I, on the other hand, couldn't move an inch without hearing the gears spinning inside my head, searching for a way out of this awkward mess. It's hard enough when a man faces his own thoughts, but having another man intrude on them is unbearable.

There is a reason humans weren't made to be mind readers. Thoughts and memories are strong weapons. They control the feelings of the heart, and the heart controls our actions. From a very young age we learn to suppress our hearts and to work with our minds, but our hearts make the decisions that matter most.

When we are deciding on the career we want to pursue or choosing the person we want to love, the heart has the final say.

Izan, a man who has spent countless days exploring his thoughts and sentiments, is in perfect unison with his psyche. His eyes are mere instruments that offer him sight; his face is a blank canvas ready to be colored; his muscles move in unison with his breathing.

Izan is in perfect sync with life. The energy of the cosmos and the grace of God pass through him, giving him peace of mind and a deep knowledge of life. He isn't afraid of life because he is living his life to the fullest. To do that, he had to leave behind him the desire to satisfy his every need.

After what seemed like hours of staring at each other, Izan finally spoke.

"Where are you from, Tommy?" he asked.

His question immediately threw me off. Wasn't this the same person who taught my father about God? Shouldn't he know where I was from? What was he trying to achieve?

Once again, I decided to follow his lead. I couldn't question the man at every turn. "I'm from New York. I live there with Catherine, my wife, and my two daughters, Lisa and Manna."

My answer seemed to please him. "How old are they?"

"Lisa is ten and Manna eight. They are my jewels, and I love them more than I love anything in this world."

The more I spoke, the easier it was to express my feelings. Izan's silent composure made me want to share my thoughts. He was an empty book that needed words, and I was eager to fill it with mine.

"They are growing up fast, aren't they?" he said.

"Yes, they are. In fact, two years ago, Manna and Lisa made me realize something very important about God."

"What was that?" he asks, showing his interest for the first time since I arrived.

"They asked me where God lives since we can't see Him or sense Him, and without thinking too hard about it, I told them He lives around us. But that answer didn't suffice for any of us. I realized God lives inside good people, the ones who are righteous and truthful and who are always on the lookout for ways to serve humanity."

"I realized that so-called religious people are not the only ones who have God in their hearts and that people with different beliefs, and even people with no religion, have the ability to perform small miracles. People find God out of pure love. I believe religion and God are distinct and independent."

When I finished speaking, I felt the warmth of a mysterious light leave my body. The words I just spoke, the words I thought my own, didn't belong to me. Another entity, grand and knowledgeable and beautiful, entered my body and spoke those words through me.

At least that's what I thought then. After being with the man for only a few hours, I had achieved a new level of epiphany. I now understood that the man before me was the one I had been searching for, a man close to God, a man of religion, a sage of modern times.

My answer somehow surprised him. Either he didn't expect we would have that level of communication simply by staring into each other's eyes, or my answer was incomplete. Luckily, he let me know at once.

"Why do you think God lives only in the hearts of those you call good people? I would agree with that, but who are those good people, and how does a person become one?"

In seconds, I felt my whole world crumbling around me. That was part of my answer to the girls, but I never thought it would be part of my later answer as well.

I quickly replied, "Well, good people are those who follow religion sent to us by God. They do good deeds and never hurt anyone. They contribute to God's workings, help those in need, and give their belongings to the poor. They go to services every Sunday."

"I don't go to a service every Sunday," Izan said. "Does that make me less of a good person? Does that mean I am not close to God?"

His eyes had turned from two lakes of sweet water into two raging seas.

"You are an exceptional case," I said. "You are closer to God than most people. Your mishaps are forgiven."

Izan bolted up from his armchair and looked at me from above. If his eyes had shot fire, he would have burned me to a crisp. However, he took a deep breath, raised his hand, and placed it on my shoulder. For a moment, I thought he would hit me or preach to me, but instead he left his hand there, touching me with compassion and forgiveness.

"It's not your fault you are confused, Tommy. Everything in life has two sides, and right now you are choosing to see only one. Your answer, my friend, is only half true. Stay the night, stay as long as you want, but until you realize what your mistake is, I can't help you see the other side."

Izan left the room. It was time for breakfast and, I later learned, for his morning meditation. Izan might be a lot of things, but when he is meditating, his spirit leaves this world, and what remains behind must not be disturbed.

I didn't mind that he had left the room. After all, he had left me with a heavy burden: a question to which I didn't know the answer.

To this day, I still haven't found an answer. What did I do wrong? What side don't I see? Doesn't God live in the hearts of good people? Isn't it easier to see His grace there? No matter how hard I try, I can't see the other side.

All my life I have received the kindness of good people, those I knew from Sunday services and those whose faith in God had been tested. My father was one of them, and everything I have received in my life I got from him.

During my stay in Izan's home I realized the hermit wasn't all that different from my father. He shared the same passion for the news and watched it on his ancient television with the same intensity and interest with which he meditated. Though he had decided to live the rest of his days in isolation, Izan still cared about the fate of the world and of the people inhabiting it.

However, he never commented on the news. He didn't even blink an eye at all the bad things happening around the world. Izan just observed with his ever-watchful eyes. Maybe he knows the way to help all these people but doesn't want to share it with them. However, I'm not sure the answer is that simple.

The one thing I'm certain about is that if I don't find the answer to his question, I won't be able to help the planet survive this ordeal.

***

# Chapter 32

# A Hint Of Sadness

*Few days later*
*Narrator: Tommy Russell*

As the days pass I keep wondering what I did wrong. I thought God sent me that vision because I was worthy of His cause, and now Izan thinks I have got it all wrong. What do I have left to prove? What is there I still don't understand? I was certain that after making this trip, I had rediscovered my compassion, my belief in myself, and everything I needed to finally get to the bottom of the world's problem.

But Izan thinks otherwise. Every day we discuss something new. Yesterday we talked about Buddhism and whether I believe it's a religion worth considering, and the day before that we discussed the environment and whether people have done enough to save the planet. The topics vary from religion to technology, from philosophy to art. Izan has an opinion about everything except humanity's current situation.

I'm unhappy that we spend our days chatting idly when people are dying. People are waiting for someone to save them, and God's grand plan, the one He showed me, has to do with that. Scientists will soon install the AX plates around the world, and I still have no idea what Izan was talking about when he said I made a mistake.

Today, like every day, Izan is waiting for me in the study. He has taken his usual stance and wears a calm expression. He won't talk to me until I sit down opposite him. After many days, I know how it feels to look into someone's eyes and to talk to the person. I haven't done this even with my wife. The intimacy makes it difficult to hide even the tiniest feeling. That has encouraged me speak only the truth.

After I take my seat opposite him, Izan stares straight into my eyes and smiles. He doesn't say a thing or move a muscle. He just smiles. The joy reaches his eyes. It's a miracle how a smile, even one so small and mirthless, can offer such joy.

The act is contagious, and soon I'm smiling at him. I'm not sure I understand what is going on, but this interaction calms me down and makes me leave all my doubts and second thoughts behind. After we're done, I look Izan once again and notice a hint of sadness in his eyes.

Unlike all the other sentiments he has shown during my days here, this one persists. It reveals itself in his eyes, in his smile, and in the rest of his body. Suddenly, Izan looks tired, lonely, and helpless. My first reaction is to help him, but an invisible wall exists between us.

The same light that led me here, the one that sometimes speaks through me, advises me to take my time and to watch the hermit. Today I'm present for one of those rare occasions I wouldn't want to miss; it's like a flower blooming once every ten years. The sadness has taken hold of Izan; tears are running down his face. His tears are silent, but they have a loud impact.

I'm soon crying myself. Compassion, the need to help, is bleeding me dry. If I can't help this man standing before me, whom can I help?

A minute passes as we cry but say nothing. The world feels like a lonely place. I miss my house, my family, and the safety of my routine. One day I want to return to all these things, but I don't know the way.

I miss feeling what it's like to know.

Ignorance can be a bliss, but bliss can be a drug. Before meeting Izan, I thought I knew my path in life, but now I see I couldn't be further astray. It's not that I didn't walk the right path; it's that I didn't always know what I was seeing.

The world is a big place, and this trip has made me realize that more than ever. I met a woman to whom I felt close after exchanging only a few words, and a man who opened up to me about losing his family. I met an old friend who spoke with the clarity of a sage. I have answered questions and questioned my answers. I have followed the vision God sent me and have fought everyone who tried to stop me.

In the end, I arrived here and met this man, my father's mentor and the cornerstone of a plan I still know nothing about. In my search for answers, I found a man with none, and that must be why I can't let go of my old beliefs. I can't deny that God lives only in the hearts of good people, because that's what made me come so far.

But what if God doesn't live only in the hearts of good people? And if He does, who in fact are those good people? Who is good enough to let Him enter?

I think God is hiding in the will of His people and in all those small, everyday actions that we take without expecting anything in return. God is living inside us, inside the good people, the ones who discover Him in the even-bigger universe inside their hearts, who understand Him, who love Him, and who would never oppose His will. And these actions and feelings are mutual. This is how love evolves between people, and this is how it must happen between a human and God.

I don't realize I have been speaking to Izan all this time. I wouldn't have learned this if my throat hadn't become dry from all that talk. The man on the receiving end of my words seems vastly different from the one I've come to know after several weeks. His eyes have the welcoming blue of the clear sky, and his lips have formed a generous smile.

"That's what I have wanted to hear, Tommy. That's the answer you have to give to your daughters when you see them again. It's all mutual. If you walk toward God, He will come running to you. His love for you is eternal. But you have to find it on your own. You will make mistakes, and you will have mixed feelings every now and then. But finally you will receive His bliss inside your heart. This requires perseverance and gratitude. I believe you have compassion, love, and every other trait needed to accept the will of God inside you.

"Now I can talk to you about His plan and about what you can do to help repair this broken world."

I can't breathe. I never expected the answer to my question to come so suddenly or so close to the end. The question my daughters posed to me so long ago was the one that helped prepare me for this moment. For the first time in years, I'm at peace. Izan hasn't told me what I can do to help the world, but right now I need to rest.

I lie back in the armchair and close my eyes. I always pray before falling asleep and first thing in the morning, and the moment I close my eyes, I start talking to God as if He is with me. I can almost feel His presence inside my heart. Our discussion soon turns into a prayer, and that prayer soothes me till I have nothing else to say and nothing left to do but sleep.

What's weird, though, is that even in my sleep I keep thinking, discovering new things to say, and walking the path of faith. And for the first time in my life, I find a reason to let go.

\*\*\*

# Chapter 33

## A Passionate Plea

*3:30 a.m., February 27, 2075*
*Narrator: Tommy Russell*

When I open my eyes, I see Izan standing over me. It's early morning, and I know I woke up because Izan nudged me awake. I feel weak and exhausted even though I must have been sleeping for many hours.

I look at him, and the old man greets me with a smile.

"It's good to have you back, Tommy. You have been sleeping for two days straight."

"I did what?" I whisper while trying to drown a yawn.

"You went through a revelation, child. Your mind needed time to process everything, and so your body shut off for a couple of days to allow that to happen."

"Then ... why do I feel so tired? Two days of sleep should have been more than enough to get me rested."

Izan smiles again. "Your mind rested but your body needs fuel to run. The only thing I could do during the past two days was wet your lips so you didn't dehydrate. You need to eat something as soon as possible to get your strength back."

The moment Izan mentions eating, my stomach growls. I'm famished. I haven't eaten for the past two days, and I want to devour the world. As always, Izan is right.

I try to get on my feet, but Izan doesn't let me. "You are far too weak to move right now. Stay there and take your time getting up. We don't have to rush, my child. Today we have all the time in the world." With that, he leaves the room.

I stare around the study. The familiar smell of the books eases my worries for a moment. I have never been a heavy sleeper, and I had never slept more than eight or nine hours. This was a first for me, and like everything else on this journey, I try to embrace it rather than shut it away.

I have no memory of my dreams during those two long days. The only thing I have kept deep inside my mind is the feeling of talking to someone, of talking in my sleep. I'll have to ask Izan about that, but my best guess is he won't know anything or he won't give me the answer so easily.

But right now my need for food surpasses my need for answers.

Just as that thought enters my head, Izan arrives in the room carrying a tray with enough food for three people. Still, it seems too little for me at the moment.

He places the tray next to me, and without waiting for him to say anything, I start eating. Izan smiles like a proud father, and it occurs to me that when I'm with him, I feel like a vulnerable son. I haven't felt like that since my father died, and I know deep inside that the moment I leave Izan's side, I won't live this carefree again.

However, the feeling persists for a little while. Izan has again put on his serious expression, and instinctively I know something changed while I was in my extended sleep.

"Tommy, there is something we need to discuss. A few days ago, the science team responsible for mending the planet announced the AX plates are in place. Because the planet's gravity has decreased significantly, the activation time has changed. They are going to set their plan in motion tomorrow."

Instead of feeling overwhelmed as I once would have, I am glad the schedule has been moved up. I can't wait to return to my family, to hug my beautiful wife and my two amazing daughters, to meet all my friends, new and old, and to talk to them about this trip.

I don't know if I'll succeed in piecing together the planet, but I know I'm staring the solution in the eyes and he seems eager to help me.

With that in mind, I stop eating, and after wiping my hands, I place them on Izan's shoulders. He seems surprised.

"What's wrong, my child? Is something troubling you?"

"I want to know how you and my father met. I want to know the truth about your relationship. Mother didn't know and couldn't help me learn the truth about my father's actions."

Exceeding my every expectation, Izan agrees to tell me everything he knows—no questions asked, no tests to pass.

"We were classmates, but we didn't know each other very well until we graduated. Your father was a very intelligent guy. He topped the class and had the highest grades ever recorded in two subjects. I only passed the exams. I met him on graduation day and offered to buy him a cup of coffee at a nearby café. He said he wanted to serve his country in some way. He said he was eager to do this because he believed a man should do what makes him happy. I asked him why he didn't want to explore what he was about, how he was different from others, or what his purpose in life might be. I explained to him that his aspiration would bring many obstacles that he might not be ready to face."

Izan stops for a moment, recollecting that time. Based on what he is saying, I no longer have any doubt that he was my father's mentor. Father always had a strong sense of duty, but he never tried to transfer that to me. He always said I had to discover myself before throwing myself headfirst into my dreams.

"Your father then asked me what I meant when I told him to be ready for what he would face," Izan says. "I wanted him to know what he was capable of, to foresee the situations he would face, and to be ready for them. I thought I would be able to help him."

Izan smiles at the last sentence. I know my father's reply. He asked Izan to help him, and that must have been what triggered their spiritual trip together.

A second later, Izan says, "Come. I will tell you everything I know about myself, this place, this world, and our true Master. So listen to me carefully. God created the universe with a purpose. The purpose was to see who loves Him. He sent many prophets who loved Him and did everything He wanted them to do. Some people, having come to know about God from these prophets, fell in love with Him. Many followed them and many went astray. God bestowed His special attention and love on these followers, more than on the prophets, as they were ordinary people and came to love Him out of their innocence. They thought of their Lord every moment of their lives, leaving their worries behind. This love gave them the strength and the courage to stand firmly against evil, and with God's help they succeeded. So if you believe in God for whatever you want to do in your life, He will help you." Izan says and looks at me.

"This is what I told your father back then, and this is what I say to you now. There is nothing else to the story of how your father and I met. I was and am very spiritual about God, and no one else knew about me. I could see a deeply hidden love in your father, and I enlightened him for God. Your father immediately rushed toward me, hugged me, and said he was not going to leave me. As we both were young, we decided to pursue our lives together."

He stops and his eyes meet mine. "I must say I have never met such a person."

"I know." He smiles.

"Did you get married?" I ask.

"Yes, I married a beautiful girl. Two years later, my wife died of a lung complication that wasn't diagnosed in time."

"I am sorry. I didn't know."

"Oh, don't worry. It's part of life."

"True. Did you marry again?"

"No," Izan replies firmly.

"But why?"

"Living alone was and is all right. Whatever happens to you is for your own good. Your father lived with me for several years, and God gave him a son who is now standing in front me, having grown up to become a fine man. And that's as much a blessing to me as it would be if I had my own children."

A moment of silence passes between us. However, time is growing short. I have to convince Izan to pray for the world and to help me find a solution, so I keep digging deeper. "So you have lived most of your life alone. I imagine that has been pretty difficult, hasn't it?"

"No, it hasn't. It depends on how you see your life and yourself. Life is all about love, and if you can find your true love, everything else is secondary. I found my love in my true Master, and I have lived happily with the belief that the Lord of the universe also loves me. That's enough for me."

"I still don't understand how to achieve this bliss and peace. I would very much like those things."

Izan's expression changes to that of a teacher rather than of a friend. "They are bestowed upon you," he says. "You cannot achieve these things through struggle. It's about believing in God and in His love and letting go of all your worries. That's the true path of a hermit—to leave behind all your earthly worries and to put your trust in your faith."

I am silent but my expressions, full of curiosity, demand some explanation. Izan takes a deep breath. "Just close your eyes and think of God at some point in your day. He is connected with us spiritually. When we think of Him, His attention is drawn to us, and then we receive His blessings."

I nod when I realize we agree on so many levels, but his last thought gives me an opening to ask about what I most want to know. "So when our eyes are closed and we are thinking about Him being close to us, can we ask Him for what we want?"

"It depends on what you are asking for."

"What about the good of humanity? What if I ask Him to reverse this dangerous situation?"

A strange glimmer appears in Izan's eyes. "Why would God choose to reverse His actions merely because someone is pleading for Him to do so? Our planet has come to this point only because of humanity's insolence and its disregard for God's laws. Why would He choose to change what is obviously our punishment?"

"True! But a plea to God for humanity is a selfless act. We make mistakes; we are not perfect. We miss our chances at every turn, but once in a while, we see our mistakes and try to fix them. And that's humanity's nature—to adapt and to change. That's how we've survived all these years."

Izan contemplates my thoughts. "It is a selfless act," he says. "Tens of millions of innocent people may be pleading with Him to save humanity from this catastrophe. But the crisis had to reach this point before they sought His help. And that's what worries me the most."

"So what's the best course of action for me now?"

The connection Izan and I had built quickly vanishes. "This is my meditation time, child. I need some privacy if you don't mind. In the meantime, you may make yourself comfortable and have some soup and replenish your strength; it's in the kitchen."

Izan closes his eyes and loses himself in deep contemplation. A man of his mental stature couldn't give me the answer I was searching for, but I can't give up. There is always tonight. If I can persuade him to help humanity tonight, there is still enough time to save the planet.

\*\*\*

I decide to spend the rest of my day taking a stroll around the house. Izan's garden is abundant with vegetables even though his house is located on the edge of the Australian desert. The sun is hotter here and the ground rougher, but somehow this man has succeeded in planting and sustaining a rich garden.

Gravity has decreased significantly. The leaves of the plants move in an eerie way, like an invisible wind is shaking them. There are more bugs in the air than there were when I arrived, and dust travels higher now and in greater quantity.

Walking has become an awkward activity. I feel like I'm jumping without placing my feet on the ground. The sensation is pleasant, and

I feel ten years younger because my weight seems to have been reduced, but I also feel nauseous even while taking a short walk around the house.

I wonder how Cat and the girls are doing; I wonder if my mother will ever forgive me for dragging her out of her house and for sending her far away to another planet. I promised her we would one day return and rebuild her house together with all the memories, but without Izan's help and guidance, I won't be able to do that.

Tomorrow morning, Jonathan and his team will put their plan in motion. They will activate the plates by supplying them with enough electricity to create a massive electromagnetic field.

I know deep inside me that without God's help, they won't make it. But Izan seems eager to let that happen since he believes humanity deserves to be punished for being too cocky and materialistic. I can't share his view. I think God is forgiving and compassionate; I think God wants someone to ask Him to forgive humanity and to help us mend our mistakes.

A question pops into my head. I check the time and make sure Izan has completed his meditation. Then I rush into the house. He is in the kitchen, preparing our dinner. He seems lost in thought, but that's a given for this man after he completes his meditation. It's not a switch that can be turned on and off. He needs time to get in and out of this state.

Unwilling to wait any longer, I ask him, "What if you were God? What would you do?"

Izan is silent; he stares at me, unable to give me an answer.

I know I'm on the right track, so I continue. "You would definitely save the Earth and its people," I tell him.

Izan unexpectedly replies, "Why? What for? If I were God, I would have learned by this time that I am nothing to these people. I don't live among them. They don't respect my words, my people, or even Me. They listen to their own counsel and do whatever they think will benefit them. In fact, they are the losers. They are materialistic, they commit crimes, they hurt the people near them, and they care more about power and fame than about being modest and compassionate. They don't even follow the laws they have imposed on themselves, and they make wars and kill people in the name of politics and of invisible boundaries. Why should I care for the species that destroyed this planet? Why shouldn't I give these people what they have strived for—to damage this planet irreversibly?"

I can't speak for a moment; I have to process what Izan has just said. I have never seen him so agitated before. Maybe he is feeling the pressure of time as I am. Still, I can't give up now, not when I'm so close. "What about one last chance? What if humans have finally learned from their mistake?"

He is silent. His eyes align with mine, and I can see his anxiety recede and another sentiment prevail inside him. My grit and passion have influenced him to change his opinion. Izan is a forgiving man, and I think he sees a younger version of himself in me, a person who hopes humanity can and will prevail and will follow the one true path in the end.

I take the hermit's hand in mine and say, "Please, Izan. I know it's unfair to ask you this, but you are the only one enlightened enough to help humanity escape this calamity. God will hear the prayers of His most faithful servant, but it has to happen tomorrow. You are right about humanity. You are right to believe there is nothing to be done, because humans have proven time and time again that they don't learn from their mistakes, but maybe this time things will be different. And faith will have prevailed."

Tears in his eyes, Izan says nothing at first but nods. When he regains his calm, he says, "Okay, let's do this, my son. I hope you are right and humanity learns from its mistake this time."

***

# Chapter 34

## The Prayers And The Push

*The next day, close to the time the Planet Mending Plan is set in motion*
*Narrator: Tommy Russell*

I couldn't get even an hour's sleep last night. My mind spun for endless hours, and I couldn't calm down enough to sleep. Everything comes to a head today. Either Earth survives this ordeal and humans can return, or the planet gets destroyed and there is nothing anyone can do to stop it.

Last night, Izan assured me he will keep his promise and will pray for humanity to be given another chance, but something inside me says trusting Izan won't be enough. There must be a way I can help him, a way I can contribute to this fight, but I haven't figured it out yet.

I got up early this morning, and I have been strolling around the house, trying to find a way to calm down. I have walked every possible path many times, but I still can't feel the fatigue from losing a whole night's sleep. Maybe it has something to do with the fact that I slept for two days straight not long ago or that I won't be at ease until this crisis is over.

As I search for answers to my questions, my hand slips into one of my pockets. The pair of jeans I'm wearing is the same pair I wore the day I met Jonathan. I remember that because of the importance of our meeting that day. Last night, I was hoping to find a way to communicate with him to ask him about the status of the plan, but because everything was happening so quickly that day, we never swapped numbers.

I have one of his old numbers saved on my phone, but I have called it several times during my stay at Izan's house and Jonathan has never answered. I trust that the military gave him a new, secure number so nobody like me will be able to reach him. I'm entertaining that thought when my hand touches a paper inside my pocket.

I pull it out and see a number written on it. It's pure luck that the ink hasn't faded when my jeans have been washed, but as soon as I see it I realize luck has nothing to do with why this number has remained intact in my pocket.

God meant for it to happen this way, and knowing His grace, He probably meant it to happen at this moment.

Izan is in the study, already having fallen into deep meditation. Later this afternoon he'll start praying for the scientists' plan to work, but he told me he first has to make sure his intent is clear. He is not close to the phone and not within hearing range, meaning I won't bother him during his meditation.

I close the kitchen door behind me and push the buttons one after another. I find the ringing of the phone soothing. I don't know if he'll pick up the phone, but I have high hopes. I shut my eyes and pray.

The Lord is certain to know the answer to this question.

"Yes? Who is this?"

"Oh, thank God, it's you Jonathan," I say, finally able to breathe after all those rings.

"Tommy? Oh my God, what are you doing? You were the last person I expected to hear from today."

Jonathan sounds stressed. I can't hear even a whisper behind him. He seems to be alone.

"I just found a note with this number on it, and I thought it might be yours. It turns out I was right."

He doesn't reply. I can hear him breathing rapidly. This isn't the best time to talk to him. Still, since I've found him, it's better to speak.

"Jonathan, I'm sorry for bothering you, but there is something I wanted to share with you. I finally found the man I was talking to you about, my father's mentor. He is indeed a holy man, one who can certainly help make this plan work. I managed to make him listen to me, and he will be praying for humanity's safety as you put your plan into operation.

"I know it doesn't mean much to you, a man of science, but if you could let people know someone is watching over them, I'm sure it will give them the courage to accept whatever happens whether it is success or defeat."

Jonathan sighs. "You are right, Tommy. This isn't the best time to talk about religion and unity or anything like that. It's time for science to fix the problem science created. The plates will work, and the planet will be pieced back together. However, I am not the stubborn man I used to be. Since we met, I have been searching for answers to my own questions about religion, and every day I'm finding new things to share with the world. You and Izan pray for us, and let's hope the combination of both realms offers the solution to mankind's biggest ordeal ever."

I haven't realized tears were running down my face until Jonathan finishes speaking. The one man I never thought I would agree with just gave me the solution to my problem. Izan can't do it by himself, but I can also pray to God to help us.

Maybe God won't listen to me and maybe I'm not as enlightened as Izan, but I should ask God to save humanity. I should ask Him for an act of mercy, for another chance at life, for a loving response to humanity. The Lord is forgiving and the Lord is great. I don't know if He'll hear a peasant like me, but that shouldn't stop me from doing what my heart commands me to do.

And my heart also tells me to pray that my family will have a safe home to return to.

"Thank you, Jonathan," I tell him. "Thank you for once again showing me the way. I'll pray. And you should pray as well. I know it's not your field of expertise, but faith can't be studied or mastered. Faith can only be summoned. And at this moment, the world needs all the faith it can muster."

Jonathan laughs but not in a derogatory way. He laughs as if a load has been lifted from his chest. "Thank you, my old friend, for all your kind words and for your courage. I will pray, and let's both hope the rest of the world prays with us. I have to bid you farewell, Tommy. The time is near for the plan to be set in motion."

I nod even though I know Jonathan can't see me. I believe my message is somehow conveyed to him. However, just before he hangs up, I say, "Jonathan, one last thing."

"Make it quick, Tommy. They are calling me from the control center."

"Is there any way I can track Cat and the girls? I haven't spoken to them for months, and I would want to hear them one last time before … you know. Everything is set into motion."

Jonathan sighs once again. He sounds like he has an answer to my question but isn't sure if he wants to share it with me. "It's too late for me to help you, Tommy. If you had called me a week ago, I would have been able to do something, but now, just hours away from starting this operation, there is nothing I can do. I'm sorry."

A weight suddenly falls on my chest and I can't breathe. There is nothing I can do. That last good-bye outside our home will have to suffice. I have faith that God won't leave humanity to perish, but I'm also afraid that if He does, I have lost my chance to talk to my family one last time.

There is nothing Jonathan can do, so I feel bad about keeping him on the line any longer. "Okay. I understand. Thank you for everything you've done for me, Jonathan. I trust your plan, and I'm certain we will succeed in putting our home back together. See you around, old friend."

"See you around, Tommy," Jonathan says and hangs up.

Izan walks into the kitchen. He sees my tears of regret and fear, but he says nothing. Instead, he extends his hand, touches my shoulder, and nods.

"Family is our shelter while we are on this planet, Tommy," he finally says. "There are no stronger ties than those we share with our family. Some say those are blood ties, and others say we have to forge them using our own blood. I say family is what we choose it to be. Your family is safe somewhere far from here. And for that, you have to be grateful."

Expecting no reply, Izan abruptly leaves the room. He probably sensed my need for support after everything I've heard. My heart aches and I can still sense the dark shadow of fear towering over my head, but after this call I'm more determined than ever to save the planet. I stayed behind, away from my shelter, to make this happen.

I can't give up now, not when there are so many things I still want to show my girls. I can't give up because if I do, I'll shatter all the ties I have created with people on my journey, and I don't want to let them down.

I look at my watch. Two hours until the designated time. Two hours until the moment of truth, and I suddenly feel last night's lost sleep catching up to me. I'm not sure what changed, but I can't keep my eyes open any longer.

I head to the study and lie down on the armchair I use for my meditation. I close my eyes and quickly relax. My eyelids are heavy. I quit my resistance and decide to rest. I'm sure Izan will wake me up when the time comes to pray.

***

Light blinds me. How is it possible for so much light to exist? How is it possible for so much light not to burn me?

I don't know.

I feel like I can't breathe but at the same time like I'm breathing for the first time in my life. The pressure on my chest is unbearable and liberating. My body is ripped in two, and I don't know what to do. I try to scream, but no sound comes out of my mouth. I want to touch the ground, but I can't move. The only thing free in me right now is my thought. The last two years of my life pass in front of my eyes. My rights and wrongs, my truths and lies, my family and friends, everything is here.

I think I hear someone speaking to me from a distance, and I think I reply to that someone, but I don't know what we are talking about. My subconscious mind seems to be having a discussion with someone, and I can't help but hear the whispers.

I'm slowly able to control my eyes. I look up and see thunderous arcs of immense power between six giant plates. I'm not sure what is happening, but I sense that they're trying to move closer to each other, trying to connect. Now I'm able to control the rest of my body as well, but I don't know what to do.

I reach for the plates, but I can't touch them. That's when I start praying, asking God for His help. Right now I feel as if I have encountered no one else on this journey.

The moment I find words to speak to Him the plates start moving. They quickly draw closer to each other, the vast canyons closing in above me. The world is moving, and I'm in the middle of all this chaos, unable to move. I can't go up or down, left or right. I can only stay where I am, hands and feet moving, eyes watching the world change, hoping someone will save me.

Why should I be saved? I have forgotten my reason for being alive. The plates are moving closer to each other every second. Why should I be saved? Is someone expecting me? Do I have a family?

The question echoes in my mind. I see Catherine waking up by my side all these years, and I see Lisa and Manna being born. I see them growing up to become wonderful girls. And I see myself, a happy father, a man following his faith.

I smile at the picture and relax. The chaos slowly drowns me until only my consciousness remains. If I die here, it won't matter because the world has been saved. If I die here, my only regret will be not hearing my family speak to me one more time.

And just like that, the intense light returns, but this time it's a single ray. It doesn't hurt my eyes or burn me. It's like an anchor pulling me up instead of down, an anchor of hope and faith.

It pulls me up until there is nowhere else to go but the armchair in Izan's study.

I open my eyes and I'm there. My whole body hurts, as if I have been running for days. It's dark outside, and Izan is nowhere to be found. Something in the back of my mind tells me I have been sleeping for days again. I try to get up but it's impossible. My limbs are too weak.

I muster all my strength and succeed into getting up. I head to the kitchen. As I suspected, Izan is waiting for me there. When I enter, he turns and stares at me. That unique smile appears on his face.

Before I can say anything, Izan rushes toward me and hugs me. I think he's crying, but I'm not sure. I hug him back. We spend a few moments like that. When Izan is calmer, he takes a step back and speaks.

"The world is safe again, Tommy. The world is safe and it's all due to you."

I have no words to describe my happiness. All I can say is, "What about my family?"

"Everyone is safe, Tommy—your family, your friends, us. Your prayers were heard and the plan worked. During the first hour, the scientists kept supplying the plates with electricity, but it didn't seem to work. There was chaos all over the world. The department said that the scientists had experimented using a miniature model and that it worked in all respects. But when they began implementing the plan, it didn't work. The entire world screamed." I am gathering what Izan is saying. And I think I know what he's saying.

"Your friend Dr. Bailey addressed the world's people and said, 'I know we are going through the worst disaster humanity has ever experienced. We have lost our loved ones. We have been punished for our mistakes. We were here for a purpose, but we went astray. We need a second chance from God, and I assure you people out there are praying for the entire world, so have faith. The plan will work. God loves them, and He will give us a chance because of them!' Then, while you were praying to God, a hum suddenly started sounding throughout the world, and the planet started moving. Later Dr. Bailey confirmed that it had nothing to do with his team's plan, that it was like a magical push happened and the pieces of the planet started to move." Izan continues.

"Tommy, that push came from you. God heard you. Your prayers saved us all. The shadow of man you saw in your vision was you, not me. I was the source connecting you to God, but this was all about you. God gave humanity a second chance because of you. And your father couldn't have been prouder of you today!"

His words touch me at the core of my being. Before this journey, before everything I endured, I wouldn't have believed that the catalyst for this outcome would be me. Now, after having witnessed God's grace in its purest form, I see everything in life has a reason, and for me, that reason was to follow my path to this moment—the moment humanity was given a second chance, the moment science was able to work with God to create a miracle, the kind of miracle only true faith can achieve.

### ***The End***

# Message from the author

It is God who created earth for us and who built the sky. The east and the west belong to Him. Wherever we turn, there is His face. God is all-pervading and all-knowing. In Muslim scripture, God says that whoever from any religion believes in Him, and does good deeds, will be blessed. People preach their religions in absurd ways and fail to see that it is God, not religion, whom we must worship. All religions come from the same God, so how can they be different? Any difference has to do with method and not with basic beliefs. Every religion has the same basic beliefs.

Religions have two basic sets of principles, one concerning God and the other concerning how to improve oneself and how to behave with others. If you are good with God, it's impossible for you to be bad with people. But if you are good with people, you may still be deprived of the light of love that comes from God. He is light. His love is light. When you fall in love with your Creator, you cannot follow darkness. When there is light, there is no darkness. He calls us to come to light. This light is knowledge and His love.

Humans are made of three basic spiritual elements: spirit, heart, and mind. The spirit knows God since it was there when He created each of us. The spirit does whatever God tells it to do. The heart knows nothing but how to love and how to be loved. The mind thinks and interprets and makes decisions. God created angels first. They are pure spirits. They do whatever He says. They cannot love or be loved since they don't have hearts. They cannot decide what is right and what is wrong since they don't have minds. They are pure. Then God created demons. They have minds, so they can make decisions. They can follow their lustful desires and can hurt others, but they don't have hearts, so cannot love or be loved.

Finally, God created humans, the noblest of all creations. He favored us with all His blessings. He sent messengers to guide us. They told us everything for our benefit so we could live peaceful and loving lives. They warned us that if we don't listen to God, we will suffer. He has told us to understand Him and to serve Him by loving Him. He wants nothing from us but our hearts. Why would God want anything else from us? He is the Master of the universe. He can create and destroy everything in one moment. When God decrees something, He says only, "Be," and it is.

We feel God when our hearts beat in His name. We know nothing of Him but His name. He may not be seen but felt. His name is Ilah [Arabic], Brahman [Hinduism], Elohim [biblical Hebrew], Elah [biblical Aramaic], Abba [God the Father by Jesus], Elohim [Mormonism], and Allah [Islam]. If we wish to approach Him and to seek His attention, it's only His Name we can call. The love that evolves between a human and God is only through calling His name with our hearts.

He loves all, but His beloveds are few. In the same way, if we are good people, we are generally good to all people and do good things for them whenever we get the chance. But still our beloveds are few—our family and our friends.

How can we ignore God? He created us when we did not exist. Everyone passes one day. Nobody is immortal. But God has always been and will always be. If we want to be His beloveds, we must purify ourselves of all that is wrong. A saint was asked how he found God, and he said, "It was not I who found Him, but He found me when I cleansed myself of all that was impure." We were His and He was ours. And one day I am sure we will again be His, and He will be ours.

*Buddha was not a Buddhist. Jesus was not a Christian. Muhammad was not a Muslim. They were teachers who taught love and God. Love was their religion, and God is love.*

CPSIA information can be obtained
at www.ICGtesting.com
Printed in the USA
BVHW03*1223020718
520624BV00008B/101/P